Blight
of the
Arachna

The New Heroes of Kairodor, Book One

D. Holden Kennon

Milton, Ontario

This is a work of fiction. All of the characters, events, and organizations portrayed in this novel are either products of the author's imagination or are used fictitiously.

Brain Lag Publishing
Milton, Ontario
http://www.brain-lag.com/

Library and Archives Canada Cataloguing in Publication

Title: Blight of the arachna / D. Holden Kennon.
Names: Kennon, D. Holden, author.
Description: Series statement: The new heroes of Kairodor ; book one
Identifiers: Canadiana (print) 20220131759 | Canadiana (ebook) 20220131767 | ISBN 9781928011699
  (softcover) | ISBN 9781928011705 (ebook)
Classification: LCC PS3611.E73 B55 2022 | DDC j813/.6—dc23

As always, for Hannah

Prologue
Opera of the Dark Peddler

The forest lied. It promised tranquility, peace and life, but nowadays only delivered noise, blood and death. An ecosystem is a fragile thing, and when the highest link in a chain breaks, everything it supports can only come crashing down. Now, monsters run rampant, and those beings powerful enough to keep them in check have all but disappeared.

One remaining individual walked leisurely through the forest, singing a ballad that had never been heard on this continent. This wasn't a solo; a cacophony of snarls, shrieks, and roars, all provided by his unwilling accompaniment, filled the air.

"How many *rou*-ble is a *dead* soul worth? Two and a *half* a head."

The man's unnaturally loud baritone shook the leaves, and on each emphasis, he swung his arm so ferociously that the air cracked in its wake, though the sound was impossible to distinguish from the breaking of bones or shells, and the squeals that accompanied it. This was the percussion that completed his song.

He replied to himself in a slightly higher tone, as if to signify that another person was singing.

"No dear *sir*, I must pro-*test*, *Sim*-ple dead souls that price may reach, but not those that *I* own."

The deafening opera attracted all manner of the forest's occupants. Some were humanoid, with misshapen limbs and bulging muscles, and many were not. They swung at him with claws, fangs and giant limbs, while those that couldn't reach the man through the crowd fought with each other for the chance to attack next. Each monster would ordinarily take at least ten fully-armoured men to slay, but now they all met the same grisly fate.

"Probka Stepan, the carpenter. He was *such* a *capable* man. With the bricklayer *Milushkin* at his side, you could *find* none better to *build*. Add the wheelwright *Michiev*; his carts could last five *years*."

His pace was unhurried, only changing his stride to step over the corpses he left behind. He wielded no weapon either, choosing to simply swat each monster like one would an annoying insect.

"Fine *souls*, to be sure, they *suit*-ed you well. But they are *no* longer, carpenters, bricklayers or *wheel*wrights. The *dead* know no trade. They weigh down your *pock*-ets, so give them to *me*. All I seek are their *names*."

His presence invited the beasts' aggression, which the traveller relished the opportunity to match. He easily could have slipped through this area unnoticed; hell, he didn't even have to walk. However, this was the only guilty pleasure he allowed himself to indulge in. Every monster he now faced was a symptom of a much greater problem, and, since he couldn't take his anger out on those who were truly responsible, he was forced to settle for these creatures' lives.

Normally, the man conducted himself with the utmost dignity, prided himself on his cunning and ability to keep a level head. Those weren't traits that were commonly associated with warriors, who were often boisterous, brash and completely lacking in subtlety. But, despite his overwhelming strength, he didn't consider himself to be one. At the moment, he was just a simple peddler.

He wore a loose, dark brown traveller's cloak, which did well to hide the spattered blood of the monsters he killed. And underneath it, he kept his wares: a collection of jewellery that hung from a strap of fabric sewn into his shirt that jangled as he swung his arms.

There were bracelets, necklaces, cuffs, rings and even hair clips, and they were all made from cheap materials like leather, string, carved wood, and small bits of metal. No one would consider purchasing them for much money, so the peddler anticipated giving most of them away. No one would ever believe that a man would brave this forest, widely believed to be impassable, for the chance to sell this junk.

Very few people alive would be able to recognize each bauble's worth, and the peddler had no intention of educating them. He would instead advertise his wares as good luck charms and other bogus—whatever would keep people wearing them.

To the peddler, looking at his wares was akin to looking at a wall of light. Each one shone like a star, literally, although he was the only one who could see it. He would distribute each trinket to the populace, and hopefully events would take their course. That was how the peddler liked to operate: by planting seeds and allowing them to grow on their own. He was annoyed to have to do this much, truthfully. If he didn't distribute these trinkets, his plans would still eventually come to fruition. However, time was running out, so here he was.

His end destination was Ayzadol, a city to the east with a large population. However, he thought he might visit Toriath first, which was a much smaller village along the coast. He would reach it in half an hour, and he didn't want to draw too much attention from its citizens, which he surely would if he brought this savage contingent of monsters to their gate.

With that in mind, he reined himself in, clearing his throat and cutting off his song. Every pleasure should be taken in moderation, he believed. Besides, while it was satisfying to kill these creatures for a time, without any challenge, it grew boring. In an instant, he slew everything around him that made a sound, ending the cycle. When new monsters joined, he killed them before they could summon any others, until he was finally left in peace.

He still wasn't alone though. Many eyes gazed at him from a distance, silent, judging and eager. These were scavengers, beasts that were smart enough not to attack him and would be content to prey upon the corpses of those he had left behind. The traveller ignored them. They wouldn't bother him; he had already provided them with a feast. Plus, he valued their existence. Scavengers played a vital role, after all.

The tree line was in sight, and, with a thought, monster blood seemed to vanish from his clothes. It wasn't an illusion; he had actually changed into another, identical outfit. From across the stretch of green, between the forest and the village walls, he saw the guards give a start when they saw him emerge from between the trees. He affixed a pleasant smile to his face, and, when he was in speaking distance, he called up to them.

"Hello, Sirs and Ma'ams! My name is Volas. I am a peddler, seeking shelter for the night and an opportunity to sell my wares."

An incredulous woman, who seemed to speak for the group, called back down to him. "How in the blazes did you get here? The forest has been overrun by monsters!"

He adopted a worried expression. "Is it, now? I was travelling in a group, and our guards had to defend us several times. But since we parted ways, I haven't seen a single beast."

The guard shook her head in amazement. "Then you are the luckiest man alive. We can no longer even venture outside our walls without a substantial armed force." She peered down at him. "You said you were a peddler? I don't see a caravan."

"No caravan, I'm afraid. An axle broke and I was forced to abandon it along the road." He shook his head regretfully. "Still, I carry my most valuable pieces on my person." He pulled open his coat to reveal the jewellery he displayed underneath it. From this distance, the woman couldn't make out any of their details, and probably expected them to be crafted out of gold and jewels.

"I hate to say it after you've come so far, but I don't think anyone here would be interested in buying luxuries. Many struggle to even afford food," she remarked.

"I'm sorry to hear that. But still, I would like to try. At the very least, I would appreciate a place to spend the night. If what you say is true about the creatures in this forest, I do not relish the idea of travelling in the dark," he said, looking out at the descending sun.

The woman nodded hastily in agreement and barked an order to some of her men. The heavy gate began to open just wide enough for him to enter.

"Just so you know," she called out one last time, "we can't allow you to stay too long. As I said, we don't even have the resources to take care of ourselves, much less an outsider. I wish we could offer you our hospitality, but you will have to continue on your way tomorrow."

He shouted out his assent and thanked her once again before stepping into the village.

Just beyond the wall lay a collection of wood houses, stone fixtures and dirt roads. The village was dull and depressing, just like he imagined it to be. Since the village rested on the north coast, its people had dark skin and wore lighter clothes, both in weight and colour, to help keep cool. Therefore, the peddler stuck out like a tortoise in a cabbage patch.

He garnered some curious glances from the people he passed, which turned to derision each time he tried to give his sales pitch. However, as he walked, something curious drew his attention.

Between himself and a cluster of other buildings, he could see a light even stronger than the ones he harboured near his chest. *Oh, there's definitely a story there,* he thought in glee. His curiosity brought him to the light like a moth, until he rounded a corner and *it* ran into *him*.

"Sorry, sir," a small, unbalanced figure said to him. Then, he seemed to recognize that he bumped into someone he didn't know, which was no doubt unusual in this small town.

"Who are you?" the boy asked, a bit rudely.

"My name is Volas," the bemused man replied, keeping the same pseudonym he had adopted on a whim earlier. "I am a travelling peddler."

He looked at the boy's wrist, upon which was the source of the light. "I must say, that's a very beautiful bracelet. I specialize in jewellery, so I can recognize its value at a glance. Where did you get it?"

The boy clutched his arm to his chest defensively, as if he was uncomfortable with the man's gaze on it. "It was a gift, from a Hero. I won't sell it."

"Oh," the man waved off his concern. "I wouldn't ask you to. I was just curious as a professional. A Hero gave it to you, huh?" He gave the boy an appraising glance. "What's your name?"

"I'm Castor." He glanced around furtively, as if looking for an opportunity to escape.

Although he didn't think that his form was that intimidating, the man realized that he had come off as strange. "Well, it was nice to meet you, Castor. Take care of that bracelet; it is a beautiful piece. Could you possibly point me in the direction of the Merchant's Guild?"

Castor nodded, seemingly relieved. "All of the guilds are on the opposite side of the Keep, near the ocean."

"I'll be on my way then." The peddler turned around and walked in that direction, hearing the boy's footfalls on the packed dirt as he scampered away.

He didn't actually visit the Merchant's Guild as he had no real need to. He just wandered to the tavern in a halfhearted attempt to keep up appearances.

For the rest of his stay in Toriath, the peddler didn't try to sell any more of his trinkets, or even drop them in random places for people to find. He simply left the next morning at first light. He didn't want to interfere with whatever was going on in that slumbering village. Events would run their course here, as they always did.

"Another dead soul," he chuckled under his breath as he strolled through the gate. "I hope you prove to be valuable, so I can buy you when the time is right. Just like the others. I can wait."

Chapter One
Tale of an Errand Boy

Three Years Later

Toriath was, in a word, drab. The village consisted only of grey stone and brown dirt, and anything that was once colourful had either been destroyed or repurposed. That was half the reason Castor didn't mind delivering food to the watchers atop the wall, even though his legs burned with each treacherous step he climbed.

His job would have been much easier if the stairs had been made properly. Instead, each one varied in height and width, and many slanted downward. There was no rail or balustrade; he had to dig his fingers into crumbling, mortar-filled divots that held together chunks of stone to keep some semblance of balance. And, to make things worse, he had to climb with a sack of food hoisted over his shoulder. It wasn't heavy, per se, but it swung with each step he took and threatened to topple him backwards.

If I fell from this height, I would probably die, he thought morbidly, as he often did while climbing. The idea didn't fill him with as much dread as it probably should have. Of all the likely causes of death he now faced, this would probably be the most pleasant. Alas, like every morning, he made his way to the top unharmed.

"Castor! Oi, Castor's here!" The watchers on top of the wall rushed towards him, or, more specifically, the sack he carried. With a pained grin, Castor set it on the stone as gently as he could, released the drawstring and began distributing lunches to the starving men and women who had been sitting in the merciless sun since dawn.

His warm reception was the other half of the reason Castor didn't mind this chore. It felt good to be someone that people looked forward to seeing every day. It alleviated some of his guilt and shame.

Castor couldn't perform the same important, manual labour that many of his peers were tasked with. He had tried of course, but both the overseer in the tunnels and the farmhouse manager told him, in the most diplomatic way they could, that Castor was just too weak.

He protested these claims as strongly as he could without sounding like a brat. "If I swing a pick or a hoe long enough, I'll grow stronger eventually, right?"

Apparently, that wasn't good enough. The overseers were quick to shove other, more *suitable* chores onto him. If he wanted to help so much, he could fetch some buckets for water, right? Or rub pitch into fraying ropes? Or pick weeds?

Dohn, who was a village official and one of the most educated people in the village, gave a more coherent reply. "Hard work doesn't make you stronger. Proper nutrition after hard work is what actually helps you gain muscle. Without that, you'll only become weaker."

And that was the crux of the matter. Everything came back to that one issue; the villagers had no food, which was immediately apparent when examining the meals Castor just distributed.

"Oho, dried fish! And tubers? A feast! Lord Tolam is generous today," a portly man laughed. It was sarcasm, but good-natured. In a famine, there was no room for real animosity between villagers unless someone wasn't doing their share of work. The leader of the village, Lord Tolam, tried to emphasize unity as a solution to the ever-present terror and uncertainty that gripped each of his subjects.

"A thousand blessings on him! And Castor too, who flew up to the wall to deliver this meal with all haste. Truly magnificent, clearly a herald of the gods himself!"

Castor chuckled sheepishly at the praise, exhaustedly dropping onto the rough stone a bit harder than he intended, judging from the ache in his tailbone. "Hello, Bil," he panted, brushing away a strand of thick hair that clung to the side of his face with sweat.

Bil was once a cobbler, although the boisterous man rarely had the chance to practice his trade anymore. Looking around, Castor noticed that nearly all the watch was comprised of ordinary townsfolk. "Where are the other guards?"

"Preparing for a sea hunt," said Marian, the only member of the Noble Guard present. Castor's eyes lit up. A sea hunt was the most exciting thing that could happen in Toriath nowadays.

"When's it going to happen?" he asked eagerly.

Marian rolled her eyes. "Boys, I swear," she muttered to no one in particular. "Don't get too excited. It's not until tomorrow."

Castor wasn't too let down. It wasn't like he'd be any busier tomorrow than he was today. Marian still watched him with an eyebrow raised.

"You know, you really shouldn't watch those."

"It's okay, really!" Castor said hastily, trying to placate her. "I watch them from the roof of an old building near enough to the beach. But not too near." He corrected himself hastily, realizing that his words might have the opposite effect. "I'm not in any danger and I won't distract the hunting party, is what I'm trying to say."

She sighed. "Yeah, well, that's good. But still, I don't think that's something a kid should watch. It's really dangerous, and if it goes wrong... you shouldn't have to see that."

Castor clipped his budding frustration with a deep breath. His sister said the same thing often, and he knew that it was because she cared for him. Marian did too, in the same way any decent person cared for someone they suffered alongside for years.

"I get it. Thank you for your concern." He tried to mask his annoyance. "I'm seventeen years old though. I've watched you all hunt a million times now, and it's been months since anyone's gotten even a scratch! Besides, I want to be a Noble Guard too someday. Shouldn't I watch the Order in action?"

Though his ambition had faded in the face of reality, he still dreamed of joining the prestigious Order of the Noble Guard. Castor used to idolize the wandering Heroes that occasionally passed through the village many years ago, and after they disappeared, his admiration had transferred to the members of the Noble Guard who protected his people from monsters daily.

Marian chuckled. "I bet you think you sounded real mature just now. Only a teenager would think that being seventeen makes you an adult." Despite her levity, there was a sadness in her eyes that Castor couldn't quite place. Maybe it was because she regretted how quickly Castor was forced to grow up. Or maybe it was a fear that he, along with the rest of the village, wouldn't survive long enough for him to realize his dream.

"Oi, herald!" called out Bil. "Why don't you take a little bit of my food? I'm sure you've been running around town all day."

Castor hastily declined the offer. "Oh, no thank you, sir, I just ate." He always made sure to have lunch before this daily task, just so he wasn't tempted to steal from the watchmen on his way to the wall. He wasn't a thief by nature, but starvation did strange things to the mind.

However, even directly after lunch, he still wasn't satisfied. There wasn't enough food to go around for more than two meals a day, and even those were rather meagre. He lived in a constant state of hunger, as did everyone else.

"Sir he calls me!" Bil said raucously. "No need for that, boy. I'm not a guildmaster no more. Not with no guild to master!" Even as the portly man cackled at his joke, many others averted their gaze in discomfort. Most Torians had lost their livelihoods when the village was forced to close its gates, and few were able to laugh about it like Bil could.

"Anyway, take the food!" he continued. "You're a growing boy. You definitely need it more than I!" He laughed again and slapped his rotund belly, which was a shrinking remnant of prosperous days gone by.

Castor still declined but thanked the man profusely. Marian nodded at Bil, who must have heard the boy's optimistic words.

The cobbler was hyperaware of the state of his village. Bil knew his usefulness was dwindling. The population of the town decreased by the month, and new shoes rarely needed to be made. There was no leather and very little wood to make them out of anyway. Additionally, a lessening population left a surplus of goods, including shoes. His people had much more of a need for a young, fit body.

Castor wasn't aware of the byplay between the two adults; he was too busy catching his breath and appreciating the view from atop the wall. It overlooked a large green field that lay just outside the village, and then further behind that, a wide expanse of forest. In the very far distance, he could just make out the form of Mount Kol and, behind it, faint outlines of the other peaks of Kalival, the great mountain range that split Alaya nearly in half. Though sweltering, the day was beautiful, with just a few puffy clouds in the sky. However, he had no excuse to dawdle further, so the boy excused himself and made the much easier climb back down to the ground level.

In the past, only members of the Noble Guard took up watch duty. Now, the Order just didn't have the manpower, so they had to rely on a rotation of civilian volunteers. They still tried to keep as many members of the guard on the wall as possible, and never less than one. If there was imminent danger, someone who knew protocol and could keep a clear head needed to be there to take charge. This time, it seemed that Marian had drawn the short straw.

Toriath was located on the northern coast of Alaya, the southern continent. Its circular wall, while an eyesore, was a rather impressive construct. It was built as quickly as possible, and its architects were much more concerned with function than form, so they neglected to put any thought into aesthetics or extra features like stairs.

The stone used in its construction was rather special. It formed over the course of centuries when bits of shell calcified and merged together to create a porous rock, which, instead of breaking when struck with enough force, compacted. The stone had been mined off the coast, from large quarries still visible right outside the western side of the wall. When it came to defensible materials, shellstone was one of the most resilient, and it had been the village's saving grace against several opposing armies equipped with siege weapons in the distant past. Now, it protected them from a different form of enemy.

Empty sack in hand, Castor climbed back down the staircase, which led to the main gate, and made his way down the deserted main road. This stretch used to be known as the marketplace, where vendors would sell their merchandise to neighbours and foreigners visiting the village. The market was the first thing a person would see as they walked through the gates, and it was once characterized by its vibrant atmosphere and colourful tent awnings, neither of which were present anymore.

Truthfully, the entire concept of "selling things" and even money in general had fallen to the wayside. Gold was worthless if you couldn't eat it, and everyone in the village played a vital role in each other's survival. Besides, there were very few villagers alive still anyway, and those who survived either became very close friends or bitter enemies.

Castor walked down the marketplace until he reached the Keep, which was a massive rectangular building made out of grey shellstone that sat at the dead centre of the village. Instead of entering the building, he circled partially around it and took a right down another street that ran perpendicular to the marketplace. While not as wide, this was another main street that separated two of the four village quadrants.

Toriath was divided into four quadrants based on cardinal directions: southwest, southeast, northwest and northeast. The gate faced true south, so now Castor made his way east to complete his next errand. Soon, he had reached his destination, the Park, which was just before the eastern stretch of the village wall.

As far as parks went, this one was rather disappointing. It was basically just a slightly raised mound, not even ten square meters in diameter. However, the grass was a vibrant, deep green, and the single tree that grew in the centre—the only tree that still existed within the village walls—was large and healthy. It had to be, to support the multiple, heavy bulbs that hung down from its sturdy branches. The largest one was just bigger than his torso and would probably drop soon.

Crouched on the lawn was a woman who seemed to be playing in the grass. Truthfully, she was hard at work, and Castor sat down in the shadow of a building so as not to distract her. She was sprinkling white crystals, which Castor knew to be salt, onto the grass in certain patterns. There was a triangle around the tree, surrounded by a hexagon. Three more triangles pointed into every other side of the hexagon, the inner tips meeting with each point of the inner triangle. The woman was putting in the finishing touches by using a stencil to place angular runes that filled two gaps left inside the border of the hexagon. Castor couldn't see most of the design from his vantage point, but he was intimately familiar with it.

When the woman completed the matrix, she laid an object at each of the three outermost points of the triangles. Then, she knelt by the tree and withdrew a slip of paper and a flint and iron fire starter from a pouch she wore around her waist. She lit the slip in her right hand on fire, and hastily placed her left on the nearest side of the hexagon, in between two triangles. When the fire had nearly consumed the paper, she dropped it on the line next to her hand.

The paper seemed to explode as the fire consumed it, but in an odd way. The glowing red ember turned a metallic silver and let out a soft pop, almost like when lighting a stream of gas on fire. The woman, expecting it, didn't flinch. In a flash, the same shade of silver rushed out from the point the paper touched, along the lines and to the objects in each triangle. It was difficult to see in the noon sun, but the entire matrix glowed for a moment.

When it stopped, nothing seemed to have changed, but as he looked closely, Castor thought that the blades of grass and the leaves on the tree had become an even deeper green. That was likely confirmation bias though, as the change should be too slight to discern.

The woman seemed to shudder from her kneeling position, and Castor ran over to support her before she could fall face-first into the bark of the tree. Her hair, which was drawn together into six tight buns, roughly dug into his bicep as he tried to hold her steady.

"I'm fine, I'm fine," she said to Castor. Her words slurred a bit. "Jus' gimme a sec." The woman was named Jayna, and she was the closest thing the village had to a ritual master. As such, she was considered one of the most important people in the village. She was also Castor's sister.

Jayna had taught her brother a fair bit about her craft. She utilized a type of energy called ambiance to grant certain effects or alter the state of her surroundings. Ambiance was named so simply because it was everywhere, freely flowing through all types of matter. At least, it normally did. Centuries ago, humans learned to use rituals, like the one that Jayna just performed, to subjugate ambiance and use it for their own purposes.

The ritual that Jayna conducted was very basic. It drew ambiance from their surroundings into the matrix. Life fed off ambiance, so the trees and grass would grow faster and healthier. However, performing that ritual shouldn't have taken such a heavy toll on Jayna. Castor had assisted her in performing this same ritual every day for almost a year now, but within the last month or so, he noticed that it was affecting her a lot more than it used to. Whenever he tried to ask her about it, she had always played it off as something inconsequential, but today was by far the worst he had ever seen her react to the process.

"What's going on?" he demanded.

His sister gasped against his shoulder, trying to regain her breath, and took several large gulps of water from a skin she had attached to her belt. She seemed to be mulling over how to answer his question.

"Ambiance moves like heat," she finally began. "It drifts slowly from areas of high concentration to areas of low concentration. Each day I drag the ambiance back into this Park, but more and more of it escapes deep underground, out of my reach. A small portion is replenished from the ocean and the forest, but not at the same rate. The amount that the land can no longer supply is taken out of my own body's ambiance stores." She chuckled. "Since I've been doing this every day, I haven't had time to fully recover."

"You need a break!"

"I do," she conceded. She stood up, and Castor rose hastily as well when she swayed a bit. "I'm good, you don't need to hold me up. I've talked to Lord Tolam about it. I was gonna wait for that one to split." She gestured at the largest bulb, which, due to its weight, had pulled the branch close to the ground. Its outer membrane had turned slightly translucent, which was another sign that it was close, and Castor could see something moving inside it. "But I'll still have to conduct these rituals maybe once every other day. I don't know how that will affect the tree's growth though."

Castor took a deep breath and prepared to restart an old argument. "Let me help."

"No way."

Realizing no explanation was forthcoming, he set his shoulders and stood as tall as he could. She was the same height, but at least he could meet her in the eyes. "Look, the tree is important. I know that! It's one of the only reasons we're able to still feed ourselves! But you can't do this on your own anymore. Please, let me help!"

"No, you can't help. This ritual is too difficult for you!" This wasn't meant as a slight against Castor. Difficulty was one of two metrics used to judge the requirements of rituals. It described the amount of internal ambiance required from the activator to carry out a ritual. The other metric was cost, which referred to the physical items that were needed. While Jayna claimed that the difficulty of this ritual was high, the cost was rather low: three bones from a sea monster killed last month and the salt used to create the matrix.

"No, it's not, this isn't a difficult ritual at all!" Castor persisted.

"It is now, moron! Since there's not enough ambiance in the land, I have to supply the rest of what the tree needs. You can't hold enough ambiance to do what I need to."

Since living creatures grew to depend on ambiance, their bodies adapted to hoard the energy within them. So while it flowed into them as easily as it did through anything inorganic or dead, it was a lot slower to leave their bodies. Up to a point, at least. A being could only keep a certain amount of ambiance within themselves, and the size of any individual's reserves depended on a multitude of factors.

Castor shook his head in disbelief. "You're only seven years older than me. There's no *way* you have that much more ambiance than I do."

"*Yes,* I *do*. A person's capacity doesn't just depend on age, body type or other physical attributes. It's something you can train like a muscle. I've been doing rituals for so long, my capacity has grown a lot larger. The amount of ambiance that ritual took out of me would have drained you dry, plus some."

This too was news to Castor. "Why the *hell* didn't you tell me?" he shouted. "I could have been training earlier! I could have made my reserves big enough to help you!"

"Why the hell do you think I made you practice those channelling rituals?"

That brought him up short. Jayna used to have him perform rituals to seal away some of his body's ambiance into stones. However, "You made me stop doing that half a year ago! You said I mastered it."

She sighed wearily. "There's no such thing as mastering a ritual, it's just a matter of replication. I wanted you to deplete your reserves, so they could grow back larger. I had you stop when the problems with my rituals began. Even though you were sealing away your own body's ambiance, it still took some out of our surroundings. I couldn't afford any waste."

He didn't have anything to say to that. Still, it hurt to see his sister, who had raised him since their father died, struggling so much. There had to be something he could do. At the very least, he could start by helping with cleanup.

He went down to the side of the park and picked up a bucket where Jayna had left it. Out of the corner of his eye, he saw his sister relax, having taken this to mean that their argument was over.

"Why didn't you bring the other bucket for me?" she asked him.

"Sit down. Please, at least let me do this." It was fair, so she nodded.

Castor went around the matrix and, to the best of his ability, scooped the salt up as delicately as he could manage. Objects used in rituals became brittle, so the white flakes crumbled under his lightest touch.

Jayna used salt because it was one of the precious few resources they had that was not in short supply. Since the village was situated right next to the ocean, they could evaporate off the water and use the salt for many things, including their rituals. Any powdery material was good for making ritual matrices because it could be shaped and connected easily. Unfortunately, salt was bad for plants, so they tried to clean up as much as possible. Luckily, they had a bit of help.

After resting for a bit, Jayna left and returned with the village's only livestock, three cows that lived in a pen near the park. They were let out to feed on the verdant pasture, but, as luck would have it, they also loved to lick up salt. Between the four of them, they were done in under an hour.

As they were about to leave, Castor tried one last time. "Isn't there some way we could split the cost of the ritual?"

"No, kid. If another person is included in a ritual, the cost is split evenly. You might be able to make it through one, but at that point, why bother? Plus, I just don't want to take the risk of something happening to you."

Then, Castor made one last, terrible connection. "Jayna? What happens if you use up too much of your own ambiance in a ritual?"

She didn't answer. He felt like an idiot for never thinking about it before.

He thought of their father, who was the last ritual master. He taught Jayna everything she knew, but he died before he could pass on most of his skills. Castor was eleven at the time and was told that their father had succumbed to a deadly illness. He had never questioned it.

Castor looked at his sister, who took care of him, taught him, and provided for him all his life at the expense of her own well-being. She wouldn't meet his gaze. He knew then that she was planning to sacrifice her life for the village—for *him*—and there wasn't anything he could do about it.

Chapter Two
Whispers of Salvation

The Keep was the largest building in Toriath, and it even towered over the village's walls. It was a rectangular stone structure that sat in the dead centre of the village, and it performed a variety of functions.

Its roof was a defensible position upon which, in times of war, archers would be stationed to hold back an encroaching army. However, there were very few archers remaining, and arrows were in even shorter supply.

The upper middle part of the Keep was the lord's living quarters, which he had stopped using. Lord Tolam had decided to move to a vacant house nearby, since he spent so much time labouring amongst his subjects. He claimed that, after a hard day's work of manual labour, he didn't want to have to climb up eight flights of stairs to be able to sleep in his own bed. That may very well be true, but the people took the gesture the way it was intended: as a show of solidarity.

The next segment was the counsel and war room. Once, this space would have been used to meet with lords of neighbouring settlements or other dignitaries, and in times of conflict, it was a place for the war council to convene. Guildmasters would also use this room to occasionally meet with one another or settle disputes. Like the upper segments, this one was abandoned.

Below that, directly above the ground floor, was the

armoury. This floor was still very much in use, as the Noble Guard's extra equipment and arms were stored on tables and wall mounted racks. Even the floors were covered in weaponry because the guards ran out of room to put it all. This surplus wasn't caused by the forging of new equipment; it was because their previous owners kept dying.

The ground floor was once an open space used as a town meeting place, but several years ago it had been fashioned into a large dining hall. It was lined with mismatched tables and chairs, which had been donated by many of the villagers. A fair number of them came from Lord Tolam himself, and around half were taken out of homes left vacant.

People were allowed two visits to the dining hall daily. Those who performed jobs that required them to stay in a specific location were delivered dry food by someone else, usually Castor. However, everyone preferred to go to the dining hall because the cooks did their best to use their meagre ingredients to make tastier, or at least more filling, meals.

The siblings went up to the table that the cooks had commandeered, and were served mashed root vegetables, grilled mushrooms and a tiny portion of fish. By Castor's standards, this was a fantastic meal. He had eaten a lot worse over the last week. Plus, he loved mushrooms.

Jayna received an extra half scoop of root vegetables. She was considered to have a physically demanding job, just like the guards, the miners down below and the farmers in the southwest quadrant.

"Do you want my mushrooms?" Jayna murmured to him. Castor just glared at her in response. Even after their prior argument, she was still trying to give up her much-needed food for him. She got the message.

"Jayna!" a deep voice called from across the room. It was Lord Tolam, who was inconspicuous aside from the guard seated to his left. Jayna once told Castor that Lord Tolam made a point to eat in the dining hall at different times each day, so everyone could see that he was served the same portions as everyone else. Castor privately believed that he was scared of his own people and wanted to make sure they had no reason to revolt. He waved them over.

Lord Tolam looked like an entirely ordinary man, especially after he had stopped wearing clothes that befit his station. His hair, which was once obscured by a ceremonial headpiece, was balding, and he no longer wore the ornate robe that hid how soft his body was, although admittedly it was a lot less so now. He also stopped bothering to shave regularly, and Castor could see that his facial hair grew rather sparse.

One thing that had not changed, however, was his demeanour, which, by all accounts, should've been what changed the most. He was always a cheerful and earnest man, and he maintained that attitude even as he and his people starved. Castor, like most of the village, realized he was trying to stay optimistic and project confidence to his subjects. However, it did come across as distasteful at times.

"Jayna! And Castor too! How are you both today?"

"Good, my lord," Jayna said demurely. She was usually rather brusque, so it always came as a surprise to Castor when he saw her interact with Lord Tolam. He supposed it was more fitting, considering his title. Also, while Jayna held a lot of influence in the village, she was quite a bit younger than the guildmasters and her other peers in positions of power, which might have also contributed to her diffidence.

"Good as well, my lord." Castor tried to copy his sister's cadence.

The man sighed. "You know, that's not necessary. Not anymore."

Jayna shook her head emphatically. "I disagree. I think that showing respect to your position now is even more necessary than usual." Some of her usual steel had returned to her voice before she realized arguing with Lord Tolam made her a bit of a hypocrite, so she tacked on a sheepish, "my lord."

The man let out an unseemly snort and looked at Castor, who felt very awkward. "Quite a bit of sun today, eh? I apologize for making you climb up the wall in this heat."

"No sir. It's the least I can do."

"Still though. I know you would much prefer to be working in the tunnels."

Castor twitched. "I'm just not cut out for it, I guess. Can't swing a pick hard enough."

"Hmm." The lord looked at him in consideration. "I think it is a mark of maturity to recognize your own weaknesses. I also think that there are many other areas that you excel in."

"Like running errands?" Castor winced twice, first when his mind caught up to his mouth, and again when his sister's foot crushed his big toe. But Lord Tolam didn't seem offended, only sad.

"Perhaps in a kinder world," he muttered softly. Castor wasn't even sure he was talking to anyone. "You would be able to find your strengths and live passionately." Then his eyes focused, and he regained his usual smile.

"Let's just survive for now. I know running errands may seem trivial, but you, just like every member of this village, provide a vital service. Speaking of vital services..." He turned to Jayna. "How are preparations for tomorrow?"

"Oh, I forgot to tell you," Jayna said to her brother. "I won't be conducting the usual ritual at the tree tomorrow. I am needed elsewhere." She seemed reluctant to elaborate, but she didn't need to.

"Because of the sea hunt," Castor confirmed.

Jayna wasn't a medic, but her knowledge of rituals could stimulate healing. So, when there was a danger of serious injury, she would need to be close by with Aysomene, the village doctor.

She huffed. "So, you heard about that." Jayna tried to keep him from watching sea hunts, and, since she couldn't supervise him while they were happening, the best way to do that was by keeping him from learning they were going on. She was rarely successful.

In order to avoid a second argument today, he distracted her. "If someone does get injured, how would you heal them? With the area's ambiance the way it is."

"I have some ambiance stored in imbued crystals. I keep them in case of emergencies, but I have very few left," she said with narrowed eyes. His misdirection did not go unnoticed.

"I'm sorry, Castor," Lord Tolam interrupted. "Could I speak with your sister alone for a bit?"

Castor nodded, privately grateful. He took his plate, so far untouched, to another table across the room.

It was early evening, and the hall was mostly empty. The tunnellers, tasked to dig underground wells and retrieve water, had already finished eating and were probably asleep. They would wake up at the crack of dawn to start the cycle all over again, though Castor wondered why they bothered remaining on that strict schedule. It's not as if the rocks were going anywhere, and they worked underground so the heat was a non-issue.

Two of the last stragglers, aside from him, his sister, and Lord Tolam and his guard, were Marak and Pay, two men who sat farther down on the row of tables Castor chose. Marak was a stablehand, but his few horses had been killed and eaten long ago, so he was relegated to the role of a fisherman. It was almost a better job for him anyway, because he could sit on a boat instead of having to walk around on his weak leg, which was permanently injured by an unruly stallion before Castor was even born. Pay was another fisherman, and the two worked together frequently. They spoke in low tones, but since the room was so empty, Castor could hear them as he ate his meal.

"Don't you remember how poorly that went? The last expedition left such a heavy toll, and we didn't even get anything from it. Five guards, dead. Including my nephew."

"Look, Pay, you know I didn't mean it like that. I'm not saying we should send a lot more people to their deaths."

"Just some?" the older man bit out.

"Stop misconstruing my words," said Marak. "I'm just looking at the facts. We can't go on like this for very much longer. The crops we grow inside of our walls can't keep up with our needs, even after we burned down half of the southwest quadrant to expand our fields. The yield just isn't high enough. And you know better than anyone, we can't rely on fish anymore. Sea hunts are going to be the only way we can sustain ourselves, and that's a disaster waiting to happen. We need *something*. And that something can't be found within the village walls."

Castor was listening in on their conversation intently. Many people spoke of possible solutions to their plight, and they were always unrealistic. However, he was curious about

Marak's proposition, especially after hearing Pay's reaction.

"What could we possibly find in the woods that would improve our situation? Enough to be worth the risk?"

Marak paused before answering hesitantly. "I remember when I was a boy, back when the forest was a lot safer to travel through. My father went out to get something, I forget what. But he came back with a large sack full of fruit. It was the best fruit I ever tasted; I swear. My father told us he found them in a glade, full of bushes. He returned a couple of times and brought more and more back. Said it was like they regrew overnight. We even sold a lot of them in the market. It was the best couple years of my life. Then my father passed, and no one could ever find that meadow again. The idiot, gods rest his soul, never wrote down any directions."

The man looked at his older comrade. "If we could find that glade, and bring as many seeds back as we can, maybe we could plant them inside the village."

Pay was not convinced. "Venturing into the forest at all is a death sentence. It's been proven time and again. And, let's say this place does still exist. If we don't know where it is, we would have to wander around directionless, and that would take ages."

"Not completely directionless," Marak muttered. "I know it's east."

"Oh, east? Why didn't you say so?"

"There's no need to be like that."

"You're being a moron. There's no way an expedition party could set out on some wild goose chase through the forest. They wouldn't survive half a day."

"Well, I've been thinking. We've always sent out parties. Large groups, with armoured guards. All very slow, heavy and loud. What if we sent out, say, one or two people? Without armour, who could run quickly and hide. They might stand a much better chance."

"You want to send someone out into the forest, without armour," Pay said with derision. "If you want something so foolhardy to be done, do it yourself. Don't ask it of someone else."

"You know I could never do it, not with this leg. It was just an idea."

"A stupid one."

"We tried everything else! The way things are going, we'll all be dead in a couple of months!" Marak's voice had risen to a semi-shout.

"Keep. Your voice. Down," Pay said through gritted teeth. He looked furtively at Castor, who pretended to be engrossed in his remaining tubers.

Castor had to strain to hear his next words. "I don't care if you lost hope. Don't you dare take away anyone else's." The man pushed back his chair with a loud scrape and left. Marak followed a couple minutes later.

Jayna and Lord Tolam finished their discussion after a little longer, and then they left, putting their dirty utensils in a crate which would be taken down to the beach. Everything would be scoured with sand and salt water in preparation for tomorrow's lunch.

Jayna went home for the evening, her duties for the day complete. However, Castor still had one more task, and it was his least favourite. He walked over to the cooks and helped them take the large containers that held the last few scraps of food and put them onto a wagon. Then, he and a man named Jaram pulled it out of the hall, around the Keep, and down the road to the northwest quadrant.

As they walked, Castor's mind was abuzz. He was alarmed by Marak's words. He knew the situation in the village was bad, and he had noticed that many of the older villagers downplayed that fact around him. It infuriated him, but there was no way he would ever say so.

People likely treated Castor this way because he was the youngest person in the village. Toriath was always small, even before most of its citizens died, and thus its prosperity was never certain. Families wishing to have kids planned with one another so that they would all have children during periods of abundance. This meant that they were usually born in waves.

As a ritual master, Castor's father had the means to raise his kids no matter when they were born, so he decided not to participate in this practice, which was why Castor had no peers his age. And there were no more notably prosperous times after his birth, especially in later years. After all, it made no sense to bring a child into the world in the midst of a famine. Even if someone wanted to have a child, there was no longer any way to gather the materials to perform the Ritual of Birth.

Castor and Jaram alternated pulling the rickety cart until they reached their destination, which was a single-storey house near the centre of the quadrant. From inside, Castor could see the telltale orange glow of firelight from a candle burning. He reached out for the knob, but before he even touched it, the door seemed to open on its own accord.

Aysomene, the last medic their village had, greeted them grimly. Once upon a time, she was an unequivocally cheerful woman who would meet everyone around her with a wide smile. Castor hadn't seen that smile in years, and his sister worked with her often.

"Ah, good. You're here." Her voice was frail, as if she herself was in need of medical attention. Aysomene looked behind them at the wagon. "In the future, you can save yourself the trouble and only bring one plate. No need to lift those heavy barrels."

Castor's heart sank as he caught her hidden meaning.

"Who?" Jaram asked softly.

"Martol and Gin."

The food shortage hit the entire village hard, but none suffered as much as the elderly. Age had already weakened their bodies and starvation took an even harsher toll. Yet, the village just couldn't spare any more food, not even to save their lives. There were only three elders left, and it was with a heavy heart that Castor realized that number had fallen to one.

"Did they pass naturally?" Jaram hesitantly asked the medic.

"No," she responded, trying and failing to keep her voice steady. "No, I helped them. They decided together."

The cook gently placed a hand on her shoulder, and the woman seemed to sway, as if it weighed as much as one of the barrels he towed behind him. "The increased portion will help Basa dearly."

Aysomene didn't say anything in response, she just nodded once. Then, she shrugged off the arm and walked quickly past them, not even saying a word to Castor. In fact, she seemed unwilling to look him in the eye at all.

"Come on," Jaram said finally. "Let's not keep Basa waiting."

Leaving the wagon outside, they dished all of the food onto one plate. It looked like quite a meal by their standards; it was a triple portion after all. However, even though Castor was still hungry after his meagre dinner, he didn't think he could stomach anything.

Basa, a man nearing seventy years of age, sat upright in his bed. He stared straight ahead at the wall opposite him, even as they walked in. To his left were two other beds, each supporting two human-sized mounds wrapped in stained sheets. Castor fixed his gaze on the wall as well.

Jaram used a fork and knife to cut up the tubers and fish into bite sized pieces and crouched down next to the old man. Castor stood awkwardly by the doorway. Usually, he would do the same for another patient, but that wasn't necessary anymore.

The cook held up a first bite near Basa's mouth, but the man made no move to take it.

"I shouldn't eat any of this." The man's hoarse voice broke the heavy silence, and Jaram's hand dropped back near the plate, as if the fork had suddenly grown too heavy for him.

"That's not true!" Castor blurted out, but he couldn't articulate why he thought so.

The old man looked at him. "You're a good boy, Castor. You're very kind, you always have been." His gaze diverted back towards the wall. "My time is up. This food should go to people with a future. I've got nothing left to offer you. If I wasn't so much of a coward, I would have joined Martol and Gin."

Jaram brought the fork back up to the man's mouth. "Please just eat, for now." Then he muttered something else to the man that Castor couldn't hear, but he did notice the man's eyes flick over to where he was standing for half a second. Then, Basa took the morsel, and the next several the cook offered.

"Take the mushrooms at least," Basa said, in between bites. "They're too chewy; I couldn't eat them if I tried." He beckoned to Castor, and the boy walked mechanically to the side of the bed. With his fingers, he picked out the mushrooms and placed them into his mouth. They were hard to force down past the lump in his throat, and tears stung the corners of his eyes, although he wouldn't let them fall. He did it for Basa.

When he was finished, Castor backed away quickly and the man finished his meal in silence. Then, he and Jaram said their sombre farewells, packed up and brought the wagon back to the Keep. From there, they parted ways and Castor made his way back to his home in the northeast quadrant, knowing in his heart that he would never see Basa again.

It would be a lie to say that Castor wasn't kept up each night, drowning in despair, and tonight was even worse than usual. During the day, at least he could throw himself into his chores. There was no way to do that as he waited for sleep. For him, that was the worst part of his current way of life. Not the hunger, or the pain of strenuous labour. By far, it was the fear. Fear that he or his sister would die painfully and unavoidably. Marak was right—they were just stalling, and Castor didn't know what for.

He quashed these thoughts angrily and tried to distract himself. There was going to be a sea hunt tomorrow. Those were always fun to watch.

Any hunting or scavenging in the forest surrounding the village was perilous, so the townspeople had to turn to the ocean for most of their sustenance. Aggressive fishing had depleted the coast of most ordinary marine life, but more dangerous prey still existed just past the shallows.

A sea hunt involved luring a monster from deeper parts of the ocean onto the beach, where they would theoretically become stuck. From there, it was just a matter of killing the monster and harvesting its meat. It was still a very dangerous task, which was why only trained members of the guard were allowed to participate. Still, it was just one monster, and a much safer task than venturing beyond the walls.

The starvation and lack of resources that the village faced could all be attributed to a single truth. The entire village was under siege. Not in the traditional sense, with an enemy army that attacked and blocked all means of escape. No, the terrible force that imprisoned them within their own walls was not organized, or even human. It was an irrepressible, unending legion of giant spiders.

Chapter Three
A Plan Interrupted

Perhaps it was bias, or a narrow worldview, but the Torians wished that any kind of monster other than spiders had beset their village. Arachna, as they were properly called, varied heavily in size, and they could range from the height of a newborn calf to over twice the size of a man.

Their venom had no known antidote, and while limbs could be amputated to stop its spread, any bite to the chest, head or neck could kill in minutes. Arachna were fast too, much faster than creatures of their size had any right to be. And, their exoskeletons, while not impenetrable, could easily deflect all but the strongest and most direct blows.

They were also completely inedible, which was a terrible inconvenience for the starving village. Distasteful as it may be, other monsters, once killed, could be butchered and eaten in a pinch. Underneath this spider's armour was just a mass of foul goop, which was poisonous as well as disgusting.

One small miracle was that they were much too heavy to climb up vertical surfaces like their smaller brethren, which was the only reason Toriath hadn't been overrun already. However, if they were allowed to place their webbing, they could use it to scale any walls.

In the cover of night, the arachna would often attempt to invade the village by leaping incredibly high and connecting their thick, sticky threads to the shellstone wall before falling to the ground once again. The village had long since run out of fuel, so guards had to constantly listen for the heavy thud of spider bodies landing in the darkness. If they did, they would hastily move a boulder on a cart to the position they heard the sound from. Heavy rocks were the only ammunition available to them, and the villagers still couldn't drop them thoughtlessly. Even the slightest elevation could be a jumping point for other spiders.

Two months ago, Castor awoke to a harsh clanging late at night. It originated from an alarm bell positioned at the top of the wall, and it signified a breach in their defences. The terrified townspeople followed their set procedures and fled underground, or, in Castor and Jayna's case, into the first floor of the Keep, which they helped barricade behind them. The villagers stood pressed close together and dead silent. Castor was crammed against his sister and some other villagers he couldn't see, which only served to heighten his terror.

Over an hour passed before the guards signalled that it was safe to come out again. Though he heard varied accounts throughout the rest of the day, Castor learned what truly happened in the evening from Lord Tolam, who had called an assembly.

In the darkness, a guard identified an arachna attempting to scale the western segment of the wall. The entire watch converged upon that spot and readied themselves to defend against that attack. As that happened, another apparently struck on the exact opposite side, and somehow scaled the wall without any resistance. It attacked the guards, who were distracted by the threat below them, from behind and killed Hinor, a young man who lived very close to Castor. The guards couldn't even finish off the beast, but they did force it back over the wall.

The attack shook the entire village. Though unlikely, many were afraid that this was the first coordinated attack by the arachna, which had never shown the ability to communicate to this degree. Everyone took solace in the fact that no such attack had happened since then and hesitantly began to believe it was nothing more than bad luck.

That did little to ease anyone's grief. Even before things were so dire, the Torians were a very close-knit community, and many played at least a small part in Hinor's upbringing. Castor remembered once when Hinor and his parents came over to meet with Jayna to commission a ritual that would ward away pests. Jayna had made Castor stay and watch the proceedings, hoping to impart some of her knowledge. Hinor was in much the same boat, and they bonded over their mutual desire to get away from that boring meeting. Now he was dead.

Even beyond the tragedy of losing a well-loved member of their society, there was another layer of despair to Hinor's death. Guards were a beacon of hope for the villagers. Each of them represented a small barrier between the townspeople and the monsters that lay just beyond the gate. Losing even one was like losing a sliver of that barrier.

That was the biggest reason why Castor wanted to be a part of the Noble Guard so desperately. There were so few members left, and so many tasks around the village required their abilities. Castor wanted to join the order, not just to gain the respect that position entailed, but because he wanted to do something meaningful to help his people. Above all else, he didn't want to die here feeling useless.

He certainly felt useless when he woke up that next morning, as he joined the throng of people heading west. They were farmers, not by trade but by necessity, travelling to the southwest quadrant of the city for their hard day's work. Farms were usually held outside walled villages, but that was clearly no longer an option for the Torians.

The villagers were forced to demolish most of the houses in the southwest quadrant to make room for new fields, which was an arduous task. The houses were mostly made of wood, which was a precious commodity, so great pains were taken to extract and repurpose as much of the lumber as possible. Also, every house had at least one shellstone wall that faced the ocean. The first generation of Torians had discovered that the salty breeze that blew in from the water eroded the wood, so renovations were made to protect their homes. This, like so many other once helpful precautions, made things a lot more difficult for the starving villagers because the stone had to, at the very least, be taken away from the plots.

There were many other tasks that needed to be done to change that residential district into arable land. Castor himself had helped pick away at the compacted dirt in preparation for planting. Truly, he didn't envy the farmers in most respects. Their work was among the hardest in the village. However, their importance, just like the guards', was undeniable.

Well before reaching the farms, Castor turned right, away from the crowd, and walked towards the centre of the village. His supervisor was Dohn, a middle-aged man who was an intermediary for all the major groups in the village, including the farmers, the miners, the fishermen, the guards, Jayna, Lord Tolam himself, and, if they were active, the guilds.

Most, if not all, of these groups shared a workforce, since there were so few people to go around. Even the guild masters all helped different segments when they had no work to be done, which was most often the case since they had no materials to craft the few commodities that were still in demand. When it wasn't time to fish, the fishermen went to help farm, and when there was too little space down below, the tunnellers went to help the guard. Even Lord Tolam, when he wasn't busy with administration, spent his time floating between groups. Still, everyone had an area that they usually worked in, except for Castor. He was the only person in the village who didn't have the strength, stamina or skill to be a permanent member of any group.

Dohn first directed Castor to the fisherman's hut, which was a building that sat on the beach. The far end was open, and the small fishing boats were inside, safe from the elements, and tied to a dock that extended two hundred meters into the ocean. It had a twin as well, which was now only used by the Guards during sea hunts.

In the service of the fishermen, Castor spent his morning untangling cumbersome nets and resetting crate traps for shellfish. He was especially unenthusiastic about this chore because he knew it would be unlikely for these devices to capture even a single fish nowadays, although they would likely become tangled and activated again by the currents.

Just as he finished, Noble Guards began to trickle into the

hut to prepare for the coming sea hunt. Castor wished he had been sent to complete this chore later so that he could listen to the warriors plan and review battle tactics.

A traitorous part of him considered remaining in the hut and pretending to work on his task longer, even though he had already finished. It wasn't as if anyone would notice his absence elsewhere. However, he discarded this idea immediately. Even if a short delay wouldn't seriously hurt anyone, it went against his principles, especially since he was planning on taking a break later to watch the sea hunt. Regretfully, he left the hut, nodding respectfully to the armoured figures on the way out.

Next, he was told to collect the damaged tools that had been piled up outside the tunnel entrance below the Keep and take them to the Blacksmith's Forge, which was by far the most active guild. All of the guildhouses were located on the north half of the main street, with the Keep separating them from the marketplace.

The Keep only had one south-facing entrance, so Castor had to lug the tools around half of its perimeter before he could even make his way to the blacksmith's. He had been given a cart to do so, but it was very small with only two wheels and a short rope for him to pull. Like most appliances in the village, and people too for that matter, it was overworked and close to breaking. Its left wheel stuck often, making it turn unexpectedly, and he had to drag the whole thing until it started rolling again. And, since the cart was too small, he had to make two trips. Still, without it he would have had to make six, so it was likely worth the extra effort.

After he moved the tools, Dohn told Castor to help out the master blacksmith, who was a burly, stoic man named Musov, until noon, when he would be expected to return to complete his daily task of bringing lunch up to the villagers on the wall. Musov had him sort the tools into three categories: dull, broken metal, and broken wood. The dull tools made up the majority and would take the least amount of work, so Musov fixed those first. The other ones were much more laborious. The broken metal ones would have to be melted down again and reforged, and the broken wood ones would have to be taken apart so that the metal heads were no longer attached to the wood. Unfortunately, that last task was up to Castor.

The wooden handles had been jammed tightly into the iron heads, and this tight fit was what kept them together in the first place. It also made them incredibly difficult to disassemble. Musov told him the best way to do it was by taking one of his metal tools and hammering it into the wood from the other side. Castor found himself frequently looking up into the sky, willing noon to appear quicker. By the time he left, he had only succeeded in separating the wood from one broken tool.

Castor ate in the dining hall to stave off the worst of his gnawing hunger and picked up the food for the watchers. When he finished that errand, he would go to the park next, which was another one of his usual tasks. Since Jayna wasn't there to perform the ritual, all he had to do was let out the cattle, which would only take a short amount of time. Then, he could sneak away to watch the hunt! However, before he made it too far with the sack, Dohn called out to him again.

"When you're done at the wall, and with feeding the cattle, head to the food stores beneath the Keep for guard duty."

"What?" the young man asked incredulously. He had never been tasked with watching over the food stores before. It meant that his plans for watching the sea hunt were ruined.

"Yeah. With the Noble Guard called away for the sea hunt, we needed at least one more guard. Lord Tolam recommended you."

"Needed" was a strong word. One person could guard the food stores easily, but Lord Tolam tried to keep four guards present at a time, two common villagers and two of his guards. No one had ever tried to steal anything before, but the guards were there just to remove temptation. That was also why they tried to assign a combination of guards and other villagers.

Castor was frustrated by this turn of events, but he bit his tongue. He wouldn't dare argue with Dohn; the grim-faced man was a foot taller than him and quite imposing. Even more than that, he didn't want someone with Dohn's position to think he was a whiny brat, not when he worked so hard to be seen as dependable. Still, he was bitter about being kept from watching the sea hunt, which was probably the only exciting thing to happen in the village for the rest of the month. He was sure that his sister asked Lord Tolam to keep him busy during that time. Incensed, he went to deliver his food to those on the wall.

Making the arduous trek up the steps, he was accosted by the eager watchmen. The only two that remained the same from yesterday were Bil and Marian, who greeted him warmly, although their smiles faded when they recognized his foul mood. They didn't say anything, but they each thanked him even more sincerely than they usually did.

Then he trudged over to the park and flung open the metal gates to the cattle pens. The cows, either unnoticing or uncaring of his stormy demeanour, meandered farther up the hill to feed on the luscious grass nearest to the tree. The stubborn creatures resisted his attempts to pull them back into their places once he judged them to have eaten enough. They always walked quite well when someone gently guided them, but as soon as someone started pulling, they would dig their hooves into the ground. Castor was usually patient with them, but their behaviour only worsened his temper. By the time he got them situated and made his way to the Keep, his face was flushed, and each heartbeat felt like a crack in a pane of glass.

In the back left corner of the Keep's ground floor was a wide trapdoor that sat propped open, revealing a set of stairs that led down to the food storage room. It was a depressingly small locker that was really just an extension of the small hallway it was in, separated by an iron enforced door. This set of stairs continued down directly to the tunnels, but the food storage area had been excavated along the staircase for security and convenience, since the food was now prepared in the Keep.

In the hollowed-out alcove before the door, two other men lounged against the wall. Well, one lounged. That was Mayson, a younger fellow with a short afro and a cheery disposition. His companion couldn't have been any more different. The older man's skin was several shades lighter than that of most Torians because he rarely worked in the sun, and he bore a permanent grimace fixed above a weak chin that he tried and failed to disguise with a goatee.

This was Beesh. He was the haughty master of the Merchant's Guild, and had never lost his superiority complex even as his domain became obsolete. After all, when trade between villages became impossible, merchants were the first to lose their livelihood.

"Castor! Good to see you. You're our third, are you?"

Castor flinched from the booming tone of Mayson's voice in the narrow hall.

"*Obviously*," Beesh bit out. Castor was already in a foul mood and being forced to keep watch with Beesh would surely make it worse. He hadn't had much interaction with the man, but his sister had, and she ranted about him frequently. Even before things were this bad, Beesh had been a real piece of work. Since he and Jayna represented the heads of their sectors, they, along with the other guild masters, the captain of the guard and Dohn, made up Lord Tolam's inner council. Even though his guild was inactive, Lord Tolam still granted Beesh a position of importance, unfortunately.

Mayson either didn't hear the disrespect in Beesh's tone, or, more likely, he elected to ignore it. His dimples widened as he smiled at the boy. "I saved you a nice spot on the wall! Don't be shy."

In an exaggerated movement, he beckoned to a rough stretch of stone next to him. Despite himself, a tiny smile tugged at the corner of Castor's lips. He really did enjoy Mayson's company. The farmer was always a treat to talk to.

"You don't seem too thrilled to be here," the man rambled on. "I know, it's rather boring. But look on the bright side. It's nice and cool down here. Safe from the harsh summer sun. I suppose that would make this the dark side?"

Castor let out a long-suffering sigh. "Yeah, I suppose there's that." He crouched against the wall and rested one of his hands on the back of his neck. His skin rarely burnt, but it still radiated heat.

"I don't get much time out of the sun. I'm going to enjoy this while it lasts," Mayson said.

"You should consider enjoying it in *silence*," Beesh bit out.

Mayson shot the insufferable man a bemused glance. "Come on, Castor. Don't make me share my shift with two miserable grouches."

As Beesh glared at the farmer, Castor did feel sympathetic. "Sorry Mayson. It's just, since my sister is busy today, I had hoped to watch the sea hunt."

"I understand completely. You're a teenager, and, even more than that, you're a boy. Sorry, a man, I apologize." He waved his hands placatingly, as if expecting Castor to object to being called such. "Soldiers, fighting, monsters. That's all part of a man's romance!"

Castor wasn't too sure of that. It wasn't the blood and gore, or the actual fighting itself that was interesting to him. He loved watching the Noble Guard work in concert, almost like a dance. They all trained and rehearsed these sea hunts, and Castor appreciated their performance.

"Don't worry about missing it too much. There'll always be another, probably soon, considering how the heat is frying my plants!"

"I guess," Castor said dejectedly. They sat in silence for nearly a whole minute, and Castor messed with the leather of his bracelet, which was something he often did unconsciously when he was anxious. He found comfort in the familiar texture of the embossed leather and the metal medallion affixed to it.

"Still bummed out, huh?" At Mayson's query, Beesh whispered a curse, no doubt hoping that he had gained some peace and quiet.

"I'll tell you what," the cheerful farmer continued. "Why don't you go watch the sea hunt? Leave the guard duty to us."

Castor's eyes shot up to meet the grinning man. "I can't do that! I've been assigned a job!"

"Don't worry about it! If anyone asks, tell them that I told you to go. I'll back you up. Besides, no one's ever tried to actually steal from the stores before. It's just a precautionary thing. Us two can watch the food just fine." Mayson looked at Beesh. "Right?"

Beesh sneered back in response. "Why should I let him muck about in town when I'm stuck down here with you?"

"Because he's a kid and you're a grown-ass adult," Mayson answered pleasantly. "Why, did you have something better to do, Beesh? Important merchant business, perhaps?" The man's scowl grew even more potent.

Castor still felt hesitant, and it showed. "Ah, I know what it is!" the farmer said in mock realization. "You think we're going to steal the food as soon as you leave!" The boy hurriedly began to assure Mayson that this wasn't the case, but the mischievous man talked over him. "Fair enough, Castor, fair enough. Maybe this will convince you of my trustworthiness."

He raised his left hand to the ceiling. "I, Mayson, will not steal or otherwise disturb this village's food stores. Upon this hand, under Lior and above my heart, I swear." Then his smile grew more sincere. "Seriously, Castor. It's okay. Go on." He stepped forward and whispered into his ear, "And if Guildmaster Pig tries to stick his dirty little hooves into the food stores, I'm sure I can handle him on my own."

That was an actual concern Castor had, so he was glad Mayson had addressed it. Decision made, he thanked the cheerful man profusely and ran up the stairs.

Chapter Four
Sea Hunt

As Castor ran to the coast, he began to hear loud, irregular splashes. It seemed like the hunt had already begun.

Castor didn't set foot on the beach; at best, he would be a distraction for the Noble Guard. Instead, he went to an old house near the northwestern edge of the wall. It was the only three-storey house around, which made it considerably taller than the others surrounding it. Its owners had all perished, so it sat abandoned. Taking the shellstone steps two at a time, he went up to the roof just as a shadow flew overhead.

There was another mighty splash as the projectile landed in the ocean. Looking upwards behind him, Castor saw its source. On top of the wall was a derelict catapult, which was currently being reloaded with stone. It was a relic from a different time, when Toriath had to fear bands of marauders or even rival armies. It was useless against the spiders, who were too nimble and never attacked en masse anyway. The catapult was on wheels and had been rolled to the extreme western end of the village wall.

Since the village was situated on the coast, the original architects had decided that it was necessary to extend the semicircular wall into the shallows of the ocean, so as to discourage sea-based attacks. As far as anyone knew, it was never relied on to fulfill this function, but it came in handy under these circumstances.

The crew manning the catapult had finished reloading the weapon and fired once more, sending another stone twice as large as Castor's head into the ocean. The purpose of this seemingly futile action was to disturb a sea monster resting in the deep. If it was unsuccessful, the hunt would fail. If it did succeed in rousing a monster, and it approached anywhere except between the two piers, that was even worse.

Castor made himself comfortable on the roof, and leaned up against a raised basin, which was a feature of many houses in the village. These basins were used for collecting salt. They would be filled with seawater which the sun would evaporate off, leaving its minerals behind.

Salt was the lifeblood of the village, and its uses were numerous. Of course, the most obvious one was to season food. Even when the village was at its most prosperous, almost no one was wealthy enough to be able to afford spices or herbs, so salt was the only seasoning they had.

Another use was for rituals. Although this wasn't a huge facet in most people's lives, salt was close to a perfect material for Jayna, and occasionally Castor, to create their matrices. Since it was a powder, they could shape it in any way they pleased, and it was a good conduit for ambiance as well. Castor wasn't sure why, but salt naturally contained more ambiance than sand, dirt, ashes, sawdust or any other flexible material they had access to, although rituals could be performed with these materials or any others as far as he knew.

The greatest use the village had for salt was preservation. When meat went through special processes, such as drying, curing or brining, they could last a lot longer without rotting, even at room temperature. All these processes required salt, so it needed to be collected in large quantities. The bowl that Castor currently leaned against was for private use by the family that once called this place home, but the village had its own, much bigger collection site on top of the salt room, the building dedicated to preserving meats. Around half of their catch today would be taken to the salt room after it was butchered.

If they were successful in drawing anything's attention,

anyway. Castor kept his eyes on the water around where the rocks were being thrown. After the first couple sea hunts he watched, he realized that there was never any warning to signify a beast's approach.

Even though he was prepared for it, Castor still jumped when tentacles suddenly burst from the surface of the water. They were soon followed by the head of the beast, which let out a grating screech. The sound was cut off when the next boulder, which was already on its way, hit it directly.

Castor almost laughed. He had never seen a boulder actually hit a monster before, though he wasn't foolish enough to think that took the beast out of commission. The monster that emerged was a wadom, undoubtedly the most dangerous creature that roamed in this part of the ocean.

Two soldiers stood on each end of the pier, each armed with a crossbow. When the monster presented its bleeding head once again, the first man on the left let loose his first bolt. Immediately, he switched places with the soldier behind him, laid his instrument against the wood dock and worked quickly to reload it. The monster looked at its attacker and let out another screech as it darted towards the first dock. Then, the first soldier on the right shot at the wadom, hitting it again near its base. It redirected its attention to that woman, who again switched with the soldier behind her.

The bolts probably couldn't even penetrate its thick layer of skin and fat, but injuring the beast wasn't the archers' goal. They needed to draw it in closer, so they could lure it into just the right position.

In quick succession, the second guard on each pier shot, and these ones retreated to the rest of their force after they pulled their triggers, knowing they wouldn't have a chance to shoot again.

The first two had finished reloading and were steadily backing away as the wadom rushed forward. Each got their last shot off before they too retreated to rejoin the rest of the force, one narrowly outrunning the sharp end-spike of a tentacle that slammed into the pier behind him. Castor imagined that would leave a sizable gash in the wood.

The beast was successfully corralled in between the two

piers, but it had noticed that the ocean had become too shallow for it to manoeuvre well. It stopped approaching and screeched, its writhing tentacles hitting nothing but air. It wasn't willing to fight outside of its element, but, unfortunately for the wadom, the guards didn't give it a choice.

With a blur of grey, the soldiers released their greatest weapon. It was another battle construct, like the catapult. However, this one was made recently and had a much different effect. Instead of throwing a blunt object in an arc, this one shot a massive, deadly-sharp harpoon in a straight line.

Many had worked to build the monstrosity, but Musov, its chief architect, would cheerfully admit that it was the worst thing he ever crafted. However, it was the best they could do with the limited resources they possessed.

Musov had tried to replicate the effect of a ballista, a siege weapon that resembled an oversized crossbow. Ballista were made primarily out of flexible wood, of which they had none. The cord, from which the projectile would be fired, would be made out of rope. Again, they had none. What they did have was some repurposed lumber from old houses, a lot of stone, and, surprisingly, a fair bit of iron. While metal was usually in high demand, the massively decreased population left a surplus in the form of nails, cutlery, tools, equipment, and many other random pieces.

Everyone jokingly called the final product the Bastardista. Instead of pliable arms, to which the drawstring would be attached on a normal ballista, there was just a single channel elevated in the air upon a structure of wood and stone. Likewise, the drawstring wasn't actually a string at all, but a chain made up of rectangular links and forged out of inferior metal. When the machine was unfired, the chain was slack and drawn through each hole in the side of the channel, which formed a 'V' in the back of the machine. Nestled in the peak of the chain was a wooden block that would guide the dart. It wasn't visible because there was a metal covering over the length of the channel to ensure that the chain didn't push the block and dart up and away, causing a misfire.

The channel itself was a monstrous three meters long. The chain drawstring, as it exited the channel at its very front, ran over two pulleys, which in turn connected to a heavy stone weight underneath the contraption. When the guards chose to fire, they knocked out the wood from beneath the weight, causing it to fall towards the beach, and even further into a hole that had been dug to receive it.

The wicked dart, tipped with gigantic barbs, was dragged by the chain slowly at first, before it picked up speed as gravity accelerated the descent of the colossal stone weight. By the time it exited the contraption, it was nearly a blur.

The hunters had absolutely no way to aim the damn thing, as it was fixed at its base. That's why it was crucial for the guards to lure the monsters into the exact right location. Luckily, they had a rather large target. The dart pierced the top of the wadom's centre of mass, the sharpened barbs each slicing through its skin and blubber and preventing the dart from coming back out. The wadom screeched, in real pain for the first time, though not nearly incapacitated.

There would be no second shot. They had no other darts, and it took ages and a lot of manpower to raise the weight back up again. But, once again, the dart's main purpose was not to kill the enemy.

Attached at the tail end of it was another chain. It was completely slack when fired, but now it was near taut. It connected to a large winch, and six men struggled to reel the beast onto the beach. It was a very slow process, and some of the men had to be switched out as they reached their limit.

The wadom fought back against every centimetre they won, and its warbling cries reverberated off the beach. Less than ten meters away from the shore, the barb ripped free from the creature, dragging out a chunk of pale pink flesh, reminiscent to that of a fish.

Castor winced from atop his perch. That was not ideal. The hunters would have much preferred to get the beast closer to the sand, so that they could truly beach it, and perhaps not have to get within tentacle range at all as it eventually died. As it was, the creature could probably wriggle itself back into the sea if it was allowed to do so.

After all their effort so far, and their desperate need for food, the Guards had absolutely no intention of letting it go. The armoured figures rushed to the beast and formed a semicircle around it. Four rushed along the piers to get further behind it.

The Noble Guard had strategies for dealing with every monster that they could encounter during a sea hunt. When hunting a wadom, they had to prepare for a long, drawn out fight. The problem was those damned tentacles. There were nine of them, and they seemed to flail around randomly, which made them completely unpredictable.

To counter them, the guards formed pairs. Of each, one member focused on offence, wielding a long polearm to stab at the beast from a distance. The other was focused on defence, and wielded a heavy, rectangular shield. This one was in full command, and constantly gave directions and orders to the other. The safety of each Guard was the number one priority, even over the success of the hunt.

One of the Guard's major disadvantages was that their shields could only be worn on one arm, and they were much too heavy to switch arms in time to defend against the wadom's whiplike tentacles, which could attack from any direction. They needed to step fully in front of their partners to defend against most attacks, which was very difficult to do quickly.

By far, the most dangerous place to be was on the docks. The wooden platforms were considerably higher than the beach, and guards positioned there were far away from their fellows, which left them exposed. However, the same held true for the monster. Due to their height advantage and improved access to the wadom, they had the opportunity to deal a lot more damage. Since this position was so perilous, it only made sense to place the most skilled fighters on the pier.

On the left was Bani, who was exceptionally tall and muscular. Her skin was covered in scars, mementos of countless battles won, mostly against monsters. Her head, currently obscured by a metal helmet, was completely shaved, and Castor had never seen her entirely without armour and some weapon. She was the Captain of the Noble Guard, meaning she was a subordinate only to Lord Tolam. Her partner was Rohn, who was young but very talented. Castor watched in awe as, in a remarkable show of coordination, Bani and Rohn spun back to back and Rohn used the momentum to crash his shield into a tentacle that Castor couldn't even follow the movement of from his perch two hundred meters away.

On the right was Tomasoh, a mountain of a man. He stood at least half a head over every other member of the Noble Guard and thrust his polearm with explosive force. Castor wouldn't have been surprised if each blow could have punched a hole right through an enemy shield. He was guarded by Fanda, another veteran. He refused to wear a helmet, because he said it obscured his vision too much.

Castor couldn't really distinguish the soldiers on the beach from one another. They wore the same sets of armour, and helmets to boot, which obscured any defining features.

What *was* very apparent was that the guards were winning. They received very few injuries themselves, but the wadom's injury from the Bastardista was nearly fatal. It surely would have died without any interference, although without the guard's actions, it would have escaped back into the sea, and its body would have become unrecoverable. Its other biggest injury was delivered by Tomasoh, who was somehow able to use the minuscule axe head at the end of his polearm to sever half a meter off the end of a tentacle.

The wadom was slowing down. Its shrieks were intermixed by another harsh sound, almost like it was gasping for breath. Maybe it was, Castor realized. Did wadom have gills? They must, if they lived in the ocean. That massive form probably couldn't breathe well this far in the shallows.

Its sluggish movements finally stopped, and the soldiers all let out a massive cheer. Those that had them thrust their polearms into the air. From the roof, Castor gleefully joined them. He threw his arms up and yelled, sharing in the Guard's success.

The Guards on the beach huddled together, pounded each other on the back and revelled in their victory. Some of the bystanders on the beach began to surge forward. Most of them were fishermen preparing to butcher the wadom, but Castor also saw Lord Tolam, his sister, and a couple others.

Since Castor was so high up, and because he was still turned towards the ocean, he was the first to see the movement. Terror gripped him, and he shouted.

"Behind you!"

The monster twitched, and, quick as lightning, a single tentacle flung out around its left side. It arced, hitting Tomasoh in the back, and the hard spike at its tip pierced his armour, lifting the giant man up off the ground.

The guards roared, grabbed their dropped weapons and charged the beast in a fury, but all Castor could focus on was Tomasoh, suspended in midair, chest facing up, and head and limbs dangling limply down towards the rotting wood of the pier.

The creature was too weak to defend against the onslaught, as iron tips drove into its eyes and torso, and it soon died for real, its tentacles dropping into the sand, including the one that had speared Tomasoh. His body slid off the spike, and his peers rushed to retrieve him. Two of them dragged him to the sand, and Jayna and Aysomene ran from their places far up the beach to meet him.

Castor was too far away to hear what was being said, even as he crouched at the edge of the roof. Aysomene hurriedly fumbled with Tomasoh's armour, trying to gain access to the fount of blood that created a crimson trail against the pale-yellow sand. Castor saw his sister hurriedly laying out shapes in salt. In her hand was a round stone, which he knew to be imbued with lifesaving ambiance.

Tomasoh pushed Aysomene away, and, off balance, she fell backwards onto the bloody sand. Then he waved his hand through the salt matrix, wiping away the lines that he could reach. Castor saw Tomasoh's mouth move, and his sister and Aysomene stopped fussing over the man. Jayna put away her stone.

Castor had a good idea of what was said. He probably told them his wound was fatal, and that they shouldn't waste precious resources like Jayna's crystal. He probably told them to let him give his final service. Of course, they would.

The boy dropped to his knees, ignoring the small pain as they scraped against the rough stone roof. He cried as he realized their barrier had just gotten quite a bit thinner.

Chapter Five
Nothing to Lose

The news of Tomasoh's death spread quickly throughout the village. Lines of silent people followed the funeral procession, farmers walked back from the southwest quadrant and tunnellers climbed their way up through the basement of the Keep. Castor, eyes red, made his way to his sister at the front of the procession, right behind Tomasoh's corpse. It was supported on a makeshift stretcher, carried by a grim-faced Bani, Camah and Rikava, two other members of the guard, and Fanda, who was weeping openly.

Jayna grabbed her brother's hand. Neither was sure if it was to comfort him, or to comfort her.

"Did you see?"

Castor kept quiet, and Jayna squeezed his hand again before turning forward. Their destination was the Park, which led them all the way through the village to the near opposite side. People joined the procession; some walked alongside them for a while before leaving, while others stayed with them and stood right outside the border of the Park.

Tomasoh had no family by blood. His parents were also members of the Noble Guard and had died in service many years ago. He was the only one left of that strong line, but that didn't mean he was alone. His fellow guards were his family.

The pallbearers laid Tomasoh down at the foot of the tree. Each said their goodbyes, and Fanda took the longest before kissing the man on his forehead and stepping outside the grass. Castor felt each of Fanda's sobs permeate his body, and it spurred him to work in a frenzy. He and his sister began to construct the salt array. It was a lot like their usual matrix, with the same shapes and symbols. However, instead of three triangles pointed inward, there was only one.

Tomasoh was laid over top, both arms placed to cover the gaping hole through his stomach that still dripped blood onto the grass below. Rigor mortis had frozen his features into an expression of pain and anger so, even in death, he did not look at peace.

They didn't need any ingredients other than the salt and Tomasoh. The silent gaze of all those in mourning was fixed on the siblings and Castor worked frantically, not wanting this kind of attention. When they were finished, Jayna lit a catalyst and dropped it onto the salt next to her other hand.

The whole thing lit up with soft, silvery light. Once again, it was difficult to see anything change, except for Tomasoh's already pale skin, which lost its little remaining colour.

Though he was already dead, Tomasoh performed one final service for his village. Instead of letting it change and dissipate with time, he sacrificed all the ambiance remaining in his body to help nourish the tree.

The attendees grieved, mostly in silence. Only the sobs of his fellow soldiers could be heard. Suddenly, a loud *rip* broke the solemnity.

Startled, the villagers looked towards its source. It was the tree, or, more specifically, the bulb Jayna had pointed out the previous day as being close to splitting. Sure enough, a big tear was beginning to stretch along the crease that ran vertically down the pod. It abruptly ripped apart and a small form dropped onto the ground, which slid a bit down the gentle hill.

Jayna ran to it as the crowd began to murmur. She wiped some of the excess slime off its matted, brown fur, and supported its shaking legs as it tried to stand. It was a newborn calf.

Most of the villagers knew that it was a coincidence. The pod had been ready to split for some time now, and maybe the ambiance given by Tomasoh in his final service had given it a little push. However, to all those observing, it felt as if

Tomasoh himself was telling them not to despair. Fanda's sobs only grew louder.

The day carried on, like it always did. There was no time for everyone to grieve properly, and any mourning had to be carried out under the harsh sun, or, in the case of those working underground, with a pick in hand.

Castor stayed at the Park with his sister, helping clean up from Tomasoh's final service. Jayna tended to the newborn calf, letting it feed on sunlight and lap up water. It couldn't eat grass yet, since it was a newborn, but it was still capable of creating its own food for now.

The pallbearers were gentle as they lifted Tomasoh back up onto the stretcher. His body had lost all its ambiance, so, like the sea monster bones and the salt the day before, he became brittle. He would have to be cremated, as the ancestral burial grounds were well beyond the village walls.

Castor scooped up the crumbling salt much more meticulously than he usually did, trying to collect each particle. He felt that if any bit dissolved into the soil and hurt the tree, then it would be like he spat on Tomasoh's sacrifice. He grew frustrated as he tried and failed to pick out one particular flake that had fallen deep between the blades of grass.

He had always thought he knew how bleak his future was. All this time, he patronizingly pretended to play along with the adults when they put on a farce of cheer and hopefulness. Whatever made them happy.

How wrong he was. It turned out that there was a shred of hope he didn't even realize he still carried, which was rooted in his faith in the Noble Guard. He believed that, even as the crops failed and their fishing nets stayed empty, the Guard could continue to hunt and kill sea monsters without fail. And then Tomasoh, one of the strongest among them, died.

It was just a mistake. It won't happen again. Those thoughts rang hollow in his mind. How well would the guards fare in future hunts without one of their best members? Who would die next? How many could they lose before the guards would become unable to carry out sea hunts at all?

Everyone else in the village had already known. They *knew* how dangerous the hunts were, and how prone to failure they could be. That's why his sister, Marian and so many others didn't want him to watch them. It wasn't because they didn't want to expose him to violence. It was just an extension of their efforts to protect him from the truth.

They were all going to die.

He had known that already. Or at least, he knew it was a likely possibility. It just never sank in until now. Never before had he realized how certain his death was, and how quickly it was approaching. Castor couldn't help thinking about the conversation he had overheard in the dining hall between Marak and Pay. Looking back at it through the lens of his current understanding, Marak's words began to make a lot of sense.

There was no food in the village. There was no way to obtain any more within its walls, and they needed to look elsewhere or die.

The main obstacle was that the arachna held dominion over the forest. Any expedition outside the village walls within the last two years ended in disaster, with many casualties. Castor didn't know much about how the preparation and execution of these expeditions went though. What were their objectives? How big was the group? What equipment did they bring with them?

He was inclined to believe what Marak said, that they travelled in a large group with heavy armour. *Of course* that wouldn't work. The spiders were fast; he saw that much when he glimpsed them a couple times from atop the wall. Definitely fast enough to outpace someone burdened with twelve kilos of armour plus supplies. They were strong too; they would have to be. And armour obviously hadn't helped the slain expedition members in the past.

Now was the time to take risks, before it was too late. However, Castor believed that Pay was right as well. He couldn't ask someone to do something this risky if he wasn't willing to do it himself.

Castor was truly considering venturing out into the woods alone, seriously considering it. The more he thought about it, the more sense it made. It was a terrible idea, but it might be the only way. And he was the perfect person for the job. He was fast and had pretty good endurance. He was small too, which made him nimbler. And, most importantly, he wasn't important!

This thought should have made him sad. It certainly had in the past. But now, it brought a sense of relief, and even elation. The other people who were physically capable of performing this task were guards, or more able-bodied workers. The village would miss any of those people. If he died, well, it wouldn't be a detriment to Toriath as a whole.

Maybe this was how he could finally contribute to the village meaningfully. He could find the Glade Marak talked about and bring seeds, as many as he could, back to the village. They could plant them in their farms, and they could have more food!

The next day, as he tended to the tree, another great idea came to him. He could perform a couple rituals while he was out to trap as much ambiance as he could from out in the forest into some items, in the same fashion Jayna did with her healing stones. If he could do that, he could release the captured ambiance back into the village when he returned. That would replenish the land and make it a lot easier to perform their rituals. It could save his sister!

That solidified it. He was going to take things in his own hands and save the village. It was stupid, reckless and more than likely suicidal. But he was going to do it.

Castor spent the following week preparing. In between his daily chores, he gathered what supplies he thought he would need and kept them in his room. He made a lot of progress, but then he lost his nerve.

Paralyzed by the enormity of the task at hand, along with the overwhelming probability of violent death, he gave up. The thought of setting out into the forest without direction was terrifying, and that fear made him question whether his quest was worth the risk. In a last-ditch effort to convince himself not to quit, he decided to try and gather information from the only person he could.

As a fisherman, Marak spent most of his time out in the shallows with Pay, dropping nets into the water and setting traps. Due to their increasingly low rate of success, they had also taken to foraging around the beach for molluscs and other creatures usually considered too small to eat and too difficult to prepare. Eventually, Castor got the opportunity to speak to him alone.

The man was tending to his small boat, which was pulled up onto the sand. It was flipped face down, and he was washing its underside with a rag and fresh water from a well. When wood came in contact with salt water for long periods of time, it started to split and rot. That was why all the north facing walls of buildings close to the coast were all made of stone, as a defence against the constant sea spray. It would be unacceptable for them to lose the village's only boat to something as preventable as rot, so, every couple of trips, they tried to remove as much of the salt as possible and put on a thin coating of pitch when absolutely necessary. The man quickly accepted Castor's help when he offered.

Keeping his voice as innocent as he could, Castor began, "I've been thinking about what you said in the dining hall the other day."

Marak winced. "So, you *did* hear that."

"Yeah. It's okay though, I get what you meant. There's not much we can do to provide for ourselves here."

"Oh, I'm not sure that's true. It's the dead of summer now. Most crops won't grow too well in this heat. Once it gets cooler, the farms will probably see a lot more growth."

Castor frowned. "That's not what you said last week."

"I was just being dramatic. Pretty hungry, you know. Don't pay it any mind." His tone didn't hold the certainty that his words did, and Castor realized he was sugarcoating things for him again.

The boy forced out his frustration with a sigh. "Well. If that's true, it would be even better to have those fruit trees you were talking about."

"Bushes," the man corrected, seemingly eager to speak on the matter. "They were small fruit, smaller than an apple, but orange. You didn't have to peel the skin off. They were a bit like plums, but without a pit inside. I could eat 'em by the dozen. They were the sweetest thing I ever tasted, I'll tell you that. Yeah, it would be great to have 'em in the village."

"Definitely. Although, they might not even grow well in Toriath," Castor mused out loud. His sly words had suckered Marak in.

"They would. We saved a couple seeds and planted them in our backyard. They sprouted and bore fruit well enough."

Castor's eyes widened. He truly didn't expect that. "You grew them in the village?"

"Sure did!" The man grinned. "We kept them for a while, but then a cold snap killed them, and we didn't keep enough seeds from the last harvest. We were sure kicking ourselves for that. A real shame."

This was better than Castor even imagined. One of his big concerns was that, even if he were able to recover some seeds, they wouldn't be able to grow within the village walls. Many crops needed very specific growing conditions, after all. But Marak had proved that they could be grown here!

Castor's heart began to race. He really had to do this after all. "Maybe we should ask Lord Tolam to consider asking someone to look for the Glade your father discovered."

Marak laughed nervously. "I mean, it would be a huge boon. But I don't feel like I should bring it up to him. Pay was right, we have no right to ask someone to risk their life out in the forest. Especially when we don't really know where that glade actually is."

Castor hummed in feigned consideration. "Are you sure your father didn't mention anything about where the Glade was? No landmarks or anything?"

The fisherman pondered for a moment. "I don't think so. Wait." He glared at the wood of the boat he was rubbing down in concentration. "The first time he found it, there was a river. He fell in it; I remember he had a gash on his shoulder from a rock or something. Our ma had to treat it for infection."

"Well that's something. I'm sure Lord Tolam has a map of the surrounding area that shows rivers."

"You'd think, but no, he doesn't," Marak shot him down.

"We asked him after my father passed. Even before the monsters got too bad, it was dangerous to spend too much time in the wilds. Lord Tolam said no one had ever bothered to make a detailed map like that for this part of the continent. The only ones he's got are of cities and *major* landmarks like mountains."

That was a disappointment. "Well, we know it's to the east and it's by a river. That's something, right?"

Marak snorted. "Not enough. Especially when you consider what lies two hundred kilometres to the east." He looked at the boy in expectation and saw the puzzlement on his face. "The Umbra Bosk, kid. That's where the spiders are coming from."

Castor felt a chill crawl down his spine. Of course he knew of the place. It was a necrovale, a pocket of land that was completely impassable for ordinary folk. He didn't know that's where the spiders were coming from, though. He had assumed that they were just born in the forest.

"Is that why Ayzadol fell?" Castor asked quietly. Marak nodded solemnly.

Ayzadol was once the second largest city in Alaya, located on the northwest peninsula. It was by far the greatest economic and military power in the region, and it was widely acknowledged that, until the arachna grew too numerous, Toriath and many other small settlements only survived by Ayzadol's good will alone. Traders only ever bothered to come to Toriath on their way to or from Ayzadol, and the city's military presence deterred invasions and large bandit groups.

It was a tremendous shock to all when the great city fell. Its surviving people were forced to flee, and Toriath even hosted the refugees for a time. The Umbra Bosk was right on its doorstep, so they must have had even more arachna to contend with than Toriath.

"I think," Marak continued, "I will bring it up to Lord Tolam. As a very last resort. By the gods, I'll feel like a bastard doing so. I know that a guard would be sent out, and after Tomasoh passed yesterday... well. I hate to even bring up the idea at all."

"Does it have to be a guard?"

"Who else could it be?"

There was a pause, before Castor said hesitantly, "I could do it."

"Absolutely not," Marak answered vehemently.

"Why not?" Castor replied defensively.

"You're young. You don't have experience in the wilds or fending off spiders. You aren't trained to use weapons." Each comment Marak rattled off stung a bit, even though they were objectively true. It was the lack of faith in him personally that really hurt, especially since it echoed his own self-doubts. It must have shown on his face, and Marak sighed.

"Look. I know you want to help. You're very brave for even volunteering. But if someone's gonna go, it needs to be a person that has the absolute best chance of making it back alive. Not just for themselves, but for us as well."

Marak's words kept him up that night. He may have been right for the most part, but the more Castor thought about what he said, the more frustrated he became. He *was* a good choice, no matter what Marak said! Good at fighting and using weapons? That was irrelevant. If an arachna caught up to him, or any lone person in the village with or without armour, he would be killed immediately anyway. Even one spider was too much for any person to handle on their own, no matter their skill level. And he wasn't completely clueless about wilderness survival. That was the least of his concerns in this situation. And he was seventeen for gods' sake, it's not like he was a child!

Spite lit a fire under him, that and the knowledge he gleaned from Marak in the first part of their conversation. The bushes could be grown from a seed within the village. And the Glade was located near a river. That tidbit was huge. Rivers should be easy to find; he had heard they were often quite big and made a lot of noise. If anything, he was more confident about succeeding with this quest than he had ever been.

Castor kept everything he prepared for his quest in the bottom drawer of his dresser, which was one of the only pieces of furniture he had in his room. Since his father had been a ritual master, they had, at one time, been one of the wealthier families in the village. This same house once was tastefully furnished. Now, wealth was inconsequential. Most wooden things had been appropriated by the village and repurposed for a variety of essential uses.

He had gotten his hands on most of the supplies he needed. Castor procured a small, ratty pack, in which he put a soft waterskin, a flint and iron firestarter and a knife, not to fight with, but for utility purposes. He wanted to bring medical supplies, but all he had managed to acquire was a small wooden vial of alcohol to be used as a disinfectant and bandages that he made himself from old articles of clothing. If he tried hard enough, he may have been able to get his hands on needles and thread to stitch wounds, but he knew they were in short supply in the village, and he didn't know how to use them anyway.

For his rituals, Castor took four crystals from his sister's workstation at home. Unlike the ones she almost used to heal Tomasoh, these crystals were devoid of any ambiance aside from the small amount all inanimate objects held naturally.

Some materials could store ambiance better than others, which meant that they had a higher utility when used in rituals. Others resisted the effects of erosion that occurred after a ritual was completed and the object was drained. These crystals possessed both qualities, making them reusable storage units for ambiance. As such, they were very valuable. Technically, they were Lord Tolam's property, although he left them with Castor's father, and now Jayna, who could actually put them to use. However, since there was currently no ambiance available for them to store, they sat functionally useless. Castor planned to fill them up during his expedition and bring them back for his sister.

Aside from the crystals, he brought another waterskin full of salt to form the matrices, some bones he had also taken out of his sister's supply, and also five catalysts for his rituals. He packed a spare just in case he botched one attempt.

The only thing that he truly felt guilty for taking was dry food. Each day he was sent up to the wall, he took a tiny amount from the guards' portions. Even when all these amounts were put together at Castor's house, it was still a meagre ration. However, he refused to take any more.

Looking down at his collection, he realized that he didn't have that much to bring. That was good because any increased weight would just slow him down. Also, his pack was rather small anyway.

He patiently waited for the perfect opportunity to leave the village unnoticed. If anyone caught him trying to leave, they would invariably stop him, and Castor would never get another chance.

Soon into planning, he realized that sneaking out of the village would be quite difficult. There were several gates in the wall, big enough for a human to get through with a little difficulty, but way too small for the spiders. Physically leaving wasn't the issue.

Doing it unseen, however, was. If someone saw Castor as he left, it was likely that a group of guards would be sent to chase and retrieve him. That put everyone involved in danger, which was the last thing he wanted to happen. If they only discovered that he was missing long after he departed, they wouldn't know where to look, and it would be unlikely that they would send anyone out into the forest.

Unfortunately, Castor couldn't leave while under the cover of darkness because that's when the spiders were most active. He would have to leave during the day, when the watch could easily spot him, since there was a wide strip of open grass with no cover that he would have to cross before he could set foot in the forest. So, how could he get the guards to not look for him? The obvious answer was by using a distraction.

Well, what possible *non-destructive* distraction could he cause? The best he could come up with was lunch. The watch often migrated to where the food was when it arrived, leaving him an opening to escape from the far side of the wall. The one problem with the lunch distraction was that he was the one who brought them food every day! He would have to get someone else to take his place when it was time for him to set out.

With a loose plan designed, he next had to decide when he was going to leave. Each morning, Castor went out of his way to walk past the wall to see who was taking watch that morning. That detail, he believed, was crucial to his success. The night watch, which was comprised entirely of guards since spiders were most active at that time, was relieved of duty at dawn, which, conveniently, was also when Castor left his house to begin his chores for the day.

Usually there were around three Noble Guards stationed on the wall during the day, each of whom were a lot more disciplined than regular villagers when they were on watch. Even when Castor brought them food, they stayed on their lookout posts on the wall and alternated eating their meals, which inspired similar behaviours in the civilian members of the watch as well.

Finally, he found one morning that the dawn shift only had one guard amongst them. There must have been another task in the village that required the order's attention. Castor decided this was the best chance he could hope for, so, heart racing all the while, he put his plan into action.

He completed his morning chores and accepted the lunch sack from Dohn. However, he did not take it directly to the wall. Instead, he milled around the area near the wall, in the hopes that he would find someone wandering around outside. He eventually did. Around the outskirts of the southwest quadrant, he spotted two young men each carrying buckets of water from the nearby tunnel entrance to the farms.

"Excuse me!" Castor called out to them. He recognized the men to be Dori and Bahgi, who were each a couple of years older than himself. He rarely saw them apart.

He put on a theatrical limp as the duo looked back at him. "I'm sorry, but could one of you do me a favour? I have to bring this," he pulled up his lunch sack for them to see, "up to the guards on the wall. It's their lunches. But I twisted my ankle yesterday, and I really don't think I can make it up the stairs. Could one of you possibly do it for me? I'm sorry," he apologized again.

"I can do that," replied Dori. "That all right?" he asked Bahgi.

"No problem at all, you gimme that." Bahgi took Dori's massive bucket, which Castor doubted he could lift with both hands, with just his left. Castor couldn't help but stare at the man's arm, thick from years of manual labour, as his sleeve hiked up. He was sure that, no matter how hard he wished, he could never have muscles like that.

Castor walked with Dori the short ways to the staircase near the main gate, thanking him profusely the entire way and feeling awful as he did so. As Dori began to climb, Castor made his way to the eastern wall, at a normal pace at first, and then at a sprint once he was out of Dori's sight. Running along the wall, he soon made it to his exit point along the eastern side.

There were two postern gates along the wall, one here and another to the west. Unless you travelled out by sea, they were the only exits to the walled village aside from the main gate. The doors were wooden and attached to the inner side of the wall. However, to prevent assailants from entering, a metal portcullis could be lowered over it. That portcullis didn't exist anymore, as it had been cannibalized for its iron. Spiders had no way to break down the gate, or even fit through the narrow doorway if they could.

Castor, days prior, had stashed his pack just outside of his house. It was an easy thing to do, considering it was very close to this gate. Shoving his arms through the straps, he set to work pulling the door open. However, there was a rut of dirt and rock that made the task very difficult. Castor frantically pulled with all his might, and the old wood groaned in protest. The watch could be done eating any minute now, and there was no time to spare.

"And what do you think you're doing?"

Castor's blood turned to ice. He whipped around so fast he almost fell over. Beesh was there, leaning against an abandoned house. Why the hell was he here?

Beesh, while puzzled, seemed amused by his reaction. "Well, kid? I asked you a question. It looks like you're trying to leave the village. That's very odd indeed." The man grinned cruelly. "I can't think of any good reason to do that. Perhaps I should find a guard to talk to about this?"

"No!" he shouted reflexively. He expected someone to notice he was missing eventually of course. But this was the worst way for them to find out. If he was caught before he left on his quest, before returning with *something*, then no one would trust him ever again, and he certainly wouldn't be allowed to try and leave in the future. He did leave a note for his sister in which he explained his goals and reasons for leaving, and that painted him in a positive, if not heroic light. Of course, he wasn't doing this for the praise. Mostly. However, he did care immensely about what the Torians thought of him.

"No?" Beesh said, in an exaggeratedly incredulous tone. "Why shouldn't I?"

"I'm—" His voice broke a bit. "I'm trying to help the village!"

He explained quickly, hypervigilant of the time that passed all the while. Beesh stroked his pointed beard in consideration, and his sharp eyes still peered down at Castor.

"Oh, it seems like I must apologize. You're very brave, aren't you?" the man said, to Castor's surprise. "Hmm, well, if you're so sure. I would be remiss to get in the way of someone with your resolve." Beesh's tone was unmistakably mocking, but Castor couldn't help but feel grateful to the man. In that moment, Beesh seemed to be the only person in the village who looked at him as something more than a clueless boy who needed to be protected. The man even helped him pull open the door past the rut of dirt that obstructed it.

Thanking Beesh for his help, he cautiously slipped out, closed the door behind him and peered up at the wall from the stone doorway he hid under. He saw no watchers on this stretch of the wall. They must still be occupied with lunch.

In a dead sprint, he cleared the expanse between the village wall and the trees and slipped into the calm seclusion of the forest.

Chapter Six
Among the Monsters

Castor had been outside of the castle walls before, but it had been many years. It was very quiet, but not nearly in the same way as Toriath did. Within its walls, the quiet felt wrong.

The village was supposed to be loud from the bustle of life. Merchants and farmers were supposed to be shouting in the marketplace, trying to rustle up business. The streets were supposed to be noisy from conversation between neighbours and the patter of children's feet as they played on the packed dirt. Instead, there was no outdoor market, no conversation and no children. Fear and misery draped over the entire village and made the silence stifling.

Out here in the wild, it was quiet, and it was *supposed* to be quiet. Castor found that invigorating. He walked between the trees and watched the afternoon sun filter through the leaves like golden strings. It was so calm that Castor had to frequently remind himself to walk as silently as he could and to keep watch for the arachna. However, the deeper in he travelled, the more he saw evidence of their occupation.

Webs clung to trees like streamers, sometimes connecting the space between and sometimes freely attached to branches and blowing loosely in the wind. Also, he couldn't see any creatures one might expect to see in a forest, except for some squirrels and small birds. Castor wondered if they were too fast for the spiders to catch, or if they were just too small for them to even bother hunting.

It wasn't long before Castor caught his first glimpse of an arachna. He already knew how big and threatening they were, but there was a difference between looking down on a giant spider from atop a high wall and seeing one from eye level, knowing there was no obstacle between it and you.

The monster was relatively far away, but Castor stopped and hid behind a tree nonetheless. Logically, he knew he would see a spider out here, maybe even up close. That didn't seem to matter to his heart, which beat so hard his chest ached.

The spider's movements seemed unnatural. It crept between the tree trunks, taking one step, stopping, swaying for a moment, and then taking another. Castor knew, however, that it could move quickly when it chose to.

Castor forced himself to move. He couldn't stop every time he spotted a spider in the distance. He didn't know if they could hear him or smell him if they got close enough. He didn't even know if they had ears or a nose. They certainly did have eyes though, three dyads, as he had heard them called. Basically, that meant they had six eyes, but paired so closely together that they only appeared to have three large ones.

He also knew that they could see in the dark just as well as they could during the day, so hiding in the shadows would likely do him no favours. Plus, if he stood still, the creature might eventually get too close for him to escape from. So, taking great pains to keep as many trees in the way of the spider's line of sight as possible, he headed in the opposite direction. Only after it was far out of sight did Castor begin to move freely once again.

After his successful evasion of the monstrous arachnid, Castor began to feel more confident. Marak did seem to have some remarkable insight after all. He was sure that, if he had been armoured and in a group of ten or so people, that spider would have noticed and been on him in an instant. If he continued like this, he might be able to complete his quest!

He noticed several more spiders that day, which he avoided in much the same way as the first. However, he only managed to find more and more trees. There was no sign of a clearing, or even the telltale rush of a river nearby. Castor constantly checked the position of the sun to judge the time, as he knew travelling in the dark would be foolish at best. It wasn't precise art by any means, but he didn't need it to be.

Castor judged it to be around seven o'clock when he happened upon a fallen tree. A network of vines, now dead, had twisted around the trunk like thin snakes, which might have contributed to its demise. It had broken off near its base and toppled down, landing on a branch which prevented it from falling flush to the ground. This left a gap between it and the grass below, almost like a natural lean-to.

A part of Castor wanted to continue on his way, as it was summer, and the days were long. He still probably had a couple hours of daylight left to guide him. But he decided that this was just too convenient to pass up. A small space like this would be an ideal place for Castor to sleep in this forest, since he was alone and had no one to keep watch. It would be difficult for an arachna to pull him out, but definitely not impossible. However, the fallen tree would hide Castor from plain view as he slept, so hopefully no spider would try.

In an effort to flesh out the illusion, Castor pulled down small branches from other neighbouring trees as silently as possible and propped them against each side of the log. When the sun began to set, he hid under his improvised shelter and tried to make himself comfortable within the tiny space. He arranged himself so that his head was under the highest point of the shelter, but his feet were crammed under the point the tree met the ground. He could theoretically spread his legs out to either side, but he was terrified that they would be grabbed by a spider during the middle of the night.

Unsurprisingly, sleep did not find him quickly that evening. The hard ground was uncomfortable, and the only pillow he had was the cut strips of fabric he brought along to be used as bandages.

Though he was starving, he only allowed himself a very little bit of dried fish. He had no idea how long he would be stuck out here, and he needed to stretch out his rations. But, if there was one thing living in a long, drawn-out famine had taught him, it was perseverance, especially when food was involved.

Even worse than the gnawing hunger was the pit of fear that had taken up permanent residence within his chest. Castor rubbed his bracelet in agitation every time the wind passed through the trees and rattled their branches, or when squirrels and other small creatures scampered through the foliage. It was strange; he had never noticed these sounds all throughout the day but, as soon as his eyes were closed, he couldn't seem to block them out. Castor feared that each noise came from a spider looking to find, kill and eat him. However, he was still exhausted and, many hours into the night, he finally fell into a fitful sleep.

Castor awoke with a profound relief to be alive and a considerable amount of pain. Unthinkingly, he immediately tried to sit up and cracked his forehead against the fallen tree he had spent the night under. Cursing, he blinked away the stars and rolled out of his dwelling, knocking over the thin facade he created to obscure himself.

His back was sore from sleeping on the hard ground as well. A very minor consequence of extended starvation was that he lost all the fat that would normally cushion his bones in situations such as these. His tailbone and upper vertebrae, which were even more pronounced than they would have been if he had been properly nourished, hurt tremendously.

He ate a minuscule breakfast, more dried sea monster jerky and water from his waterskin, and repacked all of the objects he had taken out of his bag last night before deciding it was time to move on.

Castor was well into the forest now. The trees seemed to have grown closer together, and the thick canopy blotted out the sun to a much greater extent than before. He optimistically took this as a sign he was heading in the right direction, although he really had no way to tell. In fact, although he tried to continue straight ahead, he had no way of knowing if he was even still travelling east. Nevertheless, he continued moving on. There was no point in second guessing himself now.

Spiders were all around. Castor began to see more and more,

which he cautiously avoided, and bits of web littered the surrounding area. A lot more flora seemed to be knocked over or trampled as well.

Castor was horrified to happen upon a large bundle of web that must have once contained a spider's meal. It was very old; he could tell because the web was bone dry and yellowed with age. The bundle was way too big to have once contained a human; however, if anything that made Castor more terrified. It highlighted the lethality of the monsters, that they were able to take down prey of this size.

Something about the obscured corpse seemed odd to him. Underneath the aged web, its form looked more... stable than he would have thought. Castor had heard many horrific tales about arachna, and what became of their prey. Venom would melt the flesh off your bones, and the monsters would suck the sludge out like water through a straw. All that would be left were your bones and clothes.

However, in this case, Castor could count at least eight defined bulges straining against the web. If the silk wasn't obviously so old, he would have definitely left it alone, but now he was morbidly curious.

He lightly traced the tip of one bulge with his knife, and it easily frayed under the sharp metal edge. For some reason, he still gave a small start when a dark brown appendage popped through the newly made opening. Tiny hairs covered what could only be an exoskeleton, and there were dull, hooklike prongs at the end.

Apparently, the arachna were cannibals. He couldn't really say he was surprised, though he would still admit to being disgusted. He hadn't heard the watchers tell stories about spiders fighting amongst themselves, as they usually ignored each other, but the humans' views were limited from atop the village wall. Maybe, with so little prey available, the monsters had turned to eating each other to survive.

Castor frowned as he left the suspended spider husk behind, mind abuzz from the questions it raised. Amongst intelligent animals, cannibalism was a taboo of course, but it went against the instincts of most animals as well.

All creatures had one goal in life, and that was to reproduce, and that couldn't happen if their dead bodies were eaten. Aside from humans, all living things grew from plants, and had a single seed somewhere in their bodies. Their existential purpose was to grow, eat, move to a place with adequate growing conditions and die. Then, its seed would grow using the nutrients absorbed through the creature's decomposing body and the soil below it. It was a delicate process that could be thrown off by a multitude of factors.

Castor had no idea how arachna grew, he had never even really thought about it, but he was very familiar with other fauna spawning plants. Toriath relied heavily on their lone cattle tree, which he and Jayna tended to. Having even one more would have drastically increased their food supply, so they and some other villagers attempted to grow additional trees by leading cows to various prepared spots at the other side of the village, killing them, letting their bodies decompose and performing rituals around the rotting corpses to help things along, which was an unpleasant experience to say the least.

They never succeeded. The issue was that cattle trees required a lot of nutrients, and even more ambiance to thrive. If two or more of them grew too close together, they would inevitably begin competing for ambiance, which could cause them *both* to sicken and die. Lord Tolam eventually decided they couldn't continue risking their only stable source of food no matter the potential benefit, and they couldn't keep wasting beef, resources, time and manpower in their attempts either.

Remembering these failed undertakings made Castor think of home. His sister was surely inconsolable, and Castor hoped she had found his note. He left it on his bed, under his sheets. Not the most conspicuous of places, but he didn't know when he would leave the village. He didn't want to put it in a place she could discover it prematurely.

He truly felt awful. Jayna had done so much to take care of him since their father died, and it was like he was repaying her sacrifices with ingratitude. However, when he returned home with the seeds and the imbued crystals, he would finally have done something to take care of her for a change.

If, he reminded himself, as he grimly took in the landscape around him. *If I return home.*

Even ignoring the danger of the arachna, he was beginning to worry that he would never be able to find his way back to Toriath at all. The forest seemed endless, and if his concentration lapsed for even a moment, he would likely lose his bearing completely. All he could do was keep walking forward and pray to Lior that he wasn't going in circles.

The area seemed to be getting dimmer and dimmer, almost as if night was falling. For a second, Castor thought it actually was. But while he felt like he had been walking for a long time, it didn't feel like he'd been walking for *that* long.

Castor realized that the canopy was just steadily growing thicker the further east he travelled, with multiple distinct layers forming above him. The largest trees reached over thirty meters in height. Below them, shorter trees greedily drank up what little sunlight pierced through, leaving almost nothing for those on the forest floor. Even grass struggled to grow, although Castor saw many different kinds of mushrooms. He wished he knew which ones were fit for eating, but he didn't. That would have been good information to research before he left, especially considering how little food he was able to bring with him.

Then, past the veil of darkness, Castor saw a strange pillar of light. It contrasted so dramatically against its surroundings that its form almost looked like a solid statue made from quartz, and Castor's curiosity, along with his yearning to see the sun again, drew him in.

He crept closer to the light, which was almost blinding to look at, but then his foot caught something, and he stumbled. He let out a strangled shriek when he looked down and saw part of an arachna's thorax lodged into the dirt underneath him.

Castor looked around wildly, cursing under his breath when his vision just *wouldn't focus*. In the dark forest, his eyes were as dilated as they could be, and now that he was in the light, his surroundings looked even more shrouded.

When his vision finally adjusted, he cursed again. For the area around him was one giant bed of broken spider remains.

"What the hell happened here?" Castor whispered to

himself. He was on edge, furtively looking around to see if there were any survivors. Soon, though, he grew confident he was safe, from arachna at least. The corpses were mangled, with limbs ripped off, abdomens shattered and heads crushed. The forest floor was muddy from the blood that soaked into it, and everything was still.

Well, almost everything. Even stranger than the multitude of devastated bodies was the state of the trees that surrounded the lit area. They had all been broken entirely in half, but they hadn't toppled over. They couldn't. An extensive network of vines and webbing connected the trees to one another, suspending the felled trees in midair. The splintered ends closest to the ground swung minutely in the breeze, which was gentle near the ground but fierce above the leaves. The gaps between the broken trees were what allowed the column of light to pass through the otherwise impenetrable canopy.

Castor didn't understand the scene he had stumbled into, and that made him anxious. Something killed all those arachna and broke the trees, and he didn't know what. That didn't scare him so much at the moment, as whatever created this mess was clearly long gone. One thought nagged him though. *Why haven't these arachna been eaten already?*

Just earlier that day, he had discovered that arachna wouldn't hesitate to devour their own kind if given the chance. So why would they leave the veritable buffet now surrounding him alone? It seemed unlikely that the monsters just hadn't stumbled upon it yet. Was there some reason they were leaving this place alone?

He stumbled over a large rock that had probably once been flat. Now, it had been shattered into many angular pieces, some of which stabbed into the flat of his shoe. His vision had finally adjusted, and his brow furrowed as he regarded the area around him. The trees were covered by spots of what could only be described as rot. He would have attributed them to natural decay, but the spots were almost completely circular, and they even covered the webs they touched.

When he searched for them, he could find at least thirty more of these spots, each as big as his torso. And although the rot was concentrated in these spots, which were likely their points of origin, it seemed to spread all around the area.

Poison, he realized with a jolt. *Or something like it.* He needed to get out of here. The longer he lingered, the more danger he was in, and he began to panic as he looked around for an escape. His path of entry was alarmingly close to one of the spots, and Castor shuddered at the realization. He hoped none of it got on him.

As he searched, he found several large gaps between the array of poison... *things.* He made for the nearest one, twisting his body to best avoid the suspended trees. One swayed towards him, and he put one hand out to stop a branch that spun towards his face.

In that instant, he wasn't sure why he jerked his arm away and threw himself back so suddenly. He wasn't thinking exactly, but his subconscious, already on high alert, recognized that he had touched something way out of place. Branches weren't supposed to feel so smooth.

He caught sight of the thing wrapped around the branch, which looked almost like a strip of leather, but he had tripped backwards and quickly lost sight of it. Castor reached out to catch himself, but his muscles gave out as a violent spasm shot up his arm.

Castor cursed, scooting back and instinctively rubbing his arm as the strangest sensation he ever felt crept up to his forearm. It was almost like numbness, but less peaceful. He felt like he was experiencing the ache of hypothermia, the sharp pricking of cut circulation and the intense pressure of being crushed all at the same time, centralized in his right forearm.

Gritting his teeth, Castor glared up at the tree, watching as the strange rot slowly welled out of the swinging branch he had thoughtlessly touched. This place was a death trap!

He squinted around the trees, trying to find more of the leathery patches that released the poison, but his eyesight was never especially keen. Also, the bright light from above and the writhing shadows of the swinging trees played tricks on his eyes. The harder he looked, the more he found, and with so many distractions he couldn't keep track of them all.

It doesn't matter where all of them are, it only matters where they aren't, he thought incoherently. Frustrated, he looked to random areas, trying to *not* find any patches.

The flesh in his forearm was jumping involuntarily, and each spasm made the muscle feel like it was about to burst. Aside from his veins, which had grown increasingly prominent in that area, the arm looked normal. If he closed his eyes though, he would have guessed that the limb had swollen to double its actual size, such was the pressure and tightness he felt now.

There was a crack overhead, from the tree he had tried to run past. The first ripple of poison seemed to have triggered another, this one a bit farther up. And that one was connected to a sturdy vine, one of the key forces holding up that entire tree. Before his horrified eyes, the darkening fibre *snapped*.

Castor felt the groan of the wood in his bones. It tipped forward, snapping some of the thinner vines still holding it and straining the others, as the timber rolled towards the forest floor. And in its wake, clouds of poison began to puff out in sequence.

"Gods dammit!" he yelled, bolting in the opposite direction. There were poison patches there too, but he had to risk agitating them. The tree had set off a chain reaction, and if he hesitated, he would be caught in its wake.

Clutching his limp arm to his chest, Castor sprinted as fast as he could, hoping that, if he did trigger any more patches, his speed would prevent the poison from sticking. He didn't look back, but he couldn't feel any new sources of numbness.

He ran until he was far away, and hopefully out of danger, before he tripped and couldn't muster the strength to raise himself again. Taking great heaving breaths, he tried to push himself up with his one good arm but could only manage to flip over onto his back.

Most of his attention was focused on quieting his gasps and pained whimpers. He tried to massage his arm, trying to regain feeling in the way he normally would if a limb had fallen asleep. Too late, he had realized that doing so might not have been a good idea, if he wanted to keep the poison from spreading, but luckily the numbness hadn't radiated from where he had been hit at all. It was strange; he had complete control over his shoulder muscles, but he could do nothing but lightly flex his forearm, and he had no control whatsoever over any of his fingers.

He had no idea how to fix it. He'd try to wash the poison off but there were no bodies of water around. He almost pulled out his waterskin, but some rationality found him again. He couldn't afford to waste his drinking water for something that probably wouldn't even help. After all, if it was something that could be washed off, his left hand would probably be numb from rubbing the affected area.

A small mercy was that he couldn't see any arachna around here. Even though he wouldn't be able to fend one of the monsters off anyway, having one arm incapacitated made him even less optimistic about his chances. There were so many arachna corpses around the poison field, perhaps all of them in the area were killed? The vindictive part of Castor was pleased.

But as he thought about the scene he just left, he realized something else. It wasn't just a mass poisoning. Something broke all those trees and ripped the arachna to shreds as well. If they did die from the poison, another lucky—or perhaps unlucky if the poison spread—monster must have stumbled upon the helpless, or perhaps already expired, arachna and savaged their bodies.

Castor didn't exactly know what else dwelled in the forest. He, along with the other Torians, assumed that the spiders ate everything else that once dwelled here, but they had no way to prove that theory, confined within the village walls as they were.

It didn't matter, he decided. He was still surrounded by enemies, whether they be arachna, or something else. Although, now he apparently had to keep an eye out for poisonous *trees* as well.

Groaning, he pushed himself to his feet. Trying not to let his pulsating arm distract him, he examined the trees around him. They weren't broken, there were fewer vines and, most importantly, he couldn't see a single poison patch. Maybe they only grew in certain areas?

He was glad to be rid of them, and the haze of adrenaline began to clear from his mind. He knew he had to leave this place; it was past noon at least; he could tell from the position of the sun he saw through the broken trees. He wasn't especially talented at judging the time in this manner, but the sun was directly overhead, which was why it looked so solid as it pierced the darkness.

Castor began to lope onwards, legs aching and leaden from his run. The feeling loosened up the more he walked, and even at its worst it barely compared to the state his arm was in. He continued to massage it as he walked, grateful when, after a couple hours, a slight sense of feeling began to return. He at least felt the indents of his functional set of fingers as he pushed them into his larger muscle groups.

Later in the day, he was pleasantly surprised to find the mostly rotted remains of old stumps. There were plenty of stumps throughout the forest, as the arachna tended to knock trees down frequently. However, the rest of these old trees were conspicuously missing, and, underneath the lichen, Castor could see that they had been cleanly cut.

To Castor, that clearly meant there was some sort of outpost or inn nearby, and he would be eager to find whatever the lumber had contributed to.

Of course, there wouldn't be any humans there. No one could survive in this area without a wall like Toriath's. But maybe they might have supplies, of some sort. Not food, as that would have rotted a long time ago. He wouldn't have the room or strength to carry tools, or anything else his people would need. Hmm. Why was he so excited about finding an outpost again?

Castor was just grateful to find any reminder that humanity existed here, no matter how long ago the place was abandoned. The forest was foreboding; being within its bounds made him feel so alone. As if he was the only human alive, even though he had been among his people just yesterday. He decided that, as long as doing so wouldn't put him in danger, he wanted to take a look around, if only to pay respects to those who once passed through this area or called it home.

He found the place easily enough; he just had to look for an area that was lighter than its surroundings. There were just three buildings, and Castor couldn't even see much of the wood because they were almost entirely cocooned in webbing.

Why did they wrap up the entire building? Why go through all that effort? He doubted these questions had an answer. This was just what happened to an area conquered by arachna. He would hate to see Ayzadol; he bet the entire city was coated in white.

With some difficulty, Castor found the door to the nearest building and retrieved his knife, which was much more difficult than it should have been. Though he had regained some feeling, and the sharp sting of needles had tempered, he still couldn't use the entirety of his dominant hand. Dragging the shoulder strap over the lump of immobile flesh that his shoulder now was took several frustrating attempts, as did unfastening the tie of the pack.

Finally, he managed to remove the knife, and he dragged the sharp edge of the blade over the web, which split easily. That was a testament to the silk's age. When web was layered this thick, the exposed side would dry out in the heat rather quickly. However, the material at the centre would stay damp and flexible for a long time, and it would take even longer for it to fray to this extent. The web here was so old that the strands felt like thin strands of dried pasta, even at its centre. With its tension disturbed, the rest of the web on this wall fell on its own with little assistance.

Castor coughed as soon as he stepped inside. There was a lot of dust, and the whole area smelled like mould, so he pulled the neck of his shirt over his nose. He cut through the web stretching across the open windows, both for ventilation and to allow some light into the room. This building was once a pub, Castor could tell from its overall layout. There were tables with chairs stacked on top of them, and stacks of barrels rested against the back wall.

Out of curiosity, Castor opened the spigot of one, and murky liquid spilled out. Yeah, he wasn't going to drink that. He did try and manoeuvre his right arm underneath the flow, however. He was sure it tasted horrible, but the ancient grog presumably had alcohol in it, which would keep it disinfected. Grog was a staple of all settlements because safe drinking water was never guaranteed. The wells within Toriath were especially fickle, so they always kept some alcohol fermenting within the food stores. Though kids were discouraged from drinking most of the time, sometimes it was necessary.

Rinsing off his arm did nothing to alleviate the crushing numbness, not that he really thought it would at this point. With his hopes dashed, and nothing else left in this building to examine, Castor left frustrated. He made his way to the next, noting that this one was the largest of the three. The webbing was so thick that he couldn't even locate the door, so Castor was forced to cut open a window along the side and pull himself awkwardly through the sill.

It was a bit harder to discern this building's function at first. There were two floors, and the first floor he entered through was mostly empty. There were some pieces of wooden furniture scattered about, a closet with a few bits of wooden farm tools and a fireplace that was built into one wall. It wasn't until he went up the stairs that he figured out what it was.

The second floor was sectioned off into separate rooms, with most of them containing mattresses. *This was an inn,* he realized. *Well, I know where I'll be staying the night.* He glanced through the window at the sinking sun. The spiders didn't web up this floor as thoroughly since it was high enough off the ground to make the task difficult. As such, the floor wasn't nearly as musty, although the wind had blown in large piles of dead leaves.

Castor would still have to be careful about how he slept, and not just because of the arachna. This building had been abandoned for who knew how long, and parts of the ceiling and floor were likely rotted. The hay that stuffed the mattress was likely decaying as well, and bugs might have taken up residence. So, Castor spent the next half hour cutting off the fabric from spare mattresses to layer as protection, which was another task that would have been much easier with two usable hands. The fabric itself wasn't exactly sanitary, but it would hopefully block diseased insects from biting him as he slept.

He piled the sheets on the mattress he had chosen, which was located on top of the building's main support for added security, and dusted himself off. Castor still had some daylight left, so now he figured he would explore the last building.

This one was wider than the other two, but the roof was a lot lower to the ground. Castor soon realized that it was a stable, which was easy to tell from its lack of a floor and wooden partitions. There was even room to fit caravans, so that merchants' goods would be protected from the elements for the duration of their stay.

Like in the other buildings, everything remotely useful to Castor was taken. He was sincerely glad that whoever lived here was able to evacuate this outpost safely... but he was still a little disappointed that there wasn't anything for him to scavenge.

There *was* something in the stable that would have been incredibly valuable to the villagers back in Toriath. Hanging from hooks embedded into the wall were several huge coils of rope. Toriath was lacking many materials at the moment, but rope easily caused the most frustration. Both because of how useful it was, and because of how much of it existed just out of reach.

For the gods' sake, their greatest enemies were giant spiders! Arachna who left their unnaturally strong silk all over the place! It would, theoretically, be so *easy* to just go into the forest and collect it. However, in reality, anyone sent out to collect the webbing would certainly die. Toriath learned that the hard way when, almost two years ago, a group of Noble Guards were sent to fell a tree and bring it back through the gates.

They practised for weeks and ran through countless strategies. Noble Guards weren't the only ones involved either; ordinary townspeople were trained to open the gate quickly and help bring in the tree once they were close enough. Castor had even overheard a discussion atop the wall, when he came to deliver lunch, between Lord Tolam, Bani, Dohn, and Musov, who were picking out the most strategically perfect tree to cut down.

Jayna forced Castor to stay home rather than let him watch, even going so far as to ask their neighbour, Sayol, to watch over him. Castor was angry at the time, but now a large part of him was grateful. The guards didn't even reach the tree they were supposed to cut down before they were swarmed by the arachna. Only half of the group returned; the rest were eaten as the horrified Torians watched from atop the wall.

Understandably, that was the last expedition sent to gather resources outside of the village. So no, they weren't going out to collect web, even when it blew tauntingly in the wind before them. Just as the rope in front of Castor taunted him now.

He couldn't exactly bring it with him. Rope was heavy. It would slow him down too much. There was also no good way to carry it aside from slinging the coil over his shoulder, and he couldn't run like that.

"Seeds and ambiance. That's what's really important," he said out loud to remind himself before exiting once more.

One thing that Castor wanted to find out was why this outpost was built here in the first place. It seemed like an odd resting place, but it was obviously well-equipped once upon a time. There were two paths that he saw: one to his right and one leading straight ahead. The one to the right was considerably larger, which led Castor to believe it would lead to the highway that connected the two cities in Alaya: Ayzadol and Stoneheart.

Each settlement in this region had at least one path that connected them to this highway, and Toriath was no exception. Traders once used this route to travel between settlements, as their caravans needed a flat surface to move safely, and the most profitable companies often hired Heroes to protect their employees and merchandise. Then, the Heroes disappeared, and the monster populations grew a hundredfold, so trade between settlements quickly halted completely. That likely played a large hand in Ayzadol's downfall, as the city wasn't self-sufficient.

The highway ended directly at the dead city's front gate, so if this outpost was just a rest stop near the path, he was *incredibly* off course. He was supposed to be heading east, not south! He had no idea how he could have possibly messed up that badly.

Before he could truly panic, he noticed a wooden sign to his left, so obscured with web that he couldn't see what was on it at all. With trembling hands, *hand* rather, as his right still refused to follow his commands, he set to work trying to cut apart the ancient web, throwing the severed strands back over the signboard.

He was expecting to see a sign of some sort, hopefully with a name or message that might give Castor a way to orient himself. He wasn't expecting an entire *map*, painted on the old, splitting wood.

Now his heart was pounding for another reason. This was, quite possibly, the best thing he could have found, and he eagerly drank in its details. Castor let out a relieved sigh when he realized that he wasn't as lost as he feared.

It seems like this outpost is just a resting spot on a direct route to Bayla, which was a settlement near Ayzadol, but closer to the northern coast. *Hmm. Looks like I did accidentally curve south after all, damn. But I'm not near the highway at least.*

The map was narrow, and only revealed the locations its creators thought were relevant to those staying in this outpost. He could see the highway, Bayla, and some landmarks in between. In the margins, there were some other features included that were too far away to be shown on the map. He could see *Ayzadol, sixty-five kilometres* inscribed behind Bayla, with an arrow pointing east. He also saw *Toriath*, followed by an arrow pointing northwest from his current location. The creator didn't seem to find it important enough to include a distance, and Castor felt like he should take offence on behalf of his home.

Although it was limited, the map did give Castor some important information. It didn't contain most of the area he thought the Glade resided in, but it did allow him to narrow down his search. Also, the map did illustrate two rivers, both stemming from different points along the Kalival. One curled around Bayla, but the other *might* dip into his search area. Maybe. He couldn't tell because the damned map didn't show the part he needed it to.

If the river followed the course he hoped it would, he might be able to intercept it if he angled himself more towards the north. And he could now tell which way was north from the map. He even had the option to follow the smaller path, which led directly to Bayla for a couple kilometres. That would be easier on his ankles at least. Castor had always been rather active, especially lately, so his muscles weren't especially sore after only a day and a half of walking. However, the uneven terrain had already taken its toll on his joints.

Shadows were beginning to creep over the map, so Castor decided it was time to barricade himself in the inn for the night. He climbed through the window, crept up the stairs and found the bed he had chosen. The rotting mattress wasn't nearly as comfortable as the one he had at home, but it was so much better than sleeping on the ground, crammed underneath a fallen log. Even so, the steady throbbing in his arm made certain that he would gain no restful sleep that night.

Chapter Seven
The Plunge

The next morning, Castor left the outpost. With no arachna around, he made his way to the path, pausing to regard the trio of buildings behind him. He gave his best wishes, not quite a prayer, to whoever once ran this place. They had lost their livelihood when they were forced to flee their homes, probably to Bayla or Ayzadol. Neither of those settlements were around anymore either, and while there were some refugees, many of which Toriath hosted for a time, it was most likely that the owners were now all dead. But he thanked them, nonetheless.

He was grateful to find that the effects of the poison in his arm had indeed faded overnight. He could move his fingers again, though they were sluggish to obey his commands. His grip strength was weak, and he couldn't even hold anything without dropping it almost immediately. So, over the course of the morning, he continually balled his hand into a fist and clenched it as hard as he could, hoping that the repeated action would restore some of his previous mobility.

Taking this path seemed like a good idea at the time, but Castor grew more and more wary with each step he took. He could see far in front of him and behind him as well, and that clear line of sight made him feel exposed.

At least there was a bit more sun than there would have been, since there was a tiny crack in the canopy that the trees on each side of the path couldn't cover. Each ray was incredibly pronounced, especially compared to the darkness surrounding them. When it bounced off the leaves' waxy sheen, or stray bits of web, the sunlight glimmered and released spots of vivid colours that blinked in and out of existence. Then, as he walked, Castor noticed that those colours weren't just a trick of the light.

At first, he thought he was only seeing bits of plants that were carried on the wind. They didn't grow in Toriath's climate, but Castor had heard of dandelions, which released their seeds into the air for the wind to disperse. However, he soon realized that, whatever was floating in the sky above him was too big and round to be a seed.

Cautiously, Castor stopped behind a tree, suddenly realizing that, whatever these things were, they were *everywhere*. Floating above him, behind and to each side. Then his wariness turned to fear, as he realized that these orbs weren't reflecting light; they were changing colour themselves. And, even more terrifying, they were starting to drift down *towards* him.

Castor pressed himself against the tree and held his breath as his heart began to race. Three orbs, each blinking a different colour, seemed to move down towards him, coming closer and closer as Castor prepared to bolt.

One in particular seemed to be the boldest. Castor couldn't really tell how big it was, but its pale blue corona made it look to be about the size of his fist. It got too close for comfort, and Castor reflexively tried to swat it away, realizing too late that he shouldn't try to touch it at all. But something unexpected happened. The orb darted *away* from his hand.

Are these things alive? Castor thought, perplexed. Experimentally, he raised his right hand, the one that was already impaired, into the air and reached out at a smaller, mint green one. It too shied away from his touch, and Castor began to feel a bit silly for being frightened.

These things were harmless; if anything, they were afraid of *him*. The three that seemed to take an interest in Castor, the green one, the blue one, and another white one, circled around him just out of reach, as if both wary and curious. Castor doubted they had ever encountered a human out here, at least in the last five years.

He reached out a hand and laid it palm up in front of him. Castor wasn't stupid enough to let them touch him, but he wanted to see if they would even try. They didn't, although that might have been because his weakened muscles trembled violently under the strain of holding his hand in this position.

"What are you?" he whispered, and was surprised to see the orbs blink in response to his voice. "Can you understand me?" Castor asked in wonder. They responded by blinking twice.

Castor considered the beings in front of him as a new, orange orb sank towards them. They had to be alive and sentient in some capacity, right? If they could detect his voice at all, maybe even understand it. He would have to test them.

"If you can understand me," he breathed, "go to that branch," he pointed to one above his head. He was amazed when the blue one and the orange one followed his instruction.

Maybe they were just following where he pointed. "Now go to the one on the other side." Again, the same two orbs did as he asked.

Interesting. So, they do understand me. Or at least those two do, he thought, looking at the blue and orange orbs as they drifted back towards him. *Can only some of them understand speech? Or maybe those other two are just stubborn.*

"I'm looking for something," he began, pausing as he watched them blink. "Can you help me find it?" The four beings slowly leaned in towards him, as if to show they were listening. Castor suppressed a chuckle at the cute sight, as he tried to find the best way to ask his question.

"There's a place in this forest. A glade, or a clearing. Or a meadow. It has lots of bushes, full of orange fruit. Do you know where that place is?" He realized there was a huge jump between asking them to follow a simple direction and asking them for directions to a place even he didn't know how to get to. But once again he was pleasantly surprised.

The blue one shot up into the air before corkscrewing back down to him. "You do?" Castor asked in bewildered amazement. It darted back and forth in response, blinking rapidly. "Will you take me there?"

It blinked four times. The orange one that also listened to him floated towards Castor, flashing its light in a sequence, as if trying to say something. Blue cut off its dance and darted towards Orange, flashing and jerking in an even quicker pattern. For some reason, Castor got the sense that they were arguing.

Then, Blue shot forward, smashing into Orange with a muted *clack*. It sounded like two pebbles colliding.

"Whoa, whoa," Castor said, reaching out to put his hand in between the orbs, which shrank away from his touch. "Hey, there's no need to fight. It's not that big a deal." He would offer to take both of them just to keep the peace, but he had the feeling that the two would disagree and try to lead him in two directions.

"I'm gonna go with Blue, all right? It volunteered first." Blue visibly brightened at his words. "Thank you for trying to help me though!"

Orange muted its colour mournfully. It drifted towards him again but shrank back as Blue started forward. It hesitated once, before drifting back up near the canopy. At the sad sight, Castor almost called back to it, but then, without any further prompting, Blue began to drift off.

"Hey, wait up!"

The orb wandered away from the path, but its trajectory was consistent with the directions Castor received on the map. So, with only the slightest hesitation, he began to follow.

Blue floated several meters above and ahead of him, leading Castor through thick clusters of trees. Soon, they were far away from the rest of the orbs, who seemed to prefer the sunlight the path offered. Castor wondered if that was a survival instinct; the forest had grown darker once more, and that made the orb seem even more vibrant.

Castor was forced to walk more quickly than usual in order to keep up with Blue, who didn't have to worry about ground obstacles like he did. It also had the habit of weaving in between trees, and sometimes stopping when he was out of view. Castor couldn't help but wonder if it was doing it on purpose to confuse him.

His attention was focused on watching out for arachna and keeping track of his route. He had only just gotten his bearings, and he really didn't want to get lost again so soon, so every couple of steps, he dragged his heel into the ground to create as deep a rut as he could. It wasn't the most obvious clue, but it was the best he could come up with.

Though it was nearly impossible to tell for sure under the thick canopy, Castor eventually decided that it was around midday. He listened to his stomach more than anything else. He had a small dinner last night, but no breakfast this morning because he grudgingly decided that he should spread out his rations even thinner. He didn't plan on eating dinner tonight. So, he took some jerky out of his bag and chewed apart the stringy meat as he walked.

It was only a matter of time before he ran into arachna once more, and, unfortunately, he soon did. There was one in the distance, and Castor's eyes picked up on its shaky movement before his eyes even processed what he saw. Instinctively, he jumped behind a tree, and he was sure he would be far enough away to avoid the beast entirely. But Blue kept going, blinking in plain sight.

"Blue!" he hissed, and the orb stopped in its tracks. "Come back here. Hide with me, from that thing." He pointed in the direction of the arachna. "Hide!" he repeated once more, trying to convey the urgency of the situation.

Blue did not hide; it stayed still, hovering in place. Then, it let out a flare of light, much brighter than Castor had ever seen it glow. And in the distance, the arachna *stopped*.

"Stop it! Blue, turn that off!" Castor said as loud as he dared. "Blue, that thing will kill me!" The orb didn't even blink as it heard his pleas. Desperately, he pried loose a rock and threw it at the orb, but it dodged, and Castor winced at the loud sound of it hitting a tree.

The light, movement and sound truly got the arachna's attention. It shot towards them, and Castor realized he had no choice but to flee. Even if it didn't see him already from behind the tree, soon it would be too close for him to outrun once it did.

"*Traitor!*" Castor spat over his shoulder at Blue, who blinked back impassively as he took off.

The arachna changed course as soon as it saw him. The monster was fast, much faster than its size would suggest, but it seemed a lot less nimble than Castor. Its legs made it rather wide, and the vegetation provided much more of a hindrance for the spider than it did for Castor. It was odd; Castor had considered the forest to be the spider's domain, but the trees actually seemed to work *against* the beast in this instance. Nevertheless, it was fast, and it didn't allow Castor to widen the gap between them.

The pack bounced against his spine with each step, and he hurriedly tried to bunch up the straps to secure it in place with his only usable hand. His momentary distraction caused him to slam his other shoulder against the rough bark of a tree. Luckily it was still a bit numb, so the jarring force and scraping sensation felt strangely distant. Although it made him stumble, he recovered and raced on.

Castor's mind ran even faster than his legs as he desperately looked for some means of escape. But then, he was snapped out of his thoughts when he crashed into a solid mass that reached up to his waist, causing him to tumble over it. He couldn't process what was happening for a moment, and his hands felt several rods with tiny bristle-like hairs all over them. His mind finally caught back up to him as the rods moved, sending him tumbling backward. He had been so frantic to escape one spider, he had run face first into another!

He scrambled to regain his footing, but a brown leg blurred forward, hitting him in the chest and knocking the wind out of him. As he heaved, face up on the ground, another leg stepped on his hip, pinning him down.

Castor instinctively flinched out of the way, which saved his shoulder from being punctured by fangs, unsheathed from the spider's mouth in an instant. He knew that any bite would be debilitating, fatal if it was close enough to any vital organs. He hadn't been allowed to see anyone injured from a spider bite, but he heard that afflicted flesh would turn grey and slide off the bone. There were several amputees in the village who had endured spider bites inflicted before Toriath had permanently closed its gates.

He thrashed around as violently as possible, trying to knock the leg off and cursing himself for not keeping his knife on hand somewhere. Now, it rested within his bag, completely useless to him. With it, he might have been able to stab the spider in its head, and maybe force it to let him go. His erratic movement saved him from the next bite as well, and then, miraculously, there was a heavy thud and the spider was flung off of him.

The arachna from before, which had chased him at top speed, barreled right into the spider holding him captive. Castor wasn't sure if it was trying to fight the other arachna over him, or if it just couldn't stop in time. In the end, it didn't really matter. Castor rolled back onto his feet and clumsily took off once more. His sides burned, but he needed to get away fast.

The two spiders fought over him for a moment, before they realized their prey was escaping. They must have come to an agreement, and they both began to chase after him.

Castor ran on, adrenaline pushing him far beyond his limits. He had tunnel vision, barely perceiving his surroundings, and was only conscious enough to dodge the trees that appeared directly in front of him.

Then, all of a sudden, Castor was falling. Not onto solid ground, but through the air! He had been so absorbed in his escape that he didn't even notice that he was approaching a ledge until he had run completely over it.

A completely different flavor of panic overtook him as he free fell for what felt like either a second or an eternity, and then there was a shock of cold. He had plummeted into a river, and it was not a gentle one. His body and mind were unable to adapt to the drastic change of events, and he was tossed around like a leaf in the wind.

He had no control. Half the time he tried to breathe, all he took in was water. He couldn't see, as rocks and fallen branches assaulted his body without relent. Many grabbed at his backpack as well, threatening to tear it off.

There was a fallen branch, or tree, or something that hung low over the river he was uncontrollably shooting down, and he slammed into it at an angle. Castor hit it awkwardly, thigh first somehow, and it would have hurt a lot more if the cold water had not numbed his entire body. Having regained some presence of mind, he tried to grab onto the branch and was able to for a moment. Then, he was wrenched away again by the vicious current. However, that short reprieve had allowed him to regain some sense of equilibrium.

His head was above the water, and he was finally able to keep it there. His vision was blurry, and he shook his head to try and clear it. He could breathe, somewhat, though each inhale made him cough in an unconscious attempt to empty some of the liquid from his lungs.

A fuzzy mass grew larger in front of him, and Castor was able to make out a rock face quickly approaching, marking a sharp riverbend up ahead. The water would flow gracefully around it, but the current would dash Castor against the stone. It would hurt a lot, and at the speed he was travelling, it could easily break some bones. He grasped wildly at the riverbed, trying to grab hold of something to slow his momentum.

He found rocks and driftwood, and all of it came loose under his grasp or was wrenched away by the current. However, they each worked together to slow him down enough so that, when he made it to the cliff, he was able to rotate his body and use his limbs to push off it again. It hurt a lot, but he was pretty sure he didn't break anything.

Castor remained at the river's mercy for a while longer. He treaded water over to the side of the bank, but it was so high up that he couldn't get out. Finally, he found a diagonal rut in the tightly packed soil, which, with extreme effort, he used to yank himself out of the water.

Climbing up the dirt with frozen arms, one previously wounded as well, was one of the most physically difficult things he had ever done. However, even though he was currently incapable of higher thought, his innate survival instincts told him that, if he spent any more time in that river, he would certainly die. This was his last chance. So, he jammed his fingers into the earth and pulled himself up almost four meters until he was back on flat ground.

Sprawled face first into the sparse grass and dirt, Castor spent the next ten minutes vomiting fiercely. Lying on the ground as he was, most of his regurgitate ran directly down back onto his clothes. Fortunately, it consisted almost entirely of river water, which was about the only thing in his stomach anyway. At least he wasn't wasting food.

The rough coughing and gagging brought tears into his eyes, and they continued to flow freely even after he had finished. Just in the last—he didn't know how long but it couldn't have been more than an hour—he had been nearly eaten, drowned and crushed. He had run for his life and been at the mercy of a godlike and unyielding river. He knew fear that most people would never have to feel in their entire lives. His body ached, he was soaking wet, and very, very cold. Now, he just wanted to go home.

When he pulled himself together somewhat, he pushed himself up and limped back along the riverbank. He had completely lost his bearings in the river and he had no way to orient himself. He tried to look up at the sun for direction, but he couldn't find it past the canopy. His limbs were too sore, and he was much too tired to try and climb a tree so that he could search the landscape from high up.

Blearily, he wondered if he should have walked in the opposite direction, upstream. He might have been able to backtrack to the position he had fallen in and then just tried to find his way from there. Although, that might have once again put him in reach of the arachna that had nearly eaten him.

With a jolt, Castor realized that if he was attacked by a spider at this moment, he had absolutely no chance of outrunning it. Thinking back to when he was first attacked, he pulled the knife out of his pack, which had mercifully survived the trials of the day, and stuck it blade down into his belt. It dug a bit against his thigh with each step, but the minor discomfort was far outweighed by the increased sense of security it brought.

Back home in Toriath, Castor had thought that weapons were useless in this quest, since it would be futile to try and defend himself against arachna. He had only even brought a knife along to cut webs or branches if he ever needed to. His opinion hadn't changed truthfully, especially since his dominant hand was still nearly useless. But when he was pinned down with venomous fangs snapping over his head, all he could think about was how much he wished he had a knife in his hand, even if he wasn't able to use it.

Suddenly, he was blinded by a ray of light. It made him start, as he hadn't been able to see the sun so clearly for a good while, as thick as the leaves were. It shone from across the river, and Castor could see that the sun was beginning to set, as if things could get any worse. Before he lost himself in despair, he followed the beams of light it left and noticed something else interesting behind him.

There seemed to be a path that ran perpendicular to the river he was currently walking alongside. It wasn't a man-made path, Castor thought. It was a game trail, made over the course of many decades from dirt packed together by the steps of animals that lived in the forest. They all had to drink of course, so it made sense that there would be a common way for animals to reach the river. Those animals would have long since been eaten by the arachna, or at least run out of the forest. Maybe this path could lead him to a vacant den, or someplace else to spend the night. He wasn't really sure if larger animals made homes or anything similar, but he was just so exhausted. He wanted to sleep for days, but first he needed to find a safe place to do so, otherwise his efforts to survive would have all been in vain.

With no better ideas, he changed course and took the path. It also afforded him the opportunity to monitor the sun as it began its descent. Its light reflected beautifully off the leaves, which sparkled like emeralds. In his daze, Castor noticed its majesty and then promptly dismissed it. He tried to keep a lookout for someplace to sleep, but it was so hard to concentrate. His body was on autopilot.

And then, the trees opened up, and it took Castor several minutes to process what he had walked into. It was an open meadow, with a sheer cliff on the side opposite to where he had entered. The grass was lush, with blades coming halfway up his shins. Small white flowers bloomed among them, juxtaposed against the almost uniform colour of bright green. And scattered around the area were a collection of bushes, each seeming to hold many pinpricks of orange.

No, he thought. *It can't be.*

He hadn't thought about it once since he had begun his flight away from the spider. The objective, why he came out into the woods to begin with. It was his constant motivation for over a week now, searching for and finding it. Now, only after completely forgetting about its existence, he stumbled upon it.

The Glade.

Chapter Eight
A Chest Gilded in Bronze

C astor started laughing. He couldn't help it; this was just too absurd. He had travelled east and then ran into the river, quite literally. He had hurtled downstream, walked back alongside its bank for hours and not once did he realize its significance. He limped quickly over to one of the bushes and found a fruit that looked exactly like Marak described. It was orange and soft to the touch.

He realized that eating a strange fruit was not a very smart thing to do. These may be different from the ones Marak's father used to grow, and they could even be toxic. But Castor decided he just didn't care. He was so very hungry, and if it killed him, well, it would probably be a better way to go than being eaten by an arachna.

Castor popped the entire thing, which was half the size of his fist, into his mouth. It was pure bliss, sweeter by far than any fruit he had ever consumed, although he was hardly an impartial judge at the moment. The fruit was a bit too big to eat gracefully in one bite, and rivulets of juice overflowed and ran down his chin.

As he chewed, his teeth found several hard seeds, and he almost spit them out. The seeds were what he came here to collect, after all. Then, noticing how many other fruits were in the Glade, he decided that separating them from the flesh was too much work, and swallowed them.

He ate more and more, until the first bush was entirely picked clean. His knees hurt from kneeling on the hard ground, so he sat down on a large rocky mound, the only dot of grey in the otherwise lush meadow, and scoped out the Glade.

In his befuddled state, he had entered the clearing without any semblance of caution. There could have been spiders here, in plain view or hiding. Luckily, as he observed the area with more alert, although still exhausted, eyes, he saw none. In fact, he hadn't seen any arachna since he made it to this side of the river. He couldn't allow himself to become complacent though. It would be especially foolish for him to die of carelessness just after he reached the Glade.

Ironically, at that very moment, the stone outcropping underneath him shifted, knocking him off. He sank into the grass and scrambled away from the now moving rocks. He forgot that his right arm couldn't support his weight, so in doing so, he collapsed shoulder first into the ground.

Castor thought he destabilized the pile by sitting on it, and they were all about to come crashing down. But then his eyes widened when, instead of falling onto the grass, some of the stones lifted into the air. A string of them, which were connected somehow, rose and then fell again near his foot. Five more stubby rocks were attached to the end, and the entire chain seemed to push up against the ground.

That almost looks like an arm, with fingers, Castor thought in bewilderment. Then, before his very eyes, the rest of the rocks moved in concert, rising out of the ground to form a humanoid figure. Castor hadn't noticed it because of the tall grass, and the fact that it was curled up face down, but he had been sitting on some sort of primitive statue, which had seemingly come to life.

Now, it was Castor's turn to pretend to be a part of the ground. He flipped on his stomach, curled into a ball, and pressed his face into the sod, heart pounding in shock and fear. He had only gotten a quick glimpse of the thing, but it was considerably bigger than he was, and made of solid stone.

How could he defend himself against that? He *couldn't*. He would have to hope that the colossal figure didn't see him. The grass was tall, hopefully enough to obscure him from its view if he stayed completely still, which wasn't something he would have to concentrate on doing as he was frozen in fear.

He planned to run away as soon as its back was turned. Hopefully, since it was made of stone, it would be too heavy to catch up to him.

Then, something poked his back tenderly. He lay completely motionless, though, if it was possible, his heart pounded even more fiercely. Then, the thing poked him again, twice this time.

Slowly, Castor lifted his head. The behemoth was crouched over him, bearing the appearance of a curious child. It had squatted on the ground over him, with its arms resting on its knees, and its stone head was cocked to one side in confusion.

The thing had already seen him, and it was within arm's reach, so he cautiously got up, taking great pains to not make any sudden moves. The statue didn't react aggressively; it just kept staring at him.

For a being made of stone, its face was incredibly expressive. Although its head seemed to be just one domed rock, with barely any neck, it had defined features that moved freely. Its crescent mouth moved just as well as any human's, though how it did so without breaking the stone around it was beyond Castor. It had shallow pits for eyes, a raised brow that elevated and lowered to reflect its confusion, and even a bump for a nose, although there were no nostrils.

Castor flinched when the creature moved one arm from its place on its knee. It hesitated when it saw his reaction, but then continued its motion until its arm was bent at the elbow, and its grey palm faced him. Then, it waved at him.

He blinked in confusion, and then slowly waved back at it. He didn't want to seem rude, after all. The creature beamed at him, and Castor couldn't help but smile back. It was incredibly endearing. It seemed to accept his presence and got up, walking away from him.

Castor was utterly baffled. The creature, whatever it was, looked incredibly formidable but, for some reason, it no longer frightened him. It hadn't harmed him or shown any hostility at all.

Then he remembered Blue. It pretended to be friendly too, right before attempting to feed Castor to the arachna. *That was a limbless floating orb though. It wasn't physically capable of killing me itself. This thing definitely could, if it wanted to. What's to say it won't turn on me later though?*

No, Castor wouldn't let his guard down, no matter how benevolent the statue seemed to be. However, he also held no inclination to leave anymore, since it hadn't attacked him outright. He hadn't completed his quest yet.

The creature beckoned him over to where it now stood, over a fruit-laden bush. Reaching down, it plucked a fruit off its stem and held it out to Castor invitingly, who took it in bemusement. He was still hungry, and he didn't want to refuse the creature's hospitality.

The action also eased another one of Castor's concerns. He had been afraid that the creature would become aggressive if he took one of its fruits. Although, now that he thought about it, what use would a hunk of rock have for food? He doubted it had to eat.

Accepting the fruit, Castor noticed that it was just as perfect as the ones on the last bush. He had somewhat expected the creature to crush it in its massive hands when it pulled it off its stem, but it wasn't even bruised at all. The creature really seemed to be the epitome of a gentle giant.

"Can I take some more?" he asked, not knowing if it could understand him at all. It nodded enthusiastically, to his surprise. *First the orbs, and now this. Is the ability to understand humans so common?*

"Thank you!" Castor gave it a small bow, although he felt a bit silly after.

Moving around to each bush, he collected as much fruit as he could, piling them in his bag. He ate many more, hungry as he was, but he began to carefully collect the seeds, placing them in his pockets for now.

The creature seemed to turn its attention away from him, sitting near the centre of the meadow and playing in the grass, and Castor was once again reminded of a child: cheerful, immature, and easily distracted. Despite his misgivings, a wave of fondness passed over Castor, though he still refused to let it out of his sight.

Night approached, and without the warmth the sun brought, his still damp clothes felt even colder. He wanted to take them off, but he felt awkward doing so with the creature there, even though he severely doubted that the stone being would care. However, eventually his need for comfort won out, so he disrobed and hung the articles of clothing from a tree at the edge of the Glade.

He drew the line at using the restroom though, so, taking his knife for some feeling of comfort, he went out into the forest to relieve himself. He would feel bad sullying the beautiful Glade in such a manner anyway.

Castor began to grow tired as the events of the day once again caught up to him. Even though it seemed to be devoid of monsters, Castor didn't want to tempt fate by sleeping out in the open.

He did find one possible shelter rather quickly. In the cliff face on the far side of the Glade, there was a cave, easily big enough to sleep in. It would have been an ideal resting place if Castor was alone.

The creature toddled up to him, curiously looking at the cave as if it had just noticed its existence as well and Castor smiled nervously up at it. Maybe it realized he could outrun it, and was waiting for an opportunity to block his escape? This cave would be the perfect place to do it.

It didn't matter, Castor was tired enough to risk it. But he still waited until the creature lost interest and wandered away before ducking into the opening.

The sun, descending in the west, cast its light directly into the mouth of the cave, conveniently lighting up most of its interior. Still, knife in hand, Castor was cautious as he stepped into it. His body blocked the light, and he hurriedly turned sideways so he could still see. He was mostly concerned with the back right of the cave, where there was a shadowy pocket he thought might be able to hide something unpleasant. Luckily it was empty, and, with a sigh of relief, he dropped his pack on the dusty floor.

As he turned to head back out, a glint caught the corner of his eye. There was something shiny resting against the back wall of the cave. Only a metallic corner peeked out, the rest being obscured by darkness.

Curious, Castor approached the object, and found that it was a wooden chest of some kind. It was small, about the width of his forearm, and edged with bronze, which was what caused it to shine in the light. It seemed like it had rested there for ages, nestled in between two rock formations the perfect distance apart to encapsulate it.

He knelt down next to the chest. How did it get here? Did Marak's father leave it when he first found the Glade? Or did someone else? Castor expected to need a key or something to open it, so he jumped when, after softly resting a hand on the curved lid, it sprang open silently.

The lid lifted, seemingly on its own accord, and a soft light began to fill the cave, pale green, and completely unlike the fiery orange of the setting sun. Then, something slowly rose out of it.

It looked like a translucent flower, though not any Castor had ever seen. Its many overlapping petals were arranged in a spiral that began from the centre, where he would normally expect to see pollen. Although, in this case, it was smooth and the same shade as the rest of the flower. The petals looked thick as well, and each one was just a bit larger than the one before. The first, which was nearest to the centre, was only as big as the tip of his index finger, while the last one was the size of his hand.

A pattern, just a bit darker green than the space surrounding it, stretched across each petal, seeming to begin where it touched the centre and ending at its tip. It appeared to be the same sequence on each petal, although its size varied. Castor could find no meaning in the symbols.

Since the flower was floating due to forces unknown, Castor could see its underside if he crouched down. There was no stem, and where one should be, there was only a rounded nub. He did see that the patterns continued on the opposite side of the petals as well.

It was beautiful in an ethereal sort of way. His paranoia urged him to leave the flower alone, and he wasn't usually one to ignore it. However, what if it was valuable? Glowing the way it was, it obviously, in Castor's mind at least, had something to do with ambiance or rituals. Could it help his sister? He reached out to touch it.

Castor couldn't say what it felt like because, as soon as his fingers made contact, splitting pain shot through his head like an iron pick. He already had a headache before, and now it magnified one thousandfold. Two dazzling sources of light blinded him, even with his eyes scrunched shut. One he thought was the sun setting outside, the other was to the right and below him. Or was it? He felt vertigo, and he couldn't tell where anything was anymore, though he was pretty sure he had fallen to the ground. The two supernovas in his field of vision emanated a corona of innumerable, vivid colours, more than he ever knew existed. He was also acutely aware of each one of his heartbeats, which resonated throughout his entire body like giant gongs.

His mind couldn't take the sudden influx of information. Like a blown-out candle, it abruptly shut off.

Chapter Nine
Bright and Loud

Castor groaned as he finally came to. The first thing he noticed was a near ceaseless noise, as if someone was dragging a piece of heavy, wooden furniture against the ground. He opened his eyes to find the source and immediately realized that doing so was a mistake. The light flooding in from the cave opening was too damn bright, and it made his headache flare up. The agony from before he passed out had mostly subsided, but his head pounded in tandem with his heartbeat. He tried his best to cover his eyes with the crook of his elbow, and in doing so, he realized that there was something underneath his head.

It was grass, a heaping pile of it. How did it get there? Unwilling to move his right arm away from his face, he felt around the cave floor with his left, knocking into some round objects that rolled away from him. Blindly searching for them again, he found another and grabbed it. He didn't have to be able to see to know that it was one of the fruits from the Glade. Nothing else around him could be that size or shape and still be squishy. Feeling around, he found many scattered around him.

Then, a shadow fell across his face, and Castor almost audibly sighed in relief. Lowering his arm and opening his eyes a crack, he saw the creature standing in the mouth of the cave. In its arms, it cradled even more fruit, and it seemed to be having quite a bit of difficulty holding them all while not crushing them into a pulp against its hard body.

When it realized he was awake, its face lit up into a smile, and it rushed over to Castor and knelt by him. Most of the fruit cascaded onto the floor, but he offered the rest to Castor in cupped hands.

"Are these for me?" Castor asked groggily, his head still throbbing.

The creature nodded emphatically, and Castor took the offered fruit and set them on the ground. He couldn't stomach any food now.

"Thank you so much. I'm sorry, I'll eat them in a bit. My head just hurts so much," he said, pain slurring his words. "Did you make me this pillow as well?"

It nodded again, and Castor tried to smile widely at it, although it came out more as a grimace. The creature made to stand up, perhaps going to pick some more fruit for him even though there was plenty on the ground, but Castor stopped him quickly.

"Please, could you stay there? The sun is too bright; it's hurting my eyes." He had no idea how much it could understand, but he was grateful when it sat down once again.

With its massive frame blocking the entrance of the cave, Castor's eyes slowly began to adjust. The pain lessened its hold over him, and he realized that he was starving after all. He began to inhale the fruit that had been strewn across the floor, and the creature seemed to perk up when it saw him eat its gifts. Castor tried to convey his appreciation to it, but he was distracted. What the hell happened to him?

At the opposite side of the cave, the chest still lay propped open. When he felt well enough to stand, Castor edged around the perimeter of the cave and crouched near it. Whatever the glowing thing in it had been, it was gone now. Regardless, he refused to touch the chest at all, no matter how curious he was.

Even out of the punishing sunlight, his head still pounded. There was a dull roar in his ears, even though there was nothing around him to elicit such a noise. The rest of his body hurt as well, from his foray down the river and from sleeping on the hard rock floor. He was incredibly grateful that the creature tried to give him some cushioning at all, but grass could only do so much.

Then he realized something odd. He could tell that he had been unconscious for a while, both by how his body felt and by how ravenous he was. By all rights, it should be the dead of night or morning. However, the sun was shining directly at him when he woke up, and since he had already noted that the cave faced west, that meant that it was already evening. Either his body was wrong, and he had only been out for a couple minutes, or he had been unconscious for nearly an entire day!

He was inclined to believe the latter, which was upsetting to say the least. Still, so much valuable time had been wasted, and he really wanted to return home with his spoils. He rubbed the tender skin on his back, noting absentmindedly that he was still naked and needed to relieve himself.

Unfortunately, it took him a lot longer before he could bear stepping out of the cave and into the open, and even then he was forced to walk with his back to the sun, though only a sliver of it was still above the horizon.

Castor soon realized that it wasn't just his eyes that were especially sensitive at the moment. He jumped when an especially loud noise emanated from all around him. It was like a very long piece of fabric being torn, and the boy looked around wildly for the source, wincing, as doing so brought his eyes in contact with the sun's rays once again. The noise stopped for a while before starting up again, and this time the movement of the branches of trees surrounding the Glade caught his attention.

Was he hearing the breeze all this time? Was that what that dull roar in the cave was too? However, it was much louder now that he wasn't sheltered in its walls.

The wind was so loud, even louder than it was in any violent storm he had witnessed, and in Toriath there were many. What was happening to him? And, more importantly, when would it go away? He was quite frustrated, so he gathered as much fruit as he could, put it in his pack, and brought it back to the cave. If he was going to be incapacitated like this for a while, he could at least use that time to be productive, especially since he lost nearly an entire day.

A not insignificant consolation for his current predicament was the fact that the slowly fading numbness in his right arm was now completely gone. He hadn't noticed it in its absence, but when he was picking fruit, he found that he could actually keep the pack open with his right hand without any difficulty. He hadn't realized how much he depended on his dominant hand, and every action he took after losing his ability felt unnatural. He was glad to be able to use it reliably again.

As he ate, Castor discovered that the fruit each contained two to four seeds. He saved each one, using his tongue to separate the seeds from the flesh of the fruit and dropped them onto his cupped palm. When he was finished, he stuck them into his pocket.

The creature had stayed near him this entire time, seemingly scared that he would pass out again. It was such a kind creature, and Castor no longer feared that it was acting to lull him into a false sense of security. If it wanted to kill him, it would have had ample opportunity to do so while he was unconscious. It had done so much for him that he felt bad calling it—*them*—creature.

"Do you have a name?" he asked with a smile. Their eye cavities widened in surprise, but they quickly shook their head. "Would you like one?"

This time, they nodded vigorously, and Castor laughed at their enthusiasm. He searched for the perfect one for a couple minutes in his head, toying with many stupid ideas such as Pasture, Rocky, or Forest, before he decided to give them a proper name. "How about Talias?" It was the name of one of the guards back home, a young man who Castor fancied before he died. Castor had always liked the sound of it and hoped the original Talias wouldn't mind his name being bestown like this.

The newly dubbed Talias nearly bounced up and down in glee, and Castor winced at the harsh sound their stone feet made against the cave floor.

"Oh, I suppose I never told you my name. I'm Castor. It's nice to meet you, Talias." He held out his arm and was once again surprised when Talias shook it on their own accord. He wondered if they had ever spent any time with humans before.

That might also explain where they learned about pillows, since Castor doubted they ever needed one. He first found them faceplanted into the dirt, after all.

Since he was stuck in the cave for the time being, he decided he should begin to fulfill his second objective of this quest, which was to take as much ambiance as he could from the wild and bring it back to the village. The cave was big enough to fit the matrix that he wanted to create, so he got to work, Talias watching curiously over his shoulder as he did so.

Pulling out the materials he brought with him, Castor began to lay down the salt he kept in one of his waterskins. His luck had shone through just this once. When he was preparing to leave the village, he had needed to find a container to put the salt in that wouldn't allow it to leak everywhere while he was travelling. The only thing he could find that was secure enough was this waterskin, which was waterproof. If he had used some other container, his trip down the river would have completely dissolved the salt, and he wouldn't be able to create the matrix now.

Castor was intimately familiar with this ritual. In essence, it was the same as the one they used to nourish the tree, but with one simple addition. Instead of simply bringing the surrounding ambiance into an area, he needed to trap it in a specific object.

This extra step was represented in the matrix by a trapezoid, which was nestled inside the inner triangle, and new symbols were also added above and below it. A sea monster bone went in each triangle and Castor placed the core of the ritual, in this case one of his crystals, in the centre.

This process was called imbuing. Almost always, matter acted as an open gate for ambiance, meaning that energy moved in and out of its own accord. In addition to this passive action, the amount of ambiance in living things fluctuated even more dramatically from moment to moment as they took in matter and expelled it by breathing, eating, metabolizing, sweating, and through other, more subtle means.

When it came to inorganic matter, there were no extenuating circumstances to affect the flow of ambiance. However, people sometimes found it useful to imbue objects, which meant that they saturated those objects in ambiance, and then trapped the energy inside. This way, the ambiance did not autonomously flow out of it.

Castor frequently lamented the fact that he couldn't just imbue the tree so that they wouldn't have to carry out that ritual every day, especially now that he knew of Jayna's plight. However, imbuing something didn't just keep ambiance inside the object. It *froze* the ambiance altogether. Strange things happened to living organisms if the ambiance inside of them was completely frozen, or so he had been told.

With the matrix finished and the ingredients placed, Castor mentally prepared himself to start the ritual. He had imbued objects several times in practice, but he had never done it at the scale he currently planned to. Also, his sister had always been present. He wasn't really worried about accidentally hurting himself because this ritual was supposed to only use a sliver of his own ambiance, but he was afraid, nonetheless. His father and sister had impressed upon him long ago that rituals weren't something to mess around with.

Another brief worry he had was that the rituals would pull in too much ambiance and hurt the ecosystem of the Glade. It would be a real shame, he thought, to damage the one sanctuary in the middle of this gods-forsaken forest. And what if they needed to retrieve more seeds from here in the future?

After some more thought, he discounted that fear as well. His sister's rituals only hurt their village's ambiance after they were conducted every day for around two years. It was an unusual case, and the Glade would recover quickly if it was even damaged by his actions at all.

Everything was all set up. Using his fire starter, he lit one of his catalyst tags in his left hand. Putting down the instrument, Castor placed his right hand onto the salt. He needed to keep a bare part of his body on the matrix in order for it to take the little ambiance it needed from him as a toll. Without his contribution, as small as it may be, the ritual would fail, and his ingredients would be wasted. As the catalyst almost completely burned away, he placed the tag onto the salt as well, which activated the matrix with a small pop.

The catalyst was another example of an imbued object.

Usually made in bulk, they contained just a small amount of ambiance. When they were burned, the energy within was condensed into a smaller and smaller amount of space until it finally ran out of matter to inhabit and popped.

Rituals needed a sudden influx of ambiance to trigger them, which was why the natural flow of ambiance between matter would always cause them to activate prematurely. The pop caused by the catalyst, although small, was strong enough to spark the ritual.

The telltale silver glow signifying the start of the ritual ran through the matrix, originating from where the catalyst was placed. Talias clapped excitedly at the spectacle, and Castor's irrational fear fell away as he found himself to be only slightly fatigued. Inspecting the crystal, it looked just the same as it did before, but this was to be expected. He put it away, sighed, and roughly swept aside the crumbling salt and bones. There were several more crystals to fill and unfortunately, he couldn't reuse any ingredients. He picked up the waterskin filled with salt once more and began to do it all over again.

By the time he was finally done, night had begun to fall. Castor was glad he was able to finish before true darkness hit, because there was no way he could have performed his rituals in the dark. What sounded fantastic to him right now was a fire. It was cool inside the cave, just enough to make him uncomfortable.

Castor had gotten used to the light by the end of the day and his headache was finally gone. He had reasoned that, if the light was still too much for him, he could always turn around. The problem was, he didn't have any fuel to use as kindling. Although, that was easily remedied, as it didn't seem to be too dark yet. He went out of the cave to search for any sticks lying around the edge of the Glade.

The night sky was enchanting, and Castor sighed contentedly. He wasn't sure why, but the stars looked so much clearer in the Glade, and he noticed so many more than he usually would in the village.

Castor frowned in thought. It was strange; the stars were out, so it should be fully dark. But to him, it looked like it was still dusk. He blinked hard and rubbed his eyes, but nothing changed. His vision had been incredibly sensitive all day, and it seemed like there was another, possibly helpful, side effect: it improved his night vision. Still, he hoped everything would be back to normal the following morning. Castor really wanted to start his journey back home tomorrow, and he couldn't do that if he was so drastically debilitated. For now, he decided to enjoy the night.

He was easily able to gather enough sticks to make a fire, so he made a pile of them in the cave and, with difficulty, set them alight with his fire starter. His satisfaction only lasted a moment, because when the fire finally flared up all the way, the roiling smoke it produced reached the cave ceiling, and had nowhere to go. When Castor realized what was happening, he frantically tried to put out the blaze, but it was stubborn. He stamped it out as best as he could and took some of the larger branches that the fire hadn't completely encompassed and threw them out of the cave mouth. Then, he realized that was potentially an even worse idea and ran after them.

Talias just watched the whole thing in confusion, and Castor realized that he may have been overestimating their level of intelligence.

Luckily, the Glade had not immediately caught on fire as he feared. The verdant grass was full of moisture, so the embers only singed it instead of spreading. Castor looked back into the mouth of the cave and nearly let out a sob of frustration. Grey smoke lazily crept out of the mouth that it had nearly filled. He just wanted a damn fire!

He grabbed his drying clothes which still hung from a tree branch, and, taking a deep gulp of air, he went back in and tried to sweep the cloth up and down to fan the smoke out of the cave. It worked moderately well, but his eyes started to sting, and he had to stop.

Then, Talias poked him on the shoulder, and gently took the fabric out of his hands. Going back into the cave, they began to imitate him, fanning away the smoke. Since they didn't have eyes, and presumably didn't need to breathe, they were impervious to the smoke. They didn't have very good fine motor control though, so it didn't work nearly as well, but Castor's fondness for the being soared.

As he waited for his shelter to become habitable again, he took his pack and went around the Glade to harvest more of the fruit. He took the waterskin that actually held water in it and placed the seeds he had gathered so far inside. He made a mental reminder not to choke whenever he went for a drink. He wanted to put it in the empty skin that had been used to carry the salt, but he didn't know if that would ruin the seeds and he didn't want to take the chance. He would rinse that one out in the river on his way back, and that could be his new waterskin.

Soon his bag was filled completely, but he still wanted as many seeds as he could possibly carry. Though he felt guilty about wasting food, Castor started tearing up fruit for their seeds without eating them. He was just too full, and wasn't that a strange sensation? He hadn't been full for almost two years!

Castor was careful to leave several fruits on each bush, so that they could hopefully survive and reproduce naturally. By the time he was done, his waterskin was completely full of seeds, as were both of his pockets. Surely, he thought, that was enough.

The cave was mostly cleared up, although the faint smell of smoke still hung in the air. He thanked Talias and took back his clothes, not wanting to be naked anymore. They smelled heavily of campfire smoke now, but Castor didn't really mind it.

Even though he had slept for nearly twenty-four hours not too long ago, he was tired again. Still, it took him a very long time to fall asleep. The now-identified sound of the wind, which Castor had moderately adjusted to by now, reverberated throughout the cave. Frustrated, he finally took out the roll of homemade bandages and tied them around his head, blocking his ears, and grumbling as he did so. He really wanted to use those as a pillow. Instead, he slept on the grass Talias gathered for him and his pack filled with fruit, probably squashing a few in the process.

When he woke up, Castor was grateful to find that his migraine from the day before hadn't risen again with the morning sun. Still, he wasn't completely back to normal. Everything he saw still appeared to be astonishingly vivid, and for the first time, Castor truly looked around the Glade. He appreciated its beauty when he first discovered it, but he had missed so much. For example, there was a definitive border between the Glade and what lay outside of it. The colour of the grass within it was a few shades brighter, and the blades grew in thicker patches. He also noticed a natural, waxy sheen on the leaves of the fruit bushes, which reflected the sunlight into iridescent auras that surrounded each one like a halo.

The most interesting sight by far was the carvings on the cliff face near the mouth of the cave. Symbols had been etched deep into the rock, each bigger than his head or even larger when taking perspective into account. All of them were equidistant from one another and formed a rectangle around four meters wide.

Castor was sure it was a message of some kind, but it must have been written in an entirely different language, and he had no clue what it said. He had never heard of any other language besides English ever existing. The symbols were all foreign, but as he examined them, he realized that he did recognize one.

One of the bottom lines near the right was the symbol ⋊⊣, which was placed in the ritual he and his sister used every day, although here it was rotated. He had assumed that it was a meaningless symbol used to control the flow of ambiance.

The ⋊⊣ must have some significance to it besides its shape, Castor now realized. He wanted to copy the message down, as he was curious to see if Jayna or someone else could make any sense out of it. Unfortunately, he had no paper or pencil to write with. Nevertheless, he stared at the symbols, trying to commit them to memory, even though he knew it was futile.

Daylight was burning, and he couldn't rationalize staying in the Glade any longer, no matter how beautiful it was. After eating a breakfast of some of the Glade's remaining fruit, he began to say his goodbyes to Talias.

"I don't suppose you want to come with me?" Castor asked.

They shook their massive head regretfully and looked back at the Glade behind them.

"I get it," Castor said sorrowfully. "This is your home. I have to go home too." They nodded in understanding, stepped back, and opened their mouth wider than Castor had ever seen them do. Then, they stuck their whole hand in the opening. Castor, a little grossed out, was surprised to see that, when they retracted their hand, they were now holding a polished disc, with another symbol Castor didn't recognize etched roughly into it.

Talias offered the disk to Castor, who took it from them gently. Even though it came from their mouth, it was completely dry, which made sense in retrospect.

"You want me to have this?" he asked. They nodded in confirmation. "Thank you, I'll treasure it." He meant it, too. The stone was clearly important to Talias, and Castor doubted that they carved the symbol on it themselves. They didn't have the dexterity.

Stepping forward, Castor gave Talias one last, great hug. They embraced him as well, patting him on the back as gently as they could. He was surprised by how emotional leaving his new friend made him, and Talias seemed forlorn as well.

Still, he really needed to go. He set off back along the path he used to enter the Glade, looking back periodically to see his friend waving back at him. Then, they were out of view.

Chapter Ten
Back in Enemy Territory

Castor appreciated just how much better he felt on this leg of the journey. No soaking wet clothes, ravenous hunger or the plethora of injuries that littered his body.

Hold on, he thought with a frown. *That makes no sense. Why doesn't everything hurt anymore?*

He wasn't completely pain free. Castor still felt twinges, aches and sores all over his body, but that was nothing compared to what he *should* be feeling. During his flight down the river, the current had knocked him into rocks and debris, and he had suffered too many cuts, scrapes and bruises to count. Just two nights of rest couldn't have been enough for him to heal this much, right?

Castor looked at his arms and found that many of the smaller scrapes were gone completely. The deeper cuts were still there, but they were thin, and covered by scabs that looked almost a week old, not a couple days. His fingers, the skin on which had been ravaged by his wild attempts to grab hold of anything, looked mostly healed as well, although the nails were quite broken and he could see the almost black marks that signalled there was old blood trapped underneath them.

He crouched down and pulled down his pants halfway to get a better look at his outer thigh. It had taken the most damage during his plunge, when that first overhanging branch smashed into it at full force. Castor knew that, by all accounts, there should be a giant bruise there. And there was one, covering the majority of his right thigh, but it was mottled a pale green and yellow, which only happened over a fair amount of time.

The only explanation he could think of was that the weird flower in the chest healed him somehow, which was fantastic.

Castor wasn't sure that the healing made up for all the trouble the flower caused him. He lost a lot of time, and his vision and hearing were still messed up. Maybe the pain was worth it though. If he had kept those injuries, he might not be able to outrun any spiders he encountered on his trip back.

On that note, Castor looked around carefully, pulling up his pants as he did so. Seeing no threats around him, he continued. He needed to remember that he was out of the Glade, which, for whatever reason, seemed to be safe from spiders. He was back in the wild now, and he should be more alert.

Castor found his way back to the river and decided to follow it downstream. He didn't have any better ideas, and he hadn't seen any spiders since he crossed it. Maybe they couldn't make it to this side? That didn't really make sense though. If they were coming from the Umbra Bosk like Marak said, then they should be even more numerous over here on the east bank.

Perhaps I've just been lucky after all, he thought, placing a hand on the knife that rested at his hip once more.

The farther away from the Glade he travelled, the less healthy the trees seemed. Castor didn't think that the species were different, but they weren't quite as tall or robust. Also, the colours of the leaves were a bit duller, and the vines that seemed to be growing everywhere else in the forest began to reappear. It was just one more mystery about the Glade, and Castor wondered what made it so special. He doubted he would ever know.

Eventually, Castor reached a point in the river where the bank wasn't too high. The waterskin he had used for drinking water on the way here was filled with seeds now, so he took this opportunity to dump the remaining salt out from his spare, rinse it out in the river and fill it up again.

Several hours later, Castor's good fortune finally ran out. Out of the corner of his eye, he saw movement and ducked behind a tree. Much to his dismay, he realized that it was, in fact, an arachna. There was quite a bit of variability in size between the monsters, Castor had noticed. He wasn't sure if it was due to their age or other factors, but it didn't matter. This one was especially large; he could tell even at this distance. He crept away, putting as many trees as he could between him and the beast without entering its line of sight.

Unfortunately, some things were out of his control. From his right, he could hear wood snapping, and at first, he was relieved. Something was out there, hopefully not human, and it might draw away the spider's attention. Then the snapping got louder and louder and, with horror, he realized that, whatever it was, it was heading directly towards him.

The arachna picked up on the noise as he hoped it would, and Castor used its distraction to move away even more quickly. Then, there was a loud crack, almost deafening to Castor's hypersensitive ears. A whole tree had been toppled and, moments later, Castor could see what caused it.

There was another monster barrelling towards them, and this time, it wasn't an arachna. It was humanoid. At least, it had two arms and two legs, and it ran upright. No one would ever mistake it for a human though. Its body was covered in dark fur, wiry like a man's beard, though underneath it he could see pinkish skin. Even more striking was its body, specifically its left arm, which seemed to be absorbed by a giant growth that was even bigger than its torso. Eyes wide, Castor realized that it wasn't a growth, but a giant muscle.

It looked as if all the muscles in only that arm had been inflated to a ridiculous degree. It just looked wrong connected to the rest of its body, which seemed to be more properly proportioned. Its right arm looked more like that of a human, puny in comparison, but Castor's keen eye could tell it was still much more muscular than even Musov's, whose biceps had been honed by years of striking hot iron.

The giant patch of muscle didn't stop as it reached the thing's shoulder. It continued up the monster's neck, making it so broad that it obscured the monster's neck entirely. A strip even encroached on its face, closing one eye permanently and inhibiting its ability to open its mouth. Still, it managed to let out a loud yet strangled roar.

Perhaps the most frightening thing about it was its size, as it stood at a gargantuan two and a half meters tall. It moved quickly as well, which was impressive considering how unbalanced the poor creature was. Each stride almost sent it crashing to the ground, but it somehow always managed to stay upright.

Castor's eyes widened when an almost casual swat of its giant arm knocked down a branch twice as thick as his torso.

No way, he thought. *I'm getting out of here.*

Unlike the spider, that monster wouldn't care if he was here or not. It was heading straight for him and destroying everything in its path.

He half expected the giant spider to run away from it as well, but the arachna quit moving at its slow, swaying pace and scuttled towards the rampaging beast. As big as the spider was, it was still two heads shorter than the monster, and Castor wouldn't have been surprised if it was squashed immediately.

However, there was a reason the arachna had conquered this forest. In morbid curiosity, Castor watched as the spider skirted past the monster instead of meeting it head on, and in an instant, used its abdomen, the biggest part of its body, to sweep out the upright creature's legs. The monster, which was quite top-heavy, went down sprawling.

Without its big form in the way, Castor saw what was causing it to rush through the trees with such reckless abandon. It was being chased by two other spiders, which had slowed after the other one took it down. They were quite a bit smaller than the first, though Castor would probably be able to look each one dead in the eye if they were face to face. Dead in the eyes rather, as they each had six.

Both spiders seemed to decide that they couldn't challenge the much larger specimen that had stolen their meal, but they were facing Castor and saw his movement.

Castor cursed to himself. The large spider was being kept occupied by its massive prey and it was turned away from him as well, so he had slowed down to watch. He didn't expect the new spiders which faced him now. Giving the titanic clash before them a wide berth, they gave chase.

All thoughts of stealth gone out the window, Castor sprinted away with all his might. Although the fear was definitely still there, this flight felt different from his last escape from spiders. Before, everything happened so fast that he had a difficult time dodging the trees while ensuring he did not trip over a root, or fall into a river perhaps.

He had none of those issues now. With ease, he tracked each and every tree as it came before him, along with every low-hanging branch and every hazard that appeared on the ground. He wasn't any faster, and sometimes his body couldn't keep up with what he perceived, but he did find that he could keep a clearer head.

Alongside his terror, he began to feel something else. Exhilaration. He felt completely in control of his body, and even his surroundings to some extent, and it was like nothing he had ever experienced before. Even as he ran for his life, from monsters that had haunted his nightmares for years, he almost felt like he was having fun.

He couldn't become completely absorbed in those feelings though. Due to his intense focus on his surroundings, he noticed that the concentration of trees had started to thin. Was he approaching the edge of the forest? That couldn't be right, it took him well over a day to travel the distance he did. Then he remembered how fast the river current took him. He didn't know how long he was in its clutches, but it might have pulled him a lot closer to the border of the forest.

He could clearly hear the monsters on his tail, but he spared a quick backwards glance to judge their distance. They were still faster than him, but his nimbleness allowed Castor to navigate through the trees better, so the gap between them remained the same size. But he was getting tired, and his backpack was considerably heavier now than it was before from the fruit he brought back from the Glade.

Then, of course, nature decided to throw another obstacle in his path. He first noticed an opening in the trees, before his view shifted and he was able to see the ground, or rather, the lack thereof. Castor belted out a strangled curse, initially thinking it was a cliff, but then he saw the other side. Another river?

The spiders had corralled him away from the one he was travelling alongside, and it was now well out of view. However, the sound of rushing water was still fading, and the closer he got to it, the farther down he could see. It seemed to be an empty, long fissure in the ground. Deep as well, although perspective made it so that he couldn't judge to what extent. But oddly, it didn't seem all that wide.

He didn't have time to weigh his options; the ravine was approaching too quickly. He could go left or right and run alongside the ravine. However, that would rob him of a lot of his momentum, and it would allow the spiders to possibly close the gap between them. Also, the trees were a lot sparser near the ravine, so the faster spiders would likely catch up to him quickly with his one advantage nullified. His second option was to take an even greater risk and try to jump over the ravine.

A large part of Castor doubted that he could make the jump. His legs were already protesting, and it was just a little bit too wide. But he saw that there were vines that grew down from the foliage just on the other side. If he jumped with all his might, using the momentum he currently built, he could grab onto a fistful of vines even if he didn't make it across.

To him, it was the only option. Reaching the lip of the ravine, he pushed off with all the strength his calves and thighs could muster. He flew most of the way across, his toe actually touching the opposite side, and then he fell. Castor didn't have time to panic, he grabbed a fistful of small vines in his left hand, and a much sturdier one in his right. The short vines ripped off easily, and he frantically grabbed the other with both hands as tightly as he could. His weight pulled down the vine, and the tiny roots that connected it to the ground ripped away. Castor continued to fall into the ravine until the vine became taut, stopping him with a mighty jerk that threatened to pull his shoulder out of its socket.

And then, under the weight of Castor's body, along with the force of the fall, the vine snapped.

Chapter Eleven
Scar in the Land

Castor might have screamed, but he had no way of knowing. The sound itself and the breath that ushered it forth was snatched straight out of his lungs. When the vine snapped, it cancelled out most of the momentum he built up until that point, which surely saved his life. It also sent him spinning like a rag doll the remainder of the way down.

He landed on his side and became stuck in the tapered gap that made up the bottom of the ravine. Dazed for a moment, his first instinct was to pull himself out, which was rather difficult to do with one of his arms trapped. Then, a shadow passed over him.

Castor had gambled over the assumption that a spider couldn't jump very far. Their legs didn't point in the same direction as his, and he thought that their knees wouldn't have the strength to propel them. In his panicked state, he had forgotten how the spiders jumped up the village walls each night, trying to attach their webs so that they could climb up.

A spider did jump after him, quite far in fact. However, like him, it couldn't manage to clear the gap. And unlike him, it didn't have hands to grab any vines. It fell the entire depth of the ravine and landed upside down next to him. The loud crack of its hard exoskeleton against the stone walls shook Castor out of his stupor.

Twisting his neck awkwardly to look up at the arachna,

Castor was horrified to see its legs twitching. He didn't know if it was in the throes of death, or if it was just dazed, but what he did know was that, if it got up, he would have no way to escape from it in the close confines of the ravine.

Castor wriggled fiercely, trying to free himself from between the rocks. Each twitch of its legs brought another surge of panic, and he could have sworn he saw it rocking itself. Was it trying to flip itself over?

Finally, he was able to lift himself out using his exposed arm and legs. His hand flew to his waist, and he thanked the gods that his knife had not come free in the fall. He drew it and clutched the handle tightly, knowing that if he let go, the knife would fall into the gap between the rocks and he wouldn't be able to retrieve it.

He used both sides of the ravine to clumsily hop to where the spider had landed. Its fangs were unsheathed and snapping: it *was* still alive. He gripped the knife as far up the hilt as possible so that he could keep as great a distance as he could between him and the writhing creature, and, with all the force his skinny arms could muster, he brought the blade down on its head. Once, twice, three times. Then its legs twitched again and so he kept stabbing.

When he was absolutely sure that the monster was dead, he leaned against the slanting wall of rock and tried to rein in his gasping breaths. He looked up, watching for the second spider. Would it try to jump as well? Would it try to climb down?

It didn't. It must have seen the failure of it brethren, or looked and saw the depth of the ravine. When he was confident that another giant arachna wasn't going to fall on top of him, he began to take stock of his surroundings. The ravine was shaped like a wedge, wide at the top, and tapering into the narrow crevice that Castor had found himself stuck in. When he looked down, he was completely unable to see the bottom. It was just a stretch of pitch black that even the sun, which was high in the sky by this point, couldn't penetrate.

Castor had felt so much panic within the last hour, he just couldn't muster up one more ounce of fear now that he was out of immediate danger. He just felt resigned.

Better get on with it. I'm already sick of this place.

The walls of the ravine weren't smooth, but there didn't appear to be handholds either. They almost looked like frozen waves, but the surface was rough and angular—the result of an uneven fracture. There also seemed to be defined layers within the stone face, each differentiated from another by a slightly different colour.

Castor made his way down the stretch of canyon, hoping that there was an area along the wall that either had divots he could use to climb up, or was narrow enough that he could escape by pushing his arms and legs against both sides to ascend. However, he couldn't find any section that would allow him to scale the rock.

The ravine was rather long, and it took just under fifteen minutes for him to make his way to one of its edges. Of course, that was due in part to the fact that he couldn't walk on the ground normally. He had to climb over the unsteady rocks and make sure that his feet didn't get stuck in the gaps.

He hoped that the end of the ravine would be narrow enough for him to climb up all the way to the top. He thought it might be like a cut on skin, where the edge was narrow before it got larger, and then it tapered once again.

What he discovered was that the ravine collapsed in on itself. A giant part of the cliff face eroded away and blocked off this area from the rest. He knew it continued on past this point because he could see above it. The fallen rock didn't completely fill up the gap; it lay diagonally against the wall. The rubble blocked off any opening that might have been left at the bottom, but at the top he could see over the slanted stone if he stood far enough back.

Castor considered the possibility of climbing up this area, because there was debris that had fallen around it, and the top of the slanted rock was lower than the walls of the ravine. He gave climbing the piled rocks a few, halfhearted tries and he failed because, after a point, the rock became too sheer. So, he gave up on trying to escape from this point for now. It might be his best option, but he decided that it would be smarter to check what was on the opposite side of the ravine first.

He reached the point he fell in from, marked by the dead spider that lay belly-up on the rocks. He shuddered again when he saw the beast and looked at all eight of its legs, trying to judge if they had moved once he was out of sight. He needed to get around the damned thing, but it scared him even now. What if, when he stepped on it, it grabbed him with its legs and bit him? Its fangs were face up; it would be easy for it to do so.

Not so easy, considering it's dead, his rational brain reminded himself. It *was* dead, truly, but Castor still spent the next ten minutes climbing over the spider by pressing against both sides of the ravine, as high as he could before it separated too far. Then, he shifted himself across the space above the spider's corpse, giving it as wide a berth as he could, before descending.

The other end of the ravine was even farther away, and as he struggled to make his way there, he began to hear an odd noise that grew louder with each step. It sounded familiar, but he couldn't place it.

The ravine was capped off on this end as well, but in a much more mysterious way. There was a man-made wall that stretched up all the way to the top of the ravine, built out of stone, mortar and some half-rotted logs. It looked ancient.

When he stood close enough to the wall, he felt cool, and not just because he was in its shadow. Touching a hand to his face, he found that the sensation resulted from a light spray of water, and, when he looked down, he saw that the rock was slick as well. This was a dam, he realized, and suddenly he understood exactly where he was.

On the other side of this dam was the river he had been walking alongside just an hour ago. He had been chased away from it by the arachna, although if he hadn't been, he would have made it to this point anyway, albeit in a much more favourable position above the ravine.

The noise he heard right now, which was a lot louder in this spot, was the sound of the river rushing past. He didn't recognize the sound because it was distorted immensely by the acoustics of the ravine and the river's position relative to himself. It was in front of him, likely just meters away, only blocked by this dam.

Someone long ago must have built it, for whatever reason, to redirect the river, or at least block one of its tributaries. *Which means this was once a path of the old river,* he realized. *That must have been what carved out the ravine.*

Castor looked up at the dam with intensity. Was it groaning, or was that just his imagination? It would be just his luck for this dam, which had probably stood unwavering for decades if not longer, to collapse right after he found himself at its mercy. Actually, would that be so bad?

He considered the possibility. If the dam broke, maybe the water would sweep in and lift him out of the ravine. Or, much more likely, the weight of the water would crush all his bones. Still, he would consider it as a *very* last resort, not that he knew how he could bring down the dam anyway.

The sun was low, and it cast his shadow in strange patterns along the uneven rocks. With resignation, Castor prepared to spend the night in this ravine. He was hungry, so he rummaged through his pack. Unsurprisingly, he found that most of his fruit was squashed.

Then he gasped and felt around his pockets. Sure enough, most of the seeds he kept there had fallen out, insecure as they were. Still, he thought, trying to calm himself, he had an entire waterskin full of seeds in his pack, and the crystals were secure in there as well.

With that thought in mind, he kept a firm grip on the bag, holding it on his knees and opening it as little as possible to prevent anything from falling out as he withdrew bits of fruit from inside. The lining was damp and slimy from the fruit juice, which made for a wholly unpleasant experience. Also, his stomach felt weird after the meal, likely from the fear response earlier and the fact that he hadn't eaten dry food in days now. There was nothing he could do about that though, so he situated himself as best as he could and prepared for night to fall.

If he thought that his quality of sleep was poor the last few nights, it was nothing compared to camping in the ravine. Before, he at least had flat ground to rest on. Now, he had to perform a precarious balancing act so that he wouldn't become stuck in the gap like when he first fell. And even when he *did* find an orientation that provided some stability, the sharp jutting rocks made lying down almost unbearable.

It was unsurprising that Castor woke up aching, tired, and very grumpy. He ate a breakfast of fruit chunks, which were already beginning to sour, and then he paced around the ravine, examining the walls once again to try and find any feasible climbing paths he might have missed the day before. He spent half the day scrutinizing the rocks, and he even tried to climb up a couple of times. Inevitably, he failed.

The issue was that, at around the four meter mark, the ravine became too wide for him to use both sides to climb, and the protruding rocks that he could use as handholds were much too far apart for him to reach.

He tried to stay far away from the dam. Castor knew that it probably wouldn't break; it had survived this long after all. It was more of a mental thing. Hearing the odd sounds of the dam put him on edge, and it completely prevented him from concentrating. Now that he knew what the sound was, he could hear it reverberate through the ravine from many meters away and there was nothing he could do to block it out while working.

Climbing the rocks over the spider once again, he made his way back to the collapsed section of the ravine. His best strategy was to remove some of the rocks that had fallen in front of the massive boulder that came down. He hoped that, once some of the debris was cleared away, there would be a gap wide enough for him to crawl through. On the other side, there might be an area that he *could* climb out from, or possibly a dried-up lake with more gradually sloping walls.

Moving those rocks was a lot easier said than done. Because the ravine was so narrow at the bottom, Castor couldn't turn around easily, so even clearing away the dirt and smaller rocks was difficult. When he got to the mid-sized rocks, it was even more challenging, both because of their weight and their size. The largest rocks, which were his biggest obstacles, he couldn't even budge at all.

It was ironic, Castor thought. He was always too weak to

perform the most strenuous physical labour back in the village, which was part of the reason he left to complete this quest. He had thought it was more in line with his skill set. Now, he was stuck in a hole performing manual labour and once again he was too weak.

Then the day was over, and Castor felt like he accomplished nothing. He went to sleep, in a new spot this time, angry, bitter, and more than a bit hopeless.

The next day, Castor crawled over the spider once again. He still refused to touch it, even though he was absolutely sure it was dead by now. Since he hated being near the dam, he used the side it was on to relieve himself when necessary. There was a gap in the bottom of the ravine so deep that he couldn't even see the bottom of it, so he tried to pretend it was just a cramped outhouse.

When he took a break from labouring at the collapsed end, he realized that the fruit had also definitely turned bad. Crushed the way it was, its skin couldn't protect the soggy flesh inside from turning. Castor ate it anyway. He had very little options, and he could only hope that it didn't make him ill. He still needed to save his dry rations, now more so than ever.

When he reached into his bag to fish out another slimy chunk, his arm let out a sharp *jolt*. It almost felt like a muscle twitch, but he didn't actually move. Castor would have disregarded the instance immediately, except something impossible happened.

At first, he thought it was his imagination. Then, his eyes widened as he realized that his bag was getting lighter. *Much* lighter. Alarmed, Castor reached into his bag and felt around. Where were his crystals? And his fruit? And medical supplies?

His bag was getting lighter and lighter by the second, and Castor actually let out a yelp of alarm when he grabbed one of his waterskins and it *disappeared* from his grasp. Soon, the bag was completely empty.

Nearly sobbing in fear and frustration, Castor tore open the bag fully, even going so far as to pull the damned thing inside out to search for his missing, vital supplies. And on the base of the pack's lining, he found something he was sure wasn't there before.

It was a design of sorts, painted into the leather. *No, not painted,* he realized. His too sensitive eyes could clearly see the grain of the leather, including every minute crease. Paint and ink would bleed into these creases, and that wasn't happening here. He ran his fingers over the middle of the pattern and couldn't find a raised imprint of any kind. It was as if the lines had always been a part of the leather, but they *couldn't* have been. Right?

The design was complex. At its core were two hexagons, one inside the other. They were connected by a triangle that pointed downwards, and all three of its points peeked out from alternating sides of the outer hexagon. In the very centre was the number eight. Either that or the symbol for infinity.

A heptagon surrounded the three connected shapes, and seven circles were embedded in each point. These circles also included their own unique symbol. Castor didn't think they were words; it obviously wasn't English, and the symbols were curved, unlike the foreign script he saw carved into the cliff. Unless there was a third unknown language, they must be pictures or icons of some sort.

The entire thing almost looked like a ritual matrix, except for the outer part. The heptagon and circles were completely disconnected from the inner portion, which would invalidate a ritual. If parts of the matrix weren't connected, there was no way for the ambiance to travel in between them.

Also, using circles, arcs or any other curved elements in a matrix was... unorthodox. It was more difficult to produce curved lines consistently, and imprecise measurements could cause the matrix to fail, so practitioners usually stuck with straight lines.

Now how the hell was Castor supposed to get his stuff back? He considered cutting the leather apart with his knife when he angled the pack and saw what looked to be a list climbing up the side.

It was in English, thank the gods, and he pulled the leather taut so he could read the words properly.

Catalyst (x1), Fabric Strips: 13-14 grams (x5), Mundane Imbued Crystal: Forest/Meadows neutral (x4), Treasure Plum Portion: 3-4 grams (x6), Treasure Plum Portion: 4-5 grams (x9)...

It was a list of everything he lost! But how the hell did he get them out?

There were a lot of treasure plum portions; that must be what the fruit was called. He skipped much further down the list just to make sure but, as he hoped, this was a list of everything he lost! But how the hell did he get them out?

He touched the first item on the list and watched in amazement as his spare catalyst tag materialized on top of the lining. Then, once its form had solidified, it faded away once more. Castor was less focused on the tag itself. As soon as he touched the lettering, the word *Catalyst* at the top of the list disappeared altogether. And even more bizarrely, every other item below it shifted up simultaneously. When the catalyst disappeared again, every item shifted down once more, and *Catalyst* reappeared at the top of the list.

Castor swore at the inexplicable sight before him. He pressed *Catalyst* again, but then picked the tag up once it materialized. It didn't fade away again. He touched it to the outside of his pack as well, just to make sure, and it still remained.

Great. So, I just have to make sure nothing touches the inside of the bag. But then where was he going to put all his stuff? He thought about pulling his pack inside out and using it that way, but then his straps were inaccessible, and he needed his arms free to try and dig himself out.

He really didn't want to leave all his stuff... wherever it currently was. Just because he could withdraw his items freely now didn't mean he would always be able to, and he couldn't afford to lose his precious few resources. But it didn't seem like there was much of an option.

Castor carefully set the pack down on a boulder, still flipped inside out. "Treasure plum," he mused. That must be what the fruit was called. He had to admit, the name fit, considering they were what he set out on this quest to retrieve. There was one more name he didn't immediately recognize on the list as well, at the very bottom of all the fruit chunks. *True Genesis: Tohroh.*

He pressed the letters, and the stone Talias gave him appeared on the canvas, though it disappeared again the next moment. His eyes raked the unfamiliar word, genesis, and his eyes flitted to the edge of the ravine, hoping his friend would peek over the edge. They didn't, of course, and Castor sighed.

His eyes turned to the insignia that rested above the list like a crown. Wondering if touching it would make something happen as well, Castor hesitantly poked the topmost icon and immediately twitched back, blinking furiously. It felt as if he had poked himself in the eye just then, leaving only a slight, lingering twinge in the back of his head. It didn't hurt exactly, it just felt strange. When his eyes refocused, he looked down at the bag and saw that the number in the centre had dropped down to seven.

What does this mean? I had eight of something, and now I have seven? Boredom and curiosity winning out over his suspicion of the supernatural, he poked the next symbol to the left. This one caused a slight pain in the front of his head, although it also faded almost instantly, and the seven decreased to six.

Castor didn't regret touching the next one. When he pressed it, his muscles jumped, and not in a bad way. It made him feel stronger, and more refreshed. He pressed it again, and again, and again, and each time he did the strain in his body seemed to diminish.

Eventually, the icon stopped doing anything, and Castor realized the number in the centre was now zero. He ran out, of what, he had no idea. He kept touching the other icons but, predictably, nothing happened. So much for his experiment. He couldn't bring himself to regret it though, he felt great!

In a much better mood, he flipped the bag right side out, obscuring the mysterious print. Then, he eyed a boulder he couldn't manage to budge just an hour ago. He crouched down, bracing his right foot against the side of the ravine and lifted with his whole body. Castor gritted his teeth in a strained smile as he felt something move underneath him. He couldn't pick the stone up all the way, but he was able to pull it back, which was something he wasn't able to do before.

With newfound enthusiasm, he went to work, slowly moving the rocks away as best he could. His good mood didn't last for long though. Even with his small boost, he quickly ran out of stamina.

When he went back to the side with the dam, his negative feelings manifested themselves as fury toward the dead spider. Not anger about how the spider chased him into the ravine—it was actually a lot stupider than that. He was angry at its corpse and how he had to make such an effort to climb over it just to use the bathroom.

He was also irrationally afraid that he would cut his leg on the spider's exposed fangs and its venom would kill him. This was both incredibly specific and very preventable, but the thought was so intrusive that he spent a full hour trying to flip over the husk, eventually succeeding. Then, he walked away until a rock outcropping blocked his view of it and tried to settle down for the night.

The next day, Castor's remaining Treasure plums were completely rotten. Although the sun beat down upon him for most of each day, he had hoped that being inside the pack protected them from the worst of the heat. He was wrong. After he forced down his breakfast, which was so soft it was nearly liquid, Castor became violently ill. Unbidden, his stomach emptied itself, and he retched into the deep crevice for a long time. When he was finally done, he tried to settle his stomach with water and dried sea monster meat.

It almost made him even more nauseous. The flavor of the dried fish had been almost completely washed out by his trip down the river, and it had picked up the rancid taste of the fruit that had exploded in his pack. Nevertheless, he forced it down. He only had maybe two meals worth of food left, and he couldn't let it go to waste.

Desperate for some amount of good fortune, he tried pressing the icon that refreshed him the previous day, even though the number in the centre still read zero. Castor had hoped that he could use the icon again since it was a new day, but he was left disappointed. Castor cursed himself for using all its reserves at once, and not rationing it like he would food or water. He was so caught up in its magic that he hadn't even considered the possibility.

Bitterly, Castor went back to the collapsed end. He worked for hours, and then, as if his day wasn't already bad enough, he hit a roadblock. There was no more room to put the rubble he needed to excavate. All he could do was move farther away from his worksite and pull back the rocks he had already cleared to make space. In essence, he had to do all his hard work from the previous day over again before he could move forward.

In protest, Castor stopped for the rest of the day, and instead sat on a rock that jutted out like a natural seat. Reaching behind him, he massaged the small of his back, which ached from the strain of lifting the heavy rocks and his last couple nights of sleep. He closed his eyes and tried to relax, but his mind kept going back to thoughts of despair, or how worried his sister must be about him. He was sure most of the village thought he was dead, and a part of him hoped that Jayna did as well. That way, if he did make it back, it would be a pleasant surprise.

The next day, Castor grudgingly went back to work, pulling each rock back about a meter or so to make room. It was a lot easier this time around, he reflected. At least he didn't have to turn; he could just pull the rocks directly back.

Still, the task took half the day to complete, after which he took a break. Out of boredom, Castor started messing with the bag once more. The icon still wasn't refreshing him anymore but taking stuff in and out of storage hadn't gotten old yet. After a couple days of it working without issue, Castor was less wary of keeping his supplies in the pack.

He had kept the seeds from the rotting fruit, but there was no room left in the waterskin he used to store the others, so he just put the extras directly in the bag. In doing so, he noticed that the bag automatically kept count of the items within it, so he decided to just dump the seeds out of the waterskin.

Treasure Plum Seed: <1 gram, (x82)

Eighty-two wasn't bad. Gods, he wished this pack had changed before he left the Glade. He could have carried more fruit, and maybe it wouldn't have been squashed when he fell. The gnawing of hunger was quickly becoming too great to bear.

He took one seed out and rolled it in his fingers before popping it into his mouth. It tasted a bit rancid from the spoiled juice it was submerged in, but his saliva quickly dissolved the slimy film. The seed was hard like wood, and his teeth could barely sink in, but he swallowed it anyway.

Castor loathed to eat too many of the seeds—they were what motivated him to go on this foolish quest in the first place. But if he was going to starve, he might have no choice, and the seeds would probably be better for him than rocks or dirt.

He went back to work, prying out bits of collapsed earth and making some more progress. He had taken to talking and singing to himself as he worked, just so there was something to listen to aside from the raucous whistling of wind as it passed through the ravine.

Looking behind him, he could see rocks ranging from the size of his foot, to some twice as large as his head. The smallest pebbles and the loose dirt he scooped out had fallen into the inky black crack in the bottom of the ravine.

The descending sun began to sink past the western lip of the ravine, and Castor decided it was time to sleep. He had fallen asleep easier the last few nights, as worn down as he was. But tonight, he felt so alone.

Not really sure why, he stumbled all the way back to where he fell into the ravine and knelt by the spider. Its eyes looked a bit like fingernails, he noticed. They reflected the moon and starlight dully, and he wondered if arachna had eyelids. It didn't look like they did. *Maybe that's why they don't like being out during the day,* he mused deliriously.

He settled down next to the corpse and fell asleep.

Castor woke up to the sight of six eyes staring dully up at him. He gave a start, not fully remembering what happened last night or how he ended up by the arachna. However, he found that he had difficulty stringing any coherent thought together. Placing a hand on the leg closest to him, which had curled up in death, he felt the sharp, almost invisible bristles that covered it. In the sun, what captured his attention most was the glossy brown exoskeleton, which shimmered in the reflected light. The sight entranced him far longer than it should, but eventually he pulled himself away.

At the collapsed end, Castor toiled mindlessly in the hot sun. By midday, he uncovered what he thought was the last stone that obstructed the gap. It was big, way too big. He couldn't budge it at all with the feeble might his body could muster, and it probably would have been impossible for him even if he was at full strength.

He screamed and kicked the rock. He tried putting his back to the cliff and pushing with both of his legs. He even tried throwing some of the other stones behind him at it, hoping he could break parts of it off. Absolutely nothing worked, and his actions only made him more exhausted.

Angrily stabbing the bag's icon with his finger brought no relief either, no mysterious rush of strength. With frustrated tears in his eyes he drank heavily from his waterskin for a moment, tipping it all the way back.

The stream slowed to a couple of drops, and even greater horror gripped him. He was out of water! He hadn't even noticed. The waterskin, while not heavy, did have some weight to it, and he thought he still had a bit more. He was wrong. All his work in the hot sun made him so thirsty that he drank all his water, and it was all for nothing. He screamed his fury and desperation into the sky, and it echoed through the ravine like the wail of a tortured spectre.

Chapter Twelve
Yellow Marquis and the Black Book

Castor stood facing the dam, eyes closed and mouth agape. The thin spray of water caressed his face, but it wasn't enough to bring any sense of relief. In fact, his mouth felt dryer from being opened for so long.

He swayed limply in the breeze, which was amplified by the narrow confines of the ravine, completely unaware of his actions. Then, he fell and didn't even realize until the sharp pain of the rocks brought him into semi-alertness.

Dizzy from the dehydration, he looked high up at the wall in front of him. The morning sun had just begun to peek out over the stone, and he winced at the colourful corona that surrounded each beam. Still, he didn't avert his eyes.

Water was so close by. So much of it, rushing just behind this wall. He could hear its dull roar, and Castor longed for it to sweep him away. He felt at the dam, pulling at the rotted wood and digging into the crumbling mortar, ignoring splinters and abrasions.

It did him no good. No matter how ferociously he scrabbled at the wall, he could not bring it down. It had survived decades of Alayan hurricanes, and Castor posed no threat in comparison.

Giving up, Castor leaned as close to the wall as he could, hiding in the shadows. He had abandoned most of his clothes days ago, hot as it was, and the sharp rocks dug into his back. The stinging sensation was welcome; it at least took his mind off the much more unpleasant pain in his stomach, the feeling of his parched mouth and headache brought on by his extreme thirst.

His greatest enemy was heat, which robbed him of his sweat. The shade, spray and wind protected him moderately, but it was summer, and they could only do so much.

In his hands, he toyed with the knife he usually kept in his belt. With the agony he was in, he seriously began to consider slipping it between his ribs. Nobody was going to come and rescue him. If anyone tried wandering through the forest, they would be killed by the arachna. There was no hope for his survival.

His hands shook. This was the furthest thing from how he expected his quest to end. He escaped the spiders, found the Glade, gathered the seeds and the ambiance, and he was on his way home. Now, he was starving to death. Although his thirst would kill him long before.

The blade was pointed towards his left side and he began to hyperventilate. He wore no shirt, and the poorly maintained tip sank into skin without breaking the skin and drawing blood. It would though, if he pressed a bit harder.

A gentle breeze wafted through the ravine, almost as if the earth was sighing. "Oh Castor," said someone to his left.

He would have whirled around if he had the energy. Instead, all he could do was roll his head, which felt heavier than all the rocks he had lifted over the last couple days combined, to the opposite shoulder.

Jayna sat next to him, arm braced on her knee. Her hair was meticulously groomed like usual, packed into six tight buns on the top of her head, with clearly defined parts and not a single strand out of place. She sat so still that, if her skin wasn't a darker brown than the reddish cave walls, he might have thought she was part of the ravine itself.

"Jayna?" he asked in a raspy voice. His throat was filled with dust and grit, and he could produce no saliva to wash it down.

The ravine sighed again. "I'm here, Castor. Please, put down the knife." Even as she spoke, her mouth didn't move.

He had forgotten it still rested against his side. He released the pressure on the blade, and it dropped tip down away from him.

"Thank you. I missed you."

"Jay-na. I missed you too. So much."

There was a beat of silence. Then, "Why have you given up?"

Castor couldn't answer. Losing the strength to keep it up, he let his head drop between his knees, no longer able to keep looking at his sister. He was physically incapable of shedding tears, but he scrunched his eyes up and cried as best as he could.

"I didn't know you knew *how* to quit. Do you remember the Yellow Marquis?"

A Yellow Marquis was a glamorous name for an unglamorous fish that dwelled off the coast of northern Alaya. They were bottom dwellers with flat bodies, sharp protrusions on their jaws and thick yellow stripes on their backs which gave them their name.

Many years ago, Castor's father once needed one of their distinct jaws to use as a ritual ingredient. No one really tried to catch a Yellow Marquis, as their bony bodies made them unfit for eating. However, they often wandered into crab traps, much to the fishermen's annoyance. He had asked Castor to talk to them and buy the fish if they had one.

When he got to the docks, he found out that the fishermen hadn't checked the traps yet and didn't plan to for several hours. Castor didn't want to come home empty-handed; his father rarely asked anything of him.

So, Castor volunteered to retrieve the traps and bring them back on land, despite being nine, having never rowed a boat, and being small enough to fit inside one of the traps he was aiming to retrieve.

The fishermen laughed in his face but agreed to retrieve the traps early and even take Castor along with them. As a joke, he had allowed the kid to try and hoist a trap from the deep by himself, expecting him to fail and give up. He *didn't* expect Castor to pull so hard that he fell into the ocean. Jayna learned about this when he returned home sopping wet, but with a smile on his face and a Yellow Marquis clutched to his chest.

"Long time ago," he gasped.

From the corner of his eye, he thought he saw her nod. "Maybe so. But I still see that drive every day. With each person you help back home. It hasn't been so long since you left."

"I'm sorry," he said. That was the most pressing thing he wanted to tell her. "I shouldn't have gone."

She hummed in consideration. "I might be upset. But it's not for me to say whether you should or shouldn't have gone."

"So, you wanted me to leave?" he asked bitterly, even though he knew that wasn't what she meant. But her clinical tone unnerved him. Jayna was always passionate, especially when it came to matters such as these.

"It doesn't matter what I wanted. You did what you thought you had to. There's nothing more useless than regret."

His face softened and he almost chuckled. That sounded a lot more like the Jayna he knew. "You always say that."

"And you never listen. So, if you're right, and this is the end of your road, what do you regret?"

"That the spiders chased me into this ravine."

"No, no," she said. "You can't regret something you have no control over. That's called mourning. You can only regret choices you make. And a poor outcome to an otherwise good choice is no cause for regret."

Forehead still buried in the crook of his elbow, Castor considered her words. Did he regret jumping into the ravine? No, not really, it was the best option he had at the time. He remembered the sadness he felt when leaving the Glade and Talias; did he regret that? No, he needed to return to Toriath. Without taking into account the situations his choices put him in, he realized he didn't actually *have* any regrets. That is, except for...

"Leaving you," he whispered. "Leaving without saying goodbye. Without getting your blessing. Without thanking you. Without saying I love you."

His words slurred, and the fog in his mind created a gentle humming that he swayed in time with. Castor's sense of touch was all that grounded him, and he played with the sharp stones and the smooth grooves of the metal piece affixed to his bracelet.

"I think... I would like you to tell me that."

He tilted his head, eyes stinging from nonexistent tears. "I just did."

"No," Jayna replied. "Come back to Toriath. Tell me there."

Dry sobs wracked his body. "I can't! I can't, I can't—"

And suddenly she was right above him. "Look at me!"

Castor went mute, trying to regain control of his breathing as he looked up to his sister's blurry face. His eyes refused to focus.

"You must. Or do you want to die with that regret?"

He didn't. Gods, he didn't. An especially strong gust rolled through the ravine, startling him and clearing away some of his brain fog. The wind was picking up, and Castor wondered if nature itself was annoyed with his weakness.

"I've tried everything! I can't climb up the walls or collapse either end! I don't have any rope or equipment! I'm *stuck* here!"

"Everything?" Jayna questioned. "Everything logical, maybe. Have you tried throwing stones at the cliff face?" She pointed to a random spot along the rocky wall of Castor's prison. "Maybe it would cause a landslide, and you can use the debris to climb out?"

Castor looked at her incredulously. "Are... are you joking?"

She didn't laugh, just cocked her head. "No. It's unlikely, but if you haven't given up yet, and the alternative is death, then you should try *everything*, right? No matter how futile it may seem."

Without really looking, he felt along the ground, located a small rock and pried it away. He tried to throw it at the spot his sister pointed out, but he couldn't muster enough strength to reach it. He gave Jayna a baleful glare.

She hummed in consideration. "Have you tried calling for help?"

He already considered it, but he knew there couldn't be anyone around. Nonetheless, he cried out "Help," several times to ease the guilt his sister's strangely detached gaze ushered. Even with the stone walls amplifying his strained voice, he doubted it would carry past the lip of the ravine.

"Now you've tried to call humans, animals and monsters too

maybe. But what about the world?"

Castor was about to angrily retort, but then he realized what Jayna had asked him. "Rituals," he breathed. He hadn't even considered that as an option, which was embarrassing when considering his upbringing.

"Is there a ritual that can save me?"

Jayna opened her mouth to speak, but then hesitated. "I don't know," she finally admitted.

"What do you mean you don't know? You're a ritual master!"

"But I never taught you any rituals that would help," she said softly, regretfully. "And it's too late now."

Castor opened and closed his mouth several times, failing to find the words to speak. He looked closely at her, gaze narrowed, trying to see past the blurs and black spots that danced over his field of vision. He sighed, deflating both physically and mentally. "Oh. Yeah, I understand."

His sister looked sad. "I'm sorry."

Silence reigned within the ravine again, only punctured by the harsh winds.

"I wish you were shown more," Jayna said. "I remember most of the matrices you've seen. Gathering, imbuing, growth, pest repellent, even purifying water and healing flesh wounds. But..." She trailed off with a frustrated shrug.

"I know. It's okay. I'm the only one to blame."

"There is one though. I remember the matrix clearly, but we never learned what it did. It was in the black book, remember?"

The black book was one of their father's indexes. It was the smallest volume, and Castor was strictly forbidden from looking through it, even when ownership passed to Jayna. Because of that restriction, it was one of the few indexes that he had actually opened.

"You don't remember what it does?"

"No, just that the matrix looked cool."

The cardinal rule, when it came to rituals, was to never perform one without knowing its purpose. From his conversation with Jayna under the tree, he knew that rituals could easily kill someone who used them too recklessly.

However, "You were right, before. I'm going to die anyway. I need to try everything, or else I won't be able to face you in the afterlife. If there is one." Then, he realized something. "I don't have salt to form the matrix though. And even if I did, I can't make it without a flat base."

She seemed to smile, though it was hard to tell. "You don't need salt, remember what I taught you? A matrix can be made out of anything."

Castor tried to mentally compile a list of everything he had with him, but the thoughts slipped away like water through loosely cupped hands. Then, he remembered his bag, which he proceeded to clumsily pull inside out. The dark letters seemed to dance on the leather, and it wasn't clear if that was due to his flickering vision or inability to hold the leather steady.

The only things he had that were flexible enough to mould into a matrix were his strips of fabric for bandages and his clothes. He stabbed the words with his finger and pulled out the bundles of cloth. "Is this enough?" he asked hopefully.

Jayna shook her head regretfully. "If we cut them into thin enough strips, we might have enough. But there's no room to lay them out, and they'll probably fall in," she said, pointing to the dark crack that stretched through the base of the ravine.

He dropped them back into the pack, where they disappeared. "But I don't *have* anything else! And the ground's crooked, anything I put there will fall in the rocks!"

"You have your blood," she said earnestly. "And if you paint it on the side of the wall, it won't fall away."

Castor didn't have the energy to express his disbelief. "You can do that?"

She laughed, and Castor's chest felt lighter at the sound he associated so closely with home. "I don't see why not!" And now he couldn't refuse, question, or even hesitate. He didn't want to.

With extreme difficulty, Castor used the pits in the rock wall to pull himself to his feet. He swayed in the wind, almost falling back down again, but his grip didn't fail him this time. He picked up the knife he had dropped and cut a slit into his right index finger. Blood welled up, but it wasn't nearly enough.

Jayna was on his opposite side now. "Maybe here?" she

whispered, her fingers ghosting over his trapezius, a muscle strip that started at his shoulder and ran partially up his neck. He almost thought that he could feel the gentle pressure of her touch.

He brought the knife up, and slowly cut into the skin. He didn't even feel it at all. Soon, a small stream of red began to run down his arm to his fingertip, which was good. Every movement was a herculean trial, and it was nice for gravity to work for him.

He began to paint, and his sister guided him, remembering the details of this ritual that Castor had all but forgotten. His finger glided over the rough, dirt encrusted rocks, and the process was messy. Whenever he brought up his finger, the blood dripped down the tip of his elbow instead, so he constantly had to take breaks with his hand extended towards the ground.

Several times, the initially steady stream slowed to a drip and each time Castor brought up the knife to make another cut. He never felt any pain from these wounds, and if he suffered any other ill effects from the blood loss, it was impossible to tell.

The matrix began to appear before him. First, a diamond in the centre, stretched vertically so that it looked narrow. Two pentagons embedded into the top and bottom points of the diamond, which was odd as he had never seen a pentagon used in a ritual before. Two triangles connecting the pentagons to one another. Extra lines for details. Script.

"There, it's finished," Jayna pronounced as she surveyed what was surely the sloppiest matrix ever created.

"Ingredients?" Castor panted.

"It needs two, I think. One in each pentagon. You don't have much to work with." She gracefully knelt down to inspect the inside-out bag that lay on one of the jutting rocks. "I think, in these circumstances, it makes sense to offer up two things that are most important to you." Her eyes locked with his blank stare. "I can think of three options. The seeds and the crystals, which you risked your life to retrieve, and that bracelet."

His hand curled protectively over his wrist. "Do I have to use all of my seeds and crystals?"

"Probably not. Just one crystal and a couple of seeds should do the trick."

He nodded, withdrawing what he needed from the bag. He had never performed a matrix that didn't lay flat on the ground, so he hesitantly placed his two fists, closed around the ingredients, onto the tips of the pentagon. He had to hold himself awkwardly and strain to touch both at the same time, as the matrix was almost as big as Castor himself. Stretching aggravated his shoulder wounds further, and a renewed flow of blood ran over his skin. He ignored it.

"Wait," he realized, craning his head to look at Jayna. "How'm I gonna catalyze—?"

Castor's question was cut off when he felt something, almost akin to an extra strong heartbeat. The same thing he felt right before his bag changed, but all throughout his body. And suddenly, the ritual *activated*.

Silver light flashed from the tips of the pentagons, racing through the matrix, mixing together, and then flowing back *into* Castor's hands. The seeds crumbled underneath his tight grip. And the crystal *shattered*, pointed shards digging into his palm.

That's not supposed to happen. These crystals weren't supposed to break when used as ritual ingredients. He couldn't dwell on it, as he was beginning to feel strange. Perhaps it was imaginary, but there was a tingling in his hands, where he touched the activated matrix, that spread through him and settled in his torso. It wormed its way into his organs, resting at the base of his spine.

"Jay-*na*?" he croaked, but she was gone. His last drops of strength disappeared with her, and he sank to the ground with a ringing in his ears.

Castor flickered in and out of consciousness, and he couldn't quite track what state he was in. He just lay there, feeling as if some force was pressing him into the hard stone. After gods knew how long, he was finally able to keep his eyes open, though at first, he wasn't exactly sure he was properly doing so.

The sky was grey, and his eyes couldn't focus on anything. Then, something hit his forehead. He mustered his strength and wiped whatever it was off, but then it happened again, and again. Whatever it was, it was wet, and it ran down his skin.

With elation, Castor realized it was raining. With shaking limbs, he pulled himself up, letting the shock of cool water energize him. Pushing away from the rock outcroppings that blocked some of the raindrops, trying to resist the invisible force that threatened to pull him back down, he tilted his head back, mouth agape. The rain came down much harder, and he stood like that until his jaw was quite sore.

Annoyed, Castor tried to find a better way to quench his thirst. First, he cupped his hands, scooping in small mouthfuls of rain at a time. Then he got frustrated with that as well and ran to his pack, taking out the empty waterskin. He pulled out the stopper on the top and cupped his hands around the opening like a funnel.

In an hour, his thirst was quenched, both waterskins were full and the cool rain had invigorated him. And then, it didn't stop. At all. In fact, rain only poured harder, and sheets fell in almost a solid mass. Castor pressed himself against the rock wall of the ravine once again, this time to shield him from the direct raindrops.

There was an outcropping above a point near to where he fell, and he hid under it. The stone didn't protect him fully from the onslaught, and his legs still suffered the full brunt of the elements as he sat down. The splatters hit his face as well, and rivulets of water constantly streamed down his cheeks. While he was grateful that he wasn't dehydrated anymore, the cold rain was unbearable in a different way. As he fell asleep, he felt like he was drowning.

The rain didn't stop or even let up one bit. When Castor woke, he found himself ankle deep in water, which was a testament to the storm's power. Until now, the rain had drained away into the gap at the base of the ravine.

Castor didn't know exactly how far down the crack went, but

in his mind, it seemed bottomless, considering how the noon sun couldn't even penetrate its shadow. The water level rose slowly throughout the day, eventually reaching his chest, neck, and then chin. Castor had grabbed his pack and put everything in it, even his knife. Soon he was treading water, grabbing onto the angular rock wall to support himself.

For the first time in days, he felt something akin to hope. What if the water level climbed high enough, and he could ride it to the top of the ravine? It was unlikely that the storm would continue so long, or that it would fill the ravine, but as the hours dragged on, it began to seem possible. He began searching the walls once again, looking for handholds that were inaccessible to him before. They would be difficult to climb in the slick rain but, if there was a chance, no matter how small, he had to either take it or die.

Although the rain showed no sign of stopping, his optimism began to fade over the next hour. The water had risen so quickly thus far because the bottom of the ravine was narrow. As it opened up, the rate at which the ravine filled slowed exponentially even though the rain poured down with the same ferocity.

Castor's whole body had shrivelled from its constant exposure to water, and the cold sapped what little strength he had left. Even if the water reached the top of the ravine, it would take much too long, and he would drown before then.

Then, he started when something solid bumped into his back. Splashing around, he turned and saw the arachna's corpse floating on top of the water. He was struck by a sudden inspiration. *What if I used the spider's body as some kind of raft?* Would it support his weight?

He tried to climb on top of its back, which was difficult for him to do without tipping it over. Eventually he succeeded, to an extent. His legs still trailed into the water, but that wasn't important. This way, he wasn't exerting so much energy treading water constantly.

It was well past midnight, and he wanted to sleep forever. But Castor knew he couldn't. He could easily fall off the spider and drown, and he didn't have faith that he could pull himself out of the water again with his numb limbs. It was a miracle he was able to mount the arachna in the first place. So, he stayed awake to the best of his ability, although he may have involuntarily dozed off a couple of times.

The spider knocked into the rock wall, shocking him into alertness and almost capsizing him. Its husk was moving quickly, not floating around in much the same place as it had before. Where was it going? And why?

The question was soon answered. They were flowing closer to the collapsed end, and Castor remembered that the top of the eroded stone was a couple meters lower than the ravine walls on each side. The water level must have reached the top of the stone, and it was flowing over!

Before, Castor had worked hard to clear away the rock so he could make his way to its other side. However, that wasn't good enough anymore. There was no telling what the other side looked like: it might lead to somewhere that he could escape from, or it might not. Or, there was a distinct possibility that the water level on that side was considerably lower, if it wasn't confined into as small a place as the section he was currently in. He might fall a great distance to the bottom and get injured. No, what he really needed to do was to escape the ravine completely, here and now.

He was rapidly approaching the slanted rock, and there was no time to think. The spider slammed into it, nearly hard enough to send him tumbling over and onto the other side. He hung on though, with all the strength his fatigued body could muster, and he managed to pull himself on top. Hugging the stone with all four limbs, he slowly crawled up the rock, fighting both gravity and the constant stream of water threatening to push him off.

The last spot was the most difficult. There was a meter-high gap between the top of the rock and the wall of the ravine. He clawed at the top, scraping off handfuls of mud until he finally found purchase. Letting out a roar of exertion, he pulled himself up and over to freedom! The slick, amazing grass rubbed against his arms for the first time in a week, and he *finally* allowed himself to rest.

Chapter Thirteen

Ravenous

Castor awoke to an unendurable pain in his stomach. It was hunger, more intense than he had ever experienced, even back in Toriath during a famine. The only thing in sight that could maybe sate it was grass, which he grabbed by the fistful.

Chlorophyll oozed from between his fingers, staining them green as he crammed the blades into his mouth until the pain had somewhat subsided. Humans couldn't survive on grass, but he needed something to fill his stomach until he could find something with nutrients. Castor couldn't bear to look at the ravine anymore, so he shambled away, desperate to leave his once prison behind.

Concentrating in this state was nearly impossible. With frustration, Castor found his vision blurring out of focus and glossing over his surroundings. He easily could have already overlooked a berry bush, mushrooms or worse, an arachna, in his daze.

He strayed back towards the river, thinking that his best bet for finding food was in that area, and noticed that the high banks seemed to gradually slope downwards, bringing him a lot closer to the water. It was a stroke of good fortune that the floodwater had deposited him on the side of the ravine opposite to the one he had fallen in from. Now, he could continue on his path to the west without finding some other way to cross the ravine or the river again.

After some time, a new sound seemed to fade into existence. In his daze, Castor didn't notice it right away, but when he did, he jumped behind a tree to hide. It was definitely coming from up ahead, and it was barely distinguishable from the sound of the river rushing past.

It sounded like... a bird? That was odd. He hadn't heard a bird call in quite some time. Could he catch and eat it?

The harsh calls increased in volume the farther he advanced, and there was something distinctive and familiar about them. When the river straightened out, he could see several white shapes soaring through the sky. *Seagulls,* he realized. And right underneath them was the ocean, the gods damned ocean!

Castor had never been so happy to see it. Fish lived in the ocean; maybe he could catch one somehow. He didn't have a fishing rod or any other tools, but it was his best bet by far.

Luckily, he didn't even have to worry about that. Shooting off the river was a small stream that led to a pool, almost like a miniature lake. It was shallow and overflowed with water carried by the stream, while the excess poured over the side like an overfilled pot, eventually spilling into the ocean.

The only thing that Castor cared about, however, was that this pool was teeming with life. Floating plants and algae coated the rocks on the bottom of the pool, and he saw minnows, tadpoles and, to his elation, fish!

Castor took off his shoes and socks and sat at the edge of the pool, ankle deep in the cool water. He sat motionless, and eventually curious fish approached and began to nibble at his leg hair. With the prospect of food directly in front of him, his focus sharpened from a dull piece of metal to that of a razor-sharp axe. Without thinking, both of his hands flashed into the water and each caught a fish. They squirmed with all their might, but there was no *way* he would let go.

He wasn't sure how he did it. The movement was pure instinct. Usually, a fish's quick, darting movements made them too unpredictable to be caught barehanded, but now Castor's eyes could track them with ease. He didn't bother questioning how at the moment; he was single-mindedly focused on his catch. Ferociously bashing one fish on a rock before dropping the now still creature, he began to tear into the raw flesh of the other even as it still wriggled about.

In his fervour, he disregarded scales and most of its bones, even as they stabbed into his mouth. When he was done, he immediately attacked the other one, not caring that dirt now clung to its wet body.

He was still starving, but the difference was astronomical. Castor leaned back onto his hands and panted. In his haste to consume each fish, he had even forgotten to breathe. He ran his tongue against his teeth, dislodging some scales that were stuck in between them. Raw fish did not taste good, and Castor realized that he may have eaten some parts of the fish that he really shouldn't have, and not just bones. He absently made a mental note to gut the next fish he caught, though his addled mind was still mostly occupied by the sight before him.

Something about this pool was enchanting. Castor watched minnows dart around and crayfish scuttle through the algae and reeds that grew at the bottom. However, soon his eyes migrated from inside the pool to its surface, and the reflection that stared back at him.

It was rare for Castor to see his reflection. Toriath wasn't a wealthy enough village to afford much glass, even during its most prosperous times, and all the metal he usually saw was dull or shaped in such a way that the image became distorted.

Castor didn't like seeing his reflection. Or rather, it always took him by surprise. It was as if he never expected the face he saw to be his own. He didn't even have a specific picture of what he thought he looked like in his mind's eye, it just... wasn't *that*.

The face that stared back at him had high cheekbones and a low brow, making him look permanently sullen. His pores were excruciatingly visible on his brown skin, and his hair was dishevelled, although that could be excused under the circumstances. He wished he looked softer, kinder. More like his sister.

Their father used to joke that the gods mismatched their personalities with their faces. Gentle Castor was supposed to have Jayna's delicate features, while brusque, assertive Jayna was supposed to have Castor's face to match. Castor, who didn't like to be reminded that he looked like a brute, hated when he said that.

He was distracted from his reverie by an obnoxious buzzing in his ears. The still water was a breeding ground for all manner of bugs as well, and Castor had absentmindedly swatted at them as they landed on his skin. A rather large and persistent dragonfly hovered around his head, and its wingbeats were especially loud and grating to his still sensitive ears. He tried to bat it away, but the annoying insect always came back so he got up and circled the water.

With a slightly clearer head, Castor marvelled at the pool's significance. It was the last reservoir of life from the river before it was swept out to sea. It stood to reason that these fish only survived in freshwater, and all those that didn't make it here, which was doubtlessly the majority, probably died out in the open ocean.

Castor almost felt bad about hunting in this pool, since its denizens had already so narrowly escaped death. Still, he was terribly hungry. The two fish were each only as large as his hand, and he was far from satisfied. However, the other animals were wary now, and they all swam as far away from him as they could, moving as he moved. Frustrated, he leapt into the centre of the pool and tried again.

After an embarrassing amount of time, Castor was able to catch four more fish. He was reluctant to eat them raw like the last two, so he made a fire using discarded twigs and branches laying around. Luckily, he still had his flint and iron.

While Castor worked with the village fishermen a lot, he didn't actually know how to prepare a fish. He knew that he should gut it, and, after its ribs denied him access from the side, he figured out how to make the cut from below. He didn't know what to do after that, however. The scales were annoying, so he should probably take those off, but he didn't quite know how. All his attempts failed, so he resigned himself to having to eat the fish with them on.

He held the fish over the fire with some sticks he had found, at what he hoped to be the right distance. He didn't want to burn his meal, considering how hungry he was and how long it took to catch the fish. Castor had made the fire small because he wasn't sure if monsters could see the smoke, or if they were smart enough to realize that something appetizing could be the one causing it. He sat with his back to the ocean and kept watch, only periodically checking on his fish. In his paranoia, he thought he saw an arachna through the rippling smoke several times.

Soon, Castor decided that his meal was ready, mostly because his arms hurt. In addition to the strain of holding the sticks and fish for a while, the heat from the fire had stung his forearms. He was pleasantly surprised to find that a lot of the scales began to flake off on their own due to the heat. He dug in, and while it wasn't delicious, it *was* food.

His hunger was sated, but Castor still felt terrible. One good meal wasn't enough to repair the damage he suffered after a week in the ravine, and his body was sore all over, on the inside and out. His pain had two major sources. First, his shoulder, which was covered in a large scab almost the size of his palm. The second seemed to be internal and felt like a weight pressed against the small of his back. Except nothing was there. Massaging his back muscles brought no relief, and he began to question if his spine was broken. If that were true, he thought it would hurt a lot more, and he probably wouldn't be able to move either.

Nothing could be done to alleviate the sensation, so he looked back over his shoulder past the beach as he considered his next move. Distracted as he was when it first came into view, Castor had overlooked the ocean's importance. It was the greatest landmark he could have found, because his village was also located on the coast.

If he walked alongside the water, eventually he would find his way back home, no matter how long it would take. And in doing so, he might be able to avoid monsters of the forest more effectively. He couldn't be sure they wouldn't follow him out into the shallows if he tried to escape into the ocean, but he had never heard of a spider that would set foot in any body of water.

Although Castor was elated to discover an infallible method to find his way back home, he was furious with himself for not thinking to use it in the first place. When he first set out on this quest, the only landmark he knew to search for was the river, and he never thought to ask where a river could possibly lead. The ocean was the obvious answer. He should have made his way around the coast until he found this very spot, not gone on a directionless hike through the forest.

He supposed it was easy to say in hindsight, and it wasn't like Marak and presumably Lord Tolam had realized it either. He decided that he should just move on instead of punishing himself for his lack of sense, secure in his knowledge that he had succeeded in finding the Glade, retrieving the Treasure plum seeds and filling up Jayna's crystals. All he had to do now was return home.

With that in mind, he began his trek down the coast, but he couldn't help but think about what he lost along the way, especially in the ravine. Just days ago, he was slowly dying from hunger and thirst, and although his memory was spotty over the last day or so, he could distinctly remember some flashes. Lots of blood, his sister—which must have been a hallucination—and the feeling of a knife's point against his ribs. He was ready to kill himself to escape his suffering, and no matter how well things turned out in the end, he couldn't just let that go. Even though he didn't have time to grieve properly, he still cried silently as he walked.

Since he was on the north coast of Alaya, Castor knew that, if he wanted to go west, he would have to go left. There was no way he could get *that* wrong. Therefore, to get back home, he would have to cross the river.

As it met the ocean, the river's current quickly lost most of its force, and Castor was easily able to wade through the shallows and get over to the opposite side. He walked barefoot over the rocks, wincing as the sharper ones dug into his feet. He had kept his shoes and socks off because they were just starting to dry off from the flooded ravine and he didn't want them to get even more soaked. Walking in wet shoes was terrible, and he had many blisters on his feet to prove it.

There wasn't a beach on this part of the coast, which Castor found odd. He had never seen trees growing so close to the ocean before. They certainly didn't in or around his village. However, in a couple of kilometres, the forest opened to expose an open, sandy waterfront.

He guessed it had something to do with salt. Castor knew that salt killed plants, that's why he and his sister had to clean up so thoroughly after each ritual. The fresh water gave vegetation the opportunity to grow around the mouth of the river, but by the time it reached this point, it had mixed with the sea water and became potent enough to kill off any plants that tried to take root.

Castor felt conflicted about walking beyond the trees. On one hand, he was happy to be out from underneath their oppressive shade. On the other, he felt exposed. If there was a monster watching him, he didn't have anywhere to hide from it. He often thought he saw hungry eyes watching him from beyond the trunks and leaves, and he quickened his pace each time. It was only his imagination, and he didn't get a glimpse of an arachna the entire rest of the day. He slept under a jutting stone, trusting its shadow to shield him from the view of any roaming beasts.

Castor woke up at dawn, and not necessarily by choice. Facing the ocean as he was, he took the brunt of the morning sun directly to his face as it reflected off the shimmering water. He had no food for breakfast, nor did he have any way to find some, but that was fine. He had eaten yesterday, and he and hunger were well acquainted by this point.

He resumed his journey along the coast. He had no idea how far he had travelled through the forest before he found the Glade and fell into the ravine. It couldn't have been that far, right? He had reached the Glade on only his second day, after all. However, after hours of walking, he realized that his foray into the river might have taken him a lot farther away than he thought.

Castor split his focus between the forest and the horizon. The human eye could see large objects at quite a distance if there was nothing in the way, and Castor continually held hope that the village walls would magically rise out of the earth before him. Unfortunately, this part of the coast seemed to curve left as he continued. Maybe once it straightened out, he would be able to see his home.

In the afternoon, Castor came across something interesting. At first, it seemed like a small blip on the tan beach resembling a boulder. However, as he got closer, he noticed its large shape and greyish-orange colour. The farther he walked, the more features revealed themselves, like its elongated shape. One end was bulbous and faced the ocean, half submerged under the ebbing and flowing wake, and strange logs splayed onto the sand in front of it. No, not logs, tentacles. Everything about it seemed very familiar, and by the time he was a couple hundred meters away, he was sure of what it was.

It was definitely a wadom, but as to what it was doing here, Castor had no idea. Did it beach itself by accident somehow? He supposed that every creature died naturally when their time came, but for some reason it felt strange that such a fate would befall this titan of the sea. Out of all the creatures the village hunted, wadom were by far the most fearsome, and it felt strange to see one brought low like this. He remembered the monster that killed Tomasoh, how fast and brutal it was, with tentacles that flung around like whips, each ending in an organic blade that was sharper than the knife Castor wore at his hip.

Castor walked towards the thing, eager to examine it. He had never gotten close to one of the creatures before, dead or alive. Once they were killed by the Noble Guard, the beasts were always taken directly to the fisherman's station to be butchered. From there, most of the meat made its way to the salt room to be dried into jerky. Some went to the food storage area to be made into fresh meals in the dining hall, while the unsavoury bits were taken to the southwest quadrant to be used as fertilizer for the farms.

At the thought of jerky and fresh meals, Castor's stomach began to growl. He might have eaten yesterday, but he had a week's worth of meals to catch up on, and the ocean seemed to have offered up this wadom on a silver platter. He might just have dinner tonight, as long as it wasn't rotten. Unfortunately, it probably was, seeing as it had been sitting in the sun for gods knew how long.

Castor stepped over several outstretched tentacles to get a better look at the creature. The wadom looked a little like a human hand, if a hand had nine long, boneless fingers and rubbery skin. Its terrifying mouth rested upon the palm, with four connected, triangular lips. If it were to be opened, the mouth would probably look like a diamond, almost certainly filled with many sharp teeth. Now though, it was closed and resembled the letter X.

On the back of its body was a protrusion, which almost reminded him of the abdomen of a spider, although it was soft and hung limply into the water. It probably held the same function as well: to house the majority of the creature's essential organs. Three eyes rested on stumps right behind its tentacles, giving it a ferocious and alien appearance.

As distracted as he was, Castor almost didn't notice the flash of movement. A tentacle behind him had whipped up at terrifying speed and came close to impaling him, but the moment it entered his peripherals, he flinched to the side. The damned thing wasn't dead yet!

Suddenly, there was a flurry of motion as more tentacles shot up around him. One came from his left and he jumped out of the way, then, a split second later, another came from above and to the right of him. He ducked, and then hastily jumped back from that position to dodge a vertical swipe from two tentacles that swung directly towards him.

He was on the ground now, which was a horrible position to be in. He rolled to the right to escape another tentacle and was about to try and rise when he heard a whoosh of air from behind. It was a good thing he followed his instincts and dropped down again, because another tentacle shot over him, right where his neck would have been if he had stood up.

He could see and track every movement the monster made, and he could even hear each tentacle that came to strike him from his blind spot. Still, even though he could sense the monster's attacks, that didn't mean he could dodge them. His body just couldn't keep up with his eyes, and the wadom was alarmingly fast.

The sharp triangular tip of one tentacle drew a long gash down the length of his calf. He tried to back away out of reach but had to fling himself sideways to avoid another tentacle that somehow attacked from behind him. A quick glance was all he could spare before another strike came from his left, but that was all he needed.

He saw the tentacle he stepped over when he first approached the wadom, motionless except for the end, raised almost perpendicular to the ground like a rearing snake, blocking him from moving away carelessly. With barely a thought, he baited the tentacle to strike and twisted around the outstretched limb as it slashed at him. The blow meant for him instead stabbed into the soft flesh of a different flailing tentacle, and the beast wailed in pain and frustration as Castor scampered out of its reach. It tried to pull its massive body out of the water towards him, but it couldn't make it more than a couple meters.

Breathless from exertion and adrenaline, Castor collapsed onto the ground well out of the monster's reach. He watched its tentacles flail and tried to figure out just what happened after he had so carelessly approached the beast he thought to be dead. How the hell did he manage to survive? He should have been dead ten times over, but instead he had been able to dodge every single attack.

Almost every attack, he thought as hot liquid dripped down his leg. The wound bled a fair bit but didn't hurt too much, although that might have been from shock. Castor flipped his bag inside out, located *Fabric Strips* and withdrew them all. When the bandages materialized in front of him, Castor winced at the state of them. The fabric was yellowed, mouldy and smelled like spoiled fruit.

His gut told him it would be a bad idea to wrap an open wound in that, so he threw it aside and ripped the sleeves off his shirt. With the state his clothes were in, they were hardly a sanitary option either, but he needed to bind his leg in *some* way.

He remembered that he still had the alcohol disinfectant as well, which he should also use. He scoured the alphabetized list, frowning when he couldn't find alcohol or disinfectant. Did he throw it out by mistake?

Then he noticed, at the very bottom of the list, Wooden Vial.

That must be it. Seems like the bag can't tell what's inside a sealed container. Now that I think about it, it was the same way with the waterskin filled with seeds. The bag just differentiated the two waterskins by weight, although Castor hadn't given it any thought while he was slowly dying in the ravine.

Castor uncorked the vial and poured a bit on the gash, letting gravity pull the liquid down its length. It stung a lot, and Castor gritted his teeth against the pain, but he knew that meant it was working. Then, he tore the sleeves into strips and used them to bind his leg.

He zoned out as he tried to catch his breath, ignoring the steady throbbing of his calf and trying to make sense of what just happened with the wadom. Ever since he touched that flower, he could see farther and in more detail. He heard things louder and more clearly. And, more than that, he noticed things he normally wouldn't have. He remembered what it felt like when he was dodging those tentacles, and how, when fleeing the spiders before he fell in the ravine, he could see every stray obstacle in his path. He wondered if it was permanent and, if so, he wondered if that was a good thing.

The beast had stopped writhing, but Castor wasn't fooled. He hadn't hurt it at all, and the poke it gave itself probably didn't cause any real damage. If he got within its range again, it would surely attack once more. But now he was faced with a dilemma. He could leave now and continue on his way, or wait for it to die, butcher it and cook the meat. It was a tough call, because he had no idea how long he would have to linger here, and he really wanted to resume his journey back home.

If only there was some way for me to speed up the process, he mused. What if he circled around, and attacked it from behind? He disregarded that thought. Its tentacles were long enough to reach him, even if it couldn't see where he was. He toyed with the idea of finding a long branch and using his knife to sharpen it into a primitive kind of spear, but he really didn't want to do that.

Then, Castor's keen eyes noticed something, the only movement from around the creature aside from the tiny ocean waves that lapped against the shore. Against the creature's sides, below its eyes, there was a disturbance against the water.

Bubbles frothed against the surface of the ocean every time the water ebbed away.

Of course, he realized. *Those are its gills!* Just like how he observed during the sea hunt, which felt like ages ago, the wadom couldn't breathe well when its gills weren't completely submerged.

Castor remembered how it tried to pull itself after him when he escaped. If he could get it to do that again, he might be able to bait it out of the water completely, and it would drown in open air! Wincing as he pulled himself up, he limped closer to the creature and, with no better ideas, he began pelting the beast with rocks. That sure got its attention, especially when he aimed for its eyes.

Its tentacles began writhing, and some even went up to shield its eyes. Still, it didn't try to move again. Maybe it thought he was too far out of reach. He quit throwing rocks and hesitantly stepped forward. When he was close enough, the tentacles once again shot out to meet him, but he was expecting them this time, and he darted away, though his leg protested the jarring movement.

He stepped forward again, hovering just out of reach, and before long the creature began to pull itself up the beach. Finally, its gills were almost completely out of the water, and Castor watched the monster suffocate. Still, he refused to approach it hastily again, and waited until it had completely stilled, periodically pestering it with more rocks and branches.

As he waited, Castor thought back to the first strike the monster made, and how it didn't start attacking with the rest of its tentacles until it saw him dodge. Did that wadom try to use a surprise attack? And then, it kept that one tentacle behind him, preventing him from just fleeing backwards out of its range immediately. It seemed to possess a fair bit of intelligence, or at least hunting prowess. Although, he supposed he couldn't call the beast intelligent when it voluntarily left the water, the only place it could survive. It was scary to know that there were monsters out there that didn't act like simple animals.

Then, he slapped himself on the forehead in realization. That other wadom did the exact same thing during the last sea hunt! That's how it killed Tomasoh, by pretending to be dead and then attacking when everybody let their guard down. He was a moron! Why couldn't he just learn from past mistakes? He would have to be smarter if he wanted to survive in the wild, and he couldn't help thinking that the only reason he survived this long was through sheer dumb luck. With an emphasis on dumb.

Although, if it was setting a trap for him, why did the wadom keep so still long before he approached it? It couldn't have seen him coming from so far away. It must have been ready to die, trapped on the rocks as it was, and it only moved again because he was there to disturb it.

During the summer, his village suffered from cockroach infestations and he saw the insects behave like the wadom did. When they were ready to die, they flipped over on their backs and remained perfectly still, but when Castor went to kick one away, its legs and antennae would flail as if it was in perfect health. Perhaps the wadom did the same thing, just in a much more deadly manner.

Castor wondered why it attacked at all if it was already dying. It seemed like an effort in futility for it to try and eat him. Maybe to monsters, the urge to kill humans was so strong that even on death's door they would try to do so. That would explain why it was willing to effectively kill itself by leaving the water.

He threw another rock at the monster, which elicited no response. So, he cautiously approached its still form to begin harvesting its meat, starting with the tentacles. With his knife, he could only cut the last meter off each before it got too thick, but that was plenty. He cut off the sharp ends, which in his hands felt like the same material as a cow's hoof, or perhaps the shell of a shrimp. He grilled the tentacles and they didn't taste too bad, although the texture was rubbery.

Castor could only eat two tentacles worth of meat, but he cooked them all to save for tomorrow, depositing the rest in his bag. They vanished into thin air, and Castor grinned at the sight. He would be excited to show the bag to his sister. As a pseudo ritual master, Jayna was the leading expert for anything mystical in Toriath.

With all the tentacles cooked, Castor looked up at the sky and winced when he saw that the sun was starting to make its descent. He had hoped that he could make it home before nightfall. Castor considered using the body of the wadom as shelter during the night, as it was the only thing he could see as cover around him; however, he quickly dismissed this idea. The meat might draw other monsters to it, and he remembered the giant spider attacking that other humanoid monster in the forest. Also, he would have to sleep in the ocean wake, which sounded awful, and he was tired of the stench of sea monster.

He continued along the coast and eventually found another suitable resting place along the treeline within a clump of high-reaching bushes. Although the leaves were itchy, he fell asleep, pleased that he could sleep on grass instead of sharp stone.

Chapter Fourteen
Return to Toriath

With difficulty, Castor tore off bites of tentacle as he continued his journey home, morning sun at his back. In Toriath, when he looked east atop the village wall, the coast was mostly straight as far as he could see. From his current location, the shore curved to the left, so Castor hoped that when he finally rounded the bend, he would be able to see the village.

Sure enough, just over an hour later, a structure came into view. At this distance, it looked very small, just a dark dot along the ocean, but it could only be Toriath. Castor let out an audible sob of relief and couldn't help quickening his pace, almost breaking out into a jog. His home was so close, and the nightmare of the last week was finally over!

His eyes still flitted past the trees, carefully watching out for any monsters that might emerge, but Castor couldn't help but stare as his village slowly grew bigger and bigger before his very eyes. He kept up this pace for more than an hour, by which time it still only appeared to be as big as his smallest fingernail. It seemed as if his depth perception was still drastically off, and he wondered if he would have even been able to see Toriath from this distance before he found the flower.

Despite his eagerness to get home, Castor had to stop several times to rest, much to his frustration. Castor could usually walk an entire day without getting tired, which was exactly what he did during his first leg of the quest.

It appeared as though his stamina hadn't recovered from his time in the ravine, though. He felt a deep-seated weariness throughout his entire body, and his unidentifiable back injury, which didn't seem to be healing, threatened to drag him down with every step. It truly felt like he was carrying a small boulder on his back, even though nothing was there. He even took off his light, empty backpack just to make certain that he wasn't carrying anything he didn't know about. Nothing helped.

Still, he moved on, and eventually he could make out a raised building that must have been the Keep, and the walls that shone in the bright sun. Something about that nagged at the back of his mind, but he didn't realize what it was until he was much closer. It was a rock wall—nothing about it should be shiny.

Perhaps they put something on top of it, something made out of metal? A machine of some kind? A sinking feeling grew in his stomach the closer he got to his home. When he was finally near enough to make out its details, his paranoia grew into true panic as he saw giant spiderwebs coating the wall, glistening sinisterly under the cloudless sky.

Castor began to hyperventilate. Ragged gasps shook his core so quickly that even he couldn't tell if he was laughing or crying. On one hand, he was terrified that his village, his last sanctuary and only constant, had finally fallen to the murderous arachna that had plagued it for years. That his people, his *sister*, might be dead, killed painfully with their flesh liquefied by the spider's venom. That he was alone.

On the other hand, this was funny. *Hilarious*, even. He set out on this quest to help his village by bringing back the promise of food. He achieved his goal by braving the wilderness, surviving, and finding the Glade. Just like a Hero would.

Then he fell into the ravine, starved, baked in the heat and nearly died from thirst, hunger and his own hand. The only thing that kept him going was the promise that, when he returned, he would be safe amongst his neighbours and loved ones. He survived even that horrid experience and made it the rest of the way back to Toriath.

Only to find that his home had fallen in the short time he was away. Castor couldn't control his breaths, and a sharp pain bloomed through his chest. His head felt fuzzy, and in his discombobulation, he didn't even notice when he dropped to the ground.

Castor had no one left. He had always been lonely, with no friends his age to socialize with, but he had never been *alone*, not until he had left the village. There was always his sister, and the other Torians were at least physically, if not emotionally, present. Now, he would be alone forever.

One moment, he was breathing so fast that his head spun; the next, he stopped breathing altogether. Pinpricks of light blinked behind his eyelids, which were scrunched shut so tightly that his forehead ached. Then, he couldn't hold his breath any longer and gasped again.

Even after his breathing had finally settled and the hot tears stopped running down his cheeks, he lay on the beach, still except for his heaving chest. He was so, so tired, and he almost wanted to fall asleep, safety be damned. However, he couldn't, not without knowing for sure what befell his people.

Still, it took him an hour before he even had the motivation to pull himself shakily to his feet. During his episode, he involuntarily seized his muscles as hard as he was capable of, and they now protested his every movement. Eventually they began to loosen as he made his way slowly to the village wall, which was still some distance away.

It was possible, likely even, that the Torians were able to evacuate. At least, that's what he told himself to keep his legs moving. He wouldn't know until he was able to look inside the village. If his people had truly perished, and their silk-encased bodies were all that awaited him past the shellstone walls, well, he didn't know what he would do.

Reaching the wall, Castor circled around to the east-facing postern gate, the same one he had left the village from over a week ago. Then, he opened it just wide enough for him to peek through.

There weren't any spiders in the general vicinity, but evidence of their presence was abundant, even from his limited perspective. There were webs everywhere, and many houses looked worse for wear. The spiders weren't able to completely destroy a well-built house, but many features were chipped or broken, especially if they were made of wood.

From his place in the gateway, he could see a house to his right that was missing a chimney, which had been broken off and rested in pieces on the ground. Since there was no immediate threat, he opened the door as silently as possible, although he had to force it over that rut in the ground that gave him difficulty when he first left. Gods, that felt like years ago.

His own house was not far from this spot, just further down the road that separated the northeast and southeast quadrants. He wasn't ready to go there yet because he was terrified by what he might find.

Arachna preferred the dark, which was why they stayed in the forest during the day. This behaviour worked well for him now because the afternoon sun cast its light directly into the eastern wall. The spiders, Castor guessed, would likely seek shelter in the long shadows of the western half of the wall during this time of the day, or behind taller buildings if they were still in the village at all. He hoped that they had left already, since he hadn't actually seen any yet, though the pessimist in him doubted it.

Right next to him was the Park. He was justifiably hesitant to head through an open space, but it was better than taking his chances by walking in the streets, where any monster could be lying in wait. So, he skirted around the wall, feeling exposed in the bright sunlight. Although Castor supposed that it didn't matter if it was dark or light, he assumed an arachna could see him just as well either way.

The cattle pen came into view, and Castor blanched at the sight. The pen wasn't very sturdy; its purpose was simply to keep the rain off the animals. Now, it was completely destroyed. The wooden roof lay on the ground in splinters, the stone was cracked, and the flimsy metal gate was crumpled. A little ways away from the mass were three bundles of web, two large and one much smaller. Castor had little doubt that these were the cattle, and the pit in his stomach grew heavier.

Then there was the tree. Each of its bulbs, no matter how small, were plucked and webbed, and most of the tree's branches were stripped off the abused trunk. If it wasn't dead already, it would be soon. Obviously, there was no one left here to depend on it, but his sister devoted her life to caring for the tree, and to see it in this state was heart-rending. Still, he moved on.

One thing that brought Castor hope was the fact that he hadn't seen any cocoons that could feasibly hold humans. In other words, as far as he could tell, the spiders hadn't killed any villagers. That was incredibly relieving, and it painted a much more favourable depiction of the situation.

He crept around the perimeter of the wall, slowly, cautiously, until he got close enough to see the main gate. Inexplicably, it was open completely. What the hell happened here? Everything he had seen thus far was contradictory. There were no bodies, meaning the villagers probably evacuated of their own volition. Why did they open the gate though? Sure, with the Torians gone, the spiders could easily climb the gate in enough time, but why make it easier for them?

He remembered the webs on the eastern wall. Did they climb over the wall from there and open the gate? No, that was ridiculous. The gate couldn't be opened in this manner with brute force. There were mechanisms built inside the stone walls, which looked like two oversized screws, that were used to open up each door, although the guards rarely opened both due to the difficulty of the task. Arachna didn't have hands, so even if they were intelligent enough to figure out how to open the gate, they were physically incapable of doing so.

The signs so far had pointed to the idea that the villagers had evacuated, but it would have been suicide for them to do so by exiting through the front gate. There was the matter of the Park as well. If they were planning on evacuating, wouldn't they take the cattle with them? Or, they should have at least butchered the animals, as any scrap of food would be crucial for the villagers to bring with them.

Looking closer at the far side of the gate, Castor came across the first human bodies wrapped in silk. But now, he felt just as perplexed as he did horrified. There were just two of them, which Castor supposed would be enough to open the gate.

Why did they stay behind? What purpose did opening the gate serve? As Castor looked at the bundles, he unconsciously wondered who they were. In this tight knit community, Castor probably knew them well. He quashed down those thoughts and replaced them with hatred for the monsters, which burned even more fiercely than before.

Soon, Castor saw his first arachna within the village. It stood atop a house in the southeast quadrant, partially obscured in the shadows of a salt bowl. It could easily see him if he went back the way he came along the wall, and Castor cursed internally. He didn't want to risk being spotted by any of the arachna, since being chased by one would surely attract the attention of others. Instead, he changed course and quickly began to weave between the houses.

Castor moved with extreme caution, eyes picking up on every slight movement around him. More often than not, the motions originated from spiders. Within the residential area, the arachna roamed more freely. They weren't afraid of sunlight; they just preferred not to be directly under it, and the houses provided plenty of shadows for them to roam in comfort. Castor tried to travel in such a manner so that he spent the longest amount of time by the front walls of each home. That way, if need be, he could duck into the houses to escape in a moment's notice.

The spiders were too big to fit through the narrow, human-sized doorway of a house, but he wasn't sure of the lengths they would go to attack if they saw him enter one. He doubted they would just give up, and some might even be capable of breaking down a wall.

With all his caution, Castor covered ground slowly. On the street that separated the southeast and northeast quadrants, a spider scuttled over the packed dirt road and was about to turn the corner. He couldn't see it yet, as there was a house in between them, but Castor was alerted to its presence by the odd sound of its legs scuttling against the dirt road.

A second later, he saw the tips of the monster's front legs poke out from behind the wood and, not stopping to think, he went with the safest option available to him. The door was already opened, so he slipped in the house, closing it quickly so that the old hinges didn't squeak as much. Just in time too, as he saw a shadow over a portion of the window. The damn thing had stopped there, right outside!

He crawled on hands and knees below the window line, unwilling to take the chance that the spider could see him through it. Or, at least, see his shape. No one in the town could afford glass windows on their houses, so most covered the openings with oiled cloth when needed. This would protect the house from the elements to an extent, while still letting some light in. Unfortunately for Castor, the translucent cloth prevented him from clearly seeing what was going on outside. The only thing he could make out was a dark shade covering most of the frame.

The first thing he did was look for a back or side door to the house, which would conveniently allow him to slip out onto the main road, keeping the house in between him and the spider. There were none, of course. He could never be so lucky.

Castor anxiously waited, unable to control his racing thoughts. What if the spider kept him here too long, possibly until dusk? In the dark, the village would be impassable. His night vision was a lot better since he found the Glade, but he didn't trust it to see every monster. Plus, the spiders were most active in the dark. They probably wouldn't be waiting around like they were now.

To distract himself, he explored the house. He hadn't thought about it in his haste to escape the spider, but this home belonged to Mayson. The man lived here alone after his mother passed, as most of the elderly villagers did when the famine became more severe. He thought about the cheerful farmer, and prayed that he, along with Jayna and the rest of the missing villagers, were still alive.

The state of the house, however, was also quite strange. Furniture was shoved out of place, and even broken or toppled in some cases. The sparse decorations along the wall had been torn off, and smaller belongings were strewn across the floor. Even the upstairs part, including Mayson's bedroom, hadn't been spared. The sheets had been ripped off the bed and dumped onto the floor along with the pillows. The single, plain dresser was pulled away from the wall, and its drawers were all ripped out of their tracks.

This, in Castor's mind, confirmed his theory that the village had evacuated in a hurry. Mayson probably had to gather the possessions he wanted to take with him as fast as possible, which was likely why the house was now in such a state of disarray. He must have lost something important.

Making his way back down the stairs as quietly as he could manage, Castor saw that the shadow still hadn't budged. He waited for what felt like an eternity, before his impatience won out against his fear. Slowly, he crept to the windowsill, even going so far as to take off his shoes to dampen the sound of his footsteps against the wooden floorboards, and very slowly lifted up the cloth by the corner. A small ray of light poked him in the eye, and he had to blink for a moment to adjust. Then, he looked outside and almost screamed. Not in fear, but in anger.

That shadow wasn't from the spider. It was a piece of the gods-damned roof that had almost broken off and hung in front of the window. He had lurked in here for gods knew how long, scared to even look out the window for fear that a spider might see him, and the spider wasn't even there. It probably didn't even stop by the house in the first place!

It would have been funny if he was more removed from the situation, but now, all he could think about was how much of a wretch he was. When he set out on his quest, he had been willing to risk his life for the welfare of his village, the people he cared about. Then, he came so close to death so many times and somehow, his experiences had turned him into a coward. He thought that defying death should have made a person *more* courageous. Maybe, he had never been brave to begin with, just stupid.

Cowardly. Stupid. Whatever he was, it needed to change if he ever wanted to survive and rejoin his people. If they were still alive.

I will be brave. I will be strong. I won't lose my head in the face of danger. I won't back down. I will find my sister. And I will not die.

He didn't put his right hand on his heart or raise his left

because this wasn't a prayer to a god. It was a pledge to himself. So, instead, he laid a hand on his bracelet and traced the curving metal design with his thumb. He felt as if that was more appropriate, considering where it came from. Then, Castor left the damned building and once again snuck away towards his house.

Less than a minute later, Castor was walking up the front steps. Having no time to explore the flood of emotions that plagued him, he simply walked through the cracked door, a reflexive greeting lodged in his throat.

He expected to find a home as empty as Mayson's. And it *was* empty, but there was something out of the ordinary, something that confirmed his suspicions about the fate of the villagers.

On the dining room table, an ornate reminder of his father, someone had written out words in stark white paint.

Tom. Kar. Evacuate.

Chapter Fifteen

Heroes

Seven years ago, the village was a much different place. For one, it was much louder. The shouts of merchants peddling their wares at the marketplace could be heard even from the docks, and the dull buzz of conversation draped over the streets like a soft blanket. People still worked hard, of course; surviving in Alaya had always been difficult. But there was less urgency, and no oppressive sense of impending death.

Not only did they have time for entertainment, there was also a great demand for it. Travelling minstrels and jongleurs set up shop in inns, sometimes even in the streets, and they were held in almost as high regard as the Heroes that passed through the village on rare occasions.

Toriath looked a lot different physically as well. Ropes ran between buildings, and brightly coloured triangular pendants were tied to them in random sequence. They brought some life and personality to the otherwise drab village, but unfortunately, they had to be salvaged for their materials when the village closed its gates. The southwest quadrant was another residential area because the farms all existed just outside of the village walls. Small trees grew on the sides of roads and in between houses, but they would of course be cut down for lumber in years to come.

Oddly, the Park, which was presently the only spot of green in the entire village, didn't exist. Neither did the cattle tree, at least in that location. There used to be several, all growing far apart from each other outside of the village walls, surrounded by farms.

Monsters still appeared occasionally, especially within the forest. However, they were a lot fewer in number, oftentimes weaker as well, and it was rare that they would approach the village at all. When they did, it was always a solitary creature that the Noble Guard killed with relative ease. They might cause some light property damage to the farms, but it was quite manageable.

Additionally, none of these monsters in question were arachna. Toriath was far away from their nesting ground, and they were kept in check by Ayzadol's armies.

Castor lived a carefree life. His father's status allowed him privileges that most others were not afforded, such as better clothes, better food, and, most conspicuously of all, the ability to forgo chores and labour each day. While life was considerably easier at this time, young kids were still expected to work as they were able. Commonly, farm owners would ask for help planting seeds, tending animals, and performing other menial tasks, and parents would volunteer their children to assist them in return for some small amount of compensation, often in the form of food. Other times, parents who could afford to do so would pay the guilds to take on their children as apprentices to be taught their master's craft.

Since Tohm, Castor's father, was the village's ritual master, he had the luxury of choosing any future that he wanted for his children, and, predictably, he decided to take them both on as his apprentices. He wanted to begin their education when they were each thirteen, so he had already begun teaching Jayna four years ago at this point, and he wouldn't begin Castor's instruction for another three years. This would prove to be a mistake, because Tohm would pass away unexpectedly within the year. Nonetheless, Castor's current life was one of ease, and, as a result, other kids didn't welcome him into their circles. A few even went out of their way to antagonize him.

At ten years old, Castor didn't understand the cause, he only saw the effect. And the effect was that he was lonely, especially since his father and sister always seemed to be busy and he didn't have another parent. Tohm never fell in love but he desperately wanted children, so he paid a travelling merchant to perform the ritual of birth with him. Jayna was born and, years later, Tohm repeated the process with a different merchant. Neither Jayna nor Castor knew why he didn't pick someone from Toriath, and they didn't know anything about their other parents either. Tohm took that information to his grave.

Castor thought that the other kids excluded him because of his age. There was no one in the village that was exactly his age or younger: they were all at least a year older than him. A year wasn't a long time for an adult, but for a young kid it may as well have been a lifetime.

On one particular day, Castor meandered through the streets of Toriath, loosely carrying a small sack that swung with every step he took, and stopping by anything that could hold his interest, if only for a moment. He spent a couple hours looking through the tents at the marketplace, which looked the same as they had two days prior, and any guild house that had an outdoor section that would allow him to watch the masters and apprentices in their element.

He loved to watch blacksmithing the most, although Musov scared him. Which was, in all honesty, something he never fully outgrew. The rhythmic strikes of hammers on cherry-red metal was something he could, and often did, watch all day. Musov wasn't out in his outdoor forge today though, and watching Sola tan leather next door was rather disgusting. The breeze carried the terrible smell of cow skin and chemicals upwards of fifty meters away. Castor couldn't understand how Musov could bear it, but he supposed one would get used to it after decades of exposure.

With nothing else to do, Castor decided that he was tired and climbed to the roof of a building in the southwest quadrant. He liked to come up here often because it had a flat roof he could lie down on and because he knew it was vacant, so he wasn't trespassing in someone's home.

It was autumn, not that many people could tell. Since Toriath lay on the north coast of Alaya, the change in seasons was very slight. Still, it did get moderately chilly during winter and everyone in town was preparing for it. Fall harvest was approaching, and some kinds of trees were beginning to change leaf colour, while most others just shed them altogether.

Still, this was Castor's favourite time of year. The temperature was cool enough, there weren't constant rainstorms and it was sunny often. Right now, the sky was mostly blue, though several large clouds edged their way across the sky. It was the perfect weather for cloud watching. He didn't know how long he had lain there, and it was quite possible he dozed off.

Some time later, he was roused by a loud noise which emanated from the street below him. People were shouting, and for a moment he thought there was a fight, but then a couple of laughs broke out as well.

Castor walked to the edge of his resting spot and peered over the wooden edge of the roof. There were a handful of kids down below, all about two years older than him. They must have finished their duties for the day, and they seemed to be playing in the street. Castor could have guessed the game without looking, it was Heroes and Monsters. It was a childish roleplaying game, where most of the kids would pretend to be Heroes, the great warriors from another world, and some would pretend to be monsters that would inevitably be slain by the Heroes. Of course, no one ever wanted to be the monsters, so the roles were usually chosen by lots.

There was a fair amount of theatrics when playing Heroes and Monsters, otherwise it wouldn't have been any fun. The Heroes would declare what kind of Hero they would try and portray. In the children's limited understanding, there seemed to be two kinds of Heroes. The colossal ones with swords, shields or other large melee weaponry, and the other, still quite large Heroes, with bows and arrows. Then, the kids would choose what specific weapons they had. Meanwhile, the monsters got to choose what they looked like, and more often than not, they didn't end up resembling any monster that anyone in the village had ever seen. They were always gigantic.

As he watched his peers run around below him, Castor decided it was time for lunch. He opened the sack he brought with him, and found inside his lunch, half a loaf of brown bread, redbutter and a cookie. If a stranger was watching him eat, they would have been instantly able to identify him as a person of means by looking at this meal alone. Redbutter was a blend of crushed nuts, dried tomatoes, a touch of honey and, of course, butter. It was salty and sweet, meant as a condiment for the bread, and altogether way above the standard that almost everyone else in the village could ever expect to eat regularly.

The cookie was even more of a tell. Castor didn't know it, but this type of cookie was first introduced to this world by a Hero, who brought the recipe from his homeland. What made it so expensive were two of its ingredients. The first, sugar, was an expensive commodity, but one Tohm could acquire with relative ease. However, even he could rarely afford to purchase chocolate, which was the second costly ingredient. In fact, it was very rare for a merchant that sold chocolate to come to Toriath at all.

Chocolate had to be imported from Nasarali, the midwestern continent, meaning that, even for Castor, these cookies were a very rare treat. He and Jayna each got one for lunch the last couple of days, but this was his last, and he would make sure to savour it.

Castor ate his lunch sedately as he watched the game unfold below him. Sana had drawn the short straw and played the part of the monster. There was no way to tell what kind he chose because Castor was too far away to make out anything he spoke, but it hardly mattered. Sana was one of the youngest in the group, about two years older than Castor, and he was very energetic since he wasn't expected to work as hard as the older kids. Despite his reluctance at being chosen as the monster, he threw himself into the role, shouting out a feeble roar, and swiping at the others around him in slow, exaggerated movements.

The Heroes shouted as well, each calling out attacks, and pretending to wield imaginary swords or other weapons. Some even found sticks to further the illusion, and more than once saw Sana yell at one of his playmates who, in their excitement, swung their makeshift weapons a bit too hard. Meanwhile, the ones pretending to hold bows mimed pulling on drawstrings, sometimes running around to find a better position, or to flee from Sana if he rushed them.

It was a whole lot of nonsense, but Castor enjoyed the show despite being unable to understand what was going on. He popped a chunk of bread smeared in redbutter into his mouth as he watched one of the older kids, Carosa, stab at Sana with an invisible spear, who theatrically threw himself to the dirt. Oftentimes, kids picked specific Heroes who occasionally visited Toriath, and Carosa surely had chosen to play the role of Karat, who, along with his partner Tommygun, visited the village a lot more frequently than any others. They performed so many services for the benefit of the village that some people referred to them as Toriath's protectors.

In one instance, a dangerous monster once took up residence on the main road between Toriath and Ayzadol. It killed or drove away any travellers between the two settlements, which was detrimental to the Torians because they depended heavily on trade from the larger city. The Heroes not only killed the monster, but they also travelled to Ayzadol to notify the Merchant's Guild that the road was safe once more.

Another time, a group of raiders attacked the farms outside of the village wall and abducted several teenagers to use as slaves or possibly recruits. Lord Tolam begged the Heroes to help recover his lost subjects and they agreed with smiles on their faces. Days later, the raider group was no more, and those who were lost had been safely returned. Carosa was among those that were saved.

Castor mopped up the last of his redbutter with a crust of bread and smacked his lips contentedly. He was about to take a bite of his cookie when another kid came running from the direction of the marketplace. It was Jima, a boy about four years his senior who was an apprentice to Aygar, the master of the mason's guild. Castor often watched the two of them work together, and Aygar's delicate stone carvings were popular fixtures throughout the village. No one knew how to work with shellstone the way he did, and it was a detriment to the village when he died in a hastily coordinated mining project four years later.

Jima shouted to the rest of the kids, who all perked up when they saw him. From up above, Castor couldn't hear everything that was said, but he was able to make out the gist of the message. Heroes were here, visiting the village! The children dropped what they were doing, threw their makeshift weapons down onto the street, and ran off in the direction of the marketplace. They could play Hero almost anytime, but now there were real Heroes nearby that they could ogle!

Castor followed them, quickly running down the stone steps, lunch sack in hand. The dull roar of the marketplace grew in volume the closer he got to it, even louder than it was normally. When he reached the main stretch, he saw that the streets were completely filled with villagers standing shoulder to shoulder, all the way to the Keep. Kids weren't the only ones who were eager to see the Heroes. Most of the village came out to greet the figures who were so revered and, beyond that, so well liked.

He had to meekly wade through the solid wall of people gathered around in order to be able to see the street at all. Once he wasn't directly behind some taller adults, he had absolutely no problem locating the Heroes.

It was Karat, and his partner Tommygun of course. The town wouldn't have been so worked up if it was an unfamiliar Hero. The duo held a special place in the Torians' hearts. They also stuck out among the crowd like a fox in a rabbit's den. Each one stood head and shoulders over the surrounding villagers, and their heavily muscled limbs made them quite wider than anyone else as well.

Aside from their general build, the two Heroes looked and behaved quite differently. Tommygun walked ahead, grinning broadly, calling out to people he recognized and shaking hands. He was a white-skinned man who wore half of a set of armour, comprised of a breastplate to protect his chest, shoulder guards and vambraces to protect his arms and greaves to protect his shins.

It was mostly impractical, and probably wouldn't be able to provide enough protection for a normal person to survive in a difficult fight. Mostly, its job was to look impressive, and it certainly did. The amount of metal on his body could have pinned a normal human to the ground, but Tommygun moved like it wasn't even there. He wore no helmet, and atop his head was an untamed mop of blond hair.

His partner, Karat, stood back a short distance. He smiled at the villagers and waved to familiar faces, but he was a lot more subdued. Unlike Tommygun, he wore no armour, at least, none that Castor could see. He was dressed in a loose tunic that ended a little above his knees, under which he had beige pants and boots. The tunic had long sleeves, and it would have been pure white, if not for the dirt that was unavoidable when travelling. Upon his shaved head, he wore a red and white checkered headdress, and he had a full, dark beard as well. The creases above his eyes suggested that he smiled frequently. All in all, the man didn't look quite as muscular as his partner, although that could have been because his clothes weren't nearly as tight.

A couple meters in front of Castor, the group that he watched play Heroes and Monsters gathered to gawk at the Heroes. As friendly as the two men were, the children were too afraid to approach them. It was to be expected; Karat and Tommygun were incredibly imposing figures. And it wasn't just their size that made them so. For over a year these Heroes had protected Toriath, and the children heard so many stories of their great deeds. Some were exaggerated and some were completely false, but that didn't matter to a child. Even most adults felt the same way, which is why the majority waved or called out from each side of the road instead of walking up and greeting the giant men.

Castor heard all these same stories, and he saw the Heroes in front of him clearly. But he *wanted* to talk to them, desperately. They were just so amazing, and they encompassed everything he wanted to be in life. He also noticed the cowering kids as well, the same ones that always excluded him. Castor wanted to be brave enough to approach them, unlike all of the older kids.

His legs began moving before he even had time to think. Castor pushed his way into the street and walked towards the duo. "Tommygun!" he shouted out. The man was engrossed in greeting a fruit stall keeper and didn't hear him, which was just as well. His voice had broken. Castor walked closer until he was five meters away.

"Tommygun!" he called out louder, and that did the trick. The titan turned around and looked right at him. Castor knew it was ridiculous to think so, but he felt like he was about to die. Though he was smiling, the figure before him was dangerous. Every fibre of his being told him so. The man could literally squeeze his head into a fine paste, and Castor had seen a few casual feats of the unimaginable strength Tommygun possessed.

The man was still looking at him, and Castor realized a few seconds had gone by since the man saw him.

"What's up, kid?" the Hero asked.

What was Castor doing? He didn't even know what he wanted to say to the man! He didn't think about it at all before he started moving. His face felt like it was on fire, and he was acutely aware that everyone in the marketplace was staring at him now.

In an impulse he held out his lunch sack, the only thing he had on hand to the man. "Please." His voice cracked, and he tried to clear his throat. "Please take this."

Bemused, Tommygun reached out and grabbed the sack. A bit more confident, Castor gave a jerky bow to the man. "Thank you for protecting my village."

Tommygun tried to reach into the sack and failed. His hand was just too big to fit inside the narrow opening. Instead, he dumped the contents into his open hand. All that was left were a couple of breadcrumbs and Castor's special cookie. "Oooh, a chocolate chip cookie. Thanks, little man!"

The man's partner had walked over to him during the exchange. Castor's heartbeat sped up once again as the second giant approached. He cast his gaze downward. "I'm sorry, I only have one."

Castor cursed himself. This might have been worse than not saying anything at all! What if Karat was offended because Castor didn't offer him a cookie as well? Or, what if Tommygun took offence on his partner's behalf? He was so flustered; he nearly had a heart attack when Tommygun burst into laughter.

Even though it expressed joy, the sound was just as terrifying as the rest of the man. The loud, deep guffaw rattled every bone in his small body.

"That's okay," the Hero told Castor as he settled down. "We'll just share it!" He broke the morsel, which was only half as big as his palm, in half just by delicately poking it, and he held out half to Karat, who shook his head in exasperation.

"Are you really going to take a cookie from a child?" Castor realized he had never heard the man speak until this very moment. He had a very nice accent.

"I think it would be rude if we didn't." Tommygun replied good-naturedly. Karat shrugged and accepted his half. They each ate the treat in one bite.

"That was really good! What's your name, kid? And how old are you?"

Castor tried to meet the man's eye and received a grin in response. "Castor. And I'm ten."

Tommygun whistled in appreciation. "You're pretty brave for a ten-year-old. Here, take this." He held out his palm face up, murmured something under his breath, and to Castor's amazement, something materialized into his palm! One second his hand was empty, and then it faded into existence like magic.

With trembling fingers, Castor took the object out of Tommygun's hand. It was a bracelet, with a medallion shaped like a leaf fixed upon a leather cuff. The leaf was highly stylized, and the metal was shinier than any he had ever seen in his life. The leather was high quality as well, and indented designs were etched into its surface. A second, thinner band was woven through the first which kept the silver medallion in place. Castor was sure that such leatherworking was beyond the level of even Lias, the leatherworking guildmaster in Toriath. When Castor tried to put it on, it fell all the way to his elbow. It was obviously made to fit someone Tommygun's size, and Castor was a normal ten-year-old boy.

"Whoops! I guess you'll have to get that resized," the man said with a laugh. "I'm sure Lias will do it for you for free. Now." He drew himself up, and Castor realized the man had hunched over to talk to him. He honestly hadn't noticed because, even bent over, their height difference was so great. Now, when Castor tried to look at the Hero's face, he had to crane his neck so far up that he was blinded by the sun.

"Karat and I have to meet with Lord Tolam. We have some important news for him. Thanks again for the cookie!" And with that the Heroes left, continuing down the marketplace and towards the Keep. Immediately, Castor was swarmed by the other children, who had watched the entire exchange, all of whom were eager to look at his gift.

Tom. Kar. Tommygun and Karat.

Castor absentmindedly rubbed the bracelet he still wore around his right wrist. The metal had lost most of its lustre, and grime filled in the grooved designs in the leather, but after it was properly fitted, he rarely took the thing off. There was even a faint tan line that bordered the leather, which was visible if the strap was pushed up or down on his arm.

That day was the last time Castor, or anyone else in the village for that matter, saw the two Heroes. It was also the day that everything started to go to hell. As a result of his meeting with the duo, Lord Tolam ordered the construction of a massive, underground tunnel that would span the distance of the village and continue southwest for another one thousand meters. It was an enormous undertaking that was only finished less than a year ago, even with the cooperation of the entire village.

The Torians were lucky that they finished the tunnel's excavation when they did. Monster populations, which had been steadily on the rise since all Heroes vanished from Alaya, boomed, and, while the workers were safe underground, the end of the tunnel was still a potential vulnerability.

It was a mystery as to why the world changed so much in the years that followed, but Lord Tolam divulged the contents of his meeting with the Heroes soon after it took place. Apparently, there had been several attacks on other settlements, and Tommygun and Karat had implored the nobleman to create defences and evacuation plans for the village.

It seemed like a bit of an overreaction, at the time. Attacks on settlements were commonplace, both by other humans and monsters, and Toriath hardly drew the attention of any potential enemies. However, the Heroes' warning was apparently enough to convince Lord Tolam that action was necessary, so all the Torians could do was trust in their leaders and the information their two mighty champions left them. Well, some discussed a revolt when they heard the extreme measures Lord Tolam decided to take based on hearsay, but the Noble Guard put a stop to that. So, they excavated the tunnel and listened to the evacuation plans that Lord Tolam devised.

Then, for some reason, Heroes disappeared altogether, and not even Lord Tolam knew why. It took a while for the villagers to notice, because Toriath wasn't exactly a common destination for Heroes to begin with. However, to this day, no Hero had since stepped through their main gate.

Castor allowed himself to succumb to the unpleasant weight that still pressed down on him and sank into the dining room chair. The pressure he felt on his lower spine wasn't alleviated in the slightest but sitting in this chair brought a sense of sad familiarity.

His brow furrowed as he tried to make sense of what he saw. Tom. Kar. Evacuate. Toriath's evacuation plan detailed what should happen if all hope for their settlement was lost. He was relieved to know that the villagers did evacuate, even though he had already deduced as much. But why resort to such extreme measures?

Chapter Sixteen
Salt

Castor reviewed the evacuation plan in his head, hoping that doing so would give him some idea on how to proceed. First, the call to evacuate was sounded, either with a bell or through word of mouth if subtlety was required. Then they would migrate to one of three entrances to the tunnel that was built underground.

The guards would stay behind, stalling the enemy and filtering into the tunnels themselves as they were able. Or they would die trying.

But against what enemy? Did the arachna attack en masse? Did an even more powerful monster emerge? If there wasn't some enemy forcing them to leave, they wouldn't have departed in such a hurry, and they would have been more seriously considering the possibility before he left.

It seemed as if the only way Castor could answer his questions was by finding the rest of his village. He touched the paint on the table and found it to be bone dry, so the evacuation must have been at least a day ago, probably more. With any luck, his people would still be seeking refuge in the tunnels below, waiting to retake the village from the spiders. However, Castor didn't want to get his hopes up. They may have been forced to abandon the village altogether and, if so, any time he wasted here would widen the gap between them.

Castor wrenched himself to his feet and searched his house

for any other clues his sister may have left him, and for supplies he might need for another journey. It was apparent that, unlike Mayson's, his house was undisturbed. Some small belongings were missing, but there wasn't much for his sister to take. Predictably, his own room was untouched. Castor was ecstatic to finally be able to change clothes, because the one set he currently wore was in tatters, missing sleeves, and smelled absolutely disgusting.

He put on a new outfit and took two spares. Before, he had gambled on his quest being quick to conclude, either by completing his goal or dying, but he refused to be caught unprepared again.

There was only so much he could do though. Castor was sure the villagers took everything useful, and he didn't have the time to find out. Above all else, he longed to get his hands on some food to take with him. The week he spent slowly starving to death in the ravine was the worst experience of his life, and he never wanted to repeat it. However, the little food that the village possessed was in the locker below the Keep, which was easily accessible through the tunnels. There was no excuse for the villagers to have left it behind.

It would be useless to search for food within other houses because villagers were not allowed to keep private supplies. Everything of use, especially when it came to food, was kept in the diligently watched communal storage spaces, and there was no way to embezzle any food either. Farmers were examined by their supervisors at the end of each day to make sure that no one had pilfered any of the crops, and the supervisors were searched by members of the Noble Guard as well.

The fishermen were also checked, and the monsters the guards killed during sea hunts were under the strictest scrutiny. After it was butchered, half of the monster was taken to the food storage, while the other half was taken to the salt room to be preserved.

Castor's eyes lit up in realization. *The salt room! If the villagers evacuated in a hurry, they might not have had time to retrieve its contents!* That was the one place in Toriath he could feasibly find some food to bring with him. And, if the villagers were still hiding underneath the village, they could use any amount of food he could retrieve for them. Even if it wasted time, and he had no guarantee that his effort could bear fruit, he had to check.

He took one last, long look at the home he had lived his entire life in, not knowing when he would be back. He paused at the ornate dining room table, a memento of their father, which Jayna defaced to write this message.

Why did Jayna mention Tommygun and Karat? He would have gotten the message by just writing about the evacuation plan. Did the reason they left have something to do with the Heroes' warning?

Maybe he was reading too far into it. All he could do was ask Jayna when he caught up to her. Opening his front door slowly, he stole out onto the street as soon as he was sure it was safe.

The salt room was located just off the beach, and, conveniently, it was right next to one of the entrances to the tunnel. However, that was on the complete opposite side of the northeast quadrant, and Castor was reluctant to traverse that distance while there were so many spiders about. In his mind, the safest way to get to that spot was to head to the tunnel entrance under the Keep, travel underground and climb back up to his destination.

While sound in theory, his plan didn't account for one factor. The arachna. As he approached the Keep from this new angle, he saw that one side of the structure was covered with webs. The wall was almost completely covered in white, but even from this distance, Castor's keen eyes noticed some protrusions coming out of the wall that were brown and a sickly green. It looked like the spiders, for some reason, had taken branches and stuck them to the adhesive surface of their webs. What purpose did they serve? And how the hell did they manage to lift them without hands?

Castor refused to get any closer, but he traced the branches with his eyes. They were more like vines he supposed, since they flexed in ways hardwood couldn't, and they all seemed to be connected. He realized that they hadn't been stuck to the web after all, the web was actually placed over them.

That brought him up short. Was there always a system of vines climbing up the side of the Keep that he just never noticed? He didn't think so, but the system was way too extensive for it to have just popped up overnight. It already stretched nearly ten meters up the wall, and not even in a straight line.

He frowned as he saw something else unusual. Attached to different parts of the tree were globes of web. They were smaller than a human and too perfectly round, so Castor didn't think that they were the remnants of an arachna's meal. Then, everything fell into place, and he began to shake. This was an arachna plant! Castor never gave any thought as to how arachna reproduced, but it seemed like it wasn't much different from any other animal or monster. He remembered seeing these vines all over the place in the forest, and most were covered in webs just like this one. None of them were this big though.

Although, he supposed that, in the forest, none of the trees were big or sturdy enough to handle a vine system like this one. Castor thought of the toppled tree he spent his first night under in the forest. It was also covered in vines like these, although they were dead. The weight of spider eggs must have been too much for it.

Castor abhorred the idea of this monstrosity growing at the heart of his village. However, there was nothing he could do about it. If he tried to remove it, and he had no idea how he would go about doing so, the spiders would be all over him in a second. Besides, he saw a moment later that it was guarded. An arachna lumbered around the corner of the Keep, and even from this distance, he could tell that it was a gigantic specimen. By comparing it to the building nearest to the Keep, Castor was sure that it was at least as big as the spider who fought that humanoid monster in the forest before he fell into the ravine. Not only was he unable to touch the spider vine, but it seemed like the Keep was off limits to him as well. He would have to take the long way around.

He only happened upon one more arachna on his way to the salt room, but it was the most harrowing encounter since setting foot in the village. There were no doors to duck into, and he was exposed in the road. The only place he could hide was under a small wooden deck that was used as a foundation for a house, since it was built upon uneven land. What sent him into a momentary panic was that, as he tried to squeeze into the narrow gap, his backpack caught on a loose piece of wood.

He didn't have the presence of mind to untangle himself or to take off the pack. In his panic, all Castor could think to do was pull and pull until the half-rotten wood snapped off. In his ears, it sounded as loud as the crack of a whip, and he burrowed as far into the gap as he could. He was on his stomach, and with his head turned, he could see out from under the house.

Sure enough, it seemed like the spider did hear the wood breaking. Castor could see its legs through the gap, and they each lifted up and down with agitation. Castor didn't even breathe, which, in conjunction with his adrenaline rush, sent a sharp pain through his chest. Fortunately, before too long the spider seemed to decide that there was nothing and continued on its way.

Extracting himself from the space he wedged himself into was no easy feat. He always hated not being able to move any part of his body, and this reminded him of when he first fell into the ravine and got stuck between the cracks. He did eventually manage to wriggle himself to the edge of the deck and, making sure that the coast was clear, he pulled himself out and sped the rest of the distance to the salt room. He moved his pack so that it rested on his stomach instead of his back, and wrapped his arms around it tightly. He didn't want it to be caught on something again, or for it to make a sound.

Despite the fact that it now held much more than what he took with him on his first journey, it seemed completely empty because everything he put in it disappeared. This, while a good thing, did mean that the pack bounced freely against his back. If he ran, he would have to hold onto the straps so as not to risk it slipping off entirely.

The salt room was locked. Of course it was. There were very few locks that the village possessed, even when it was thriving. Locks were specialty items that were too delicate for many metalworkers to bother learning to make. However, the fact that the door was locked gave him hope. After all, why would someone bother to lock a place that was empty, especially during an evacuation?

Still, any attempt to break open the door would be much too

loud, and he didn't want to take a risk like that unless there was no other way. There were no windows, both as a safety feature and because heat from the sunlight could impair the curing process. First, Castor tried to pry the nails out of the metal piece the deadbolt slid into, but then realized that he would need some kind of tool to do so after almost ripping his entire fingernail off.

He had one more idea though, and it involved climbing to the roof. There weren't any stairs on the outside, but, since it was right next to the ocean, the north-facing wall was made from pitted shellstone to protect the structure from the sea spray. With only a little difficulty, he scaled the structure.

The roof of the salt room was flat, but along the south edge there was a trough of some kind. It spanned nearly the width of the roof and the inside walls were sloped and made out of two different materials. The slope facing him was made from the same stone as the rest of the roof. The side opposite to him was wood, which was smoothed and varnished to protect it from weathering.

This trough was similar in effect to the salt basins that dotted the roofs of many houses in the village. However, unlike the salt basins that were for personal use, this manufactured salt for the village as a whole. As such, it needed to produce a much larger volume. Buckets of water were hoisted up on pulleys attached to the side of the building and dumped into the trough, which could hold over one and a half cubic meters of water. When dried, it left quite a bit of salt at the bottom of the basin, and Castor could see the white powder that caked the inside.

Castor wasn't interested in the salt itself right now. He was interested in the trough, or rather the mechanism that was inside it. The wooden panel was actually a trap door that, when opened, would drop the harvested salt down below.

He was one of the few people in the village who knew how this mechanism worked, or that it even existed at all. Since he and his sister depended so heavily on salt for their rituals, they often needed to work the mechanism and fill up the trough themselves. Of course, they didn't have to climb up the wall each time to get to the roof to operate it. They borrowed a ladder from the village's supply room, but that was inaccessible to him now.

Still, the process of opening the trapdoor really was a two-person job. There were two levers on each side of the trough that were connected to the wooden gate through gaps in the stone. By pulling them simultaneously, the trapdoor would open. However, since Castor was by himself, he could only pull it a couple millimetres at a time before the door would become misaligned, and he would have to run over to the other side to pull from there. It was slow and frustrating work, and soon he was sweating profusely from running back and forth along the roof so many times.

Finally, Castor had fully opened the hatch. Very few people, aside from children, could fit through the gap below him, and he desperately hoped that he was one. He would be furious if he did all that work for nothing. He lay down on his side in the opening, and pushed his right hand and leg, which had fit through the gap, against the stone lip, trying to force himself through. After a minute or so, he managed to do it.

Even though it went according to plan, Castor was still somehow surprised as he dropped through the ceiling. In his head, he simply skipped from the 'get through the opening' part to the 'be inside the salt room' part. He crashed down onto a wheelbarrow that was positioned to collect the salt, and the contraption, which was not built to support the weight of a free falling human, toppled underneath him.

Castor cursed and rubbed his bruised tailbone and right shoulder. It was a good thing he closed his eyes instinctively upon impact, because otherwise he might have gotten salt in them, which he knew from experience was excruciating. Falling through the ceiling wasn't the most elegant solution, but he was finally inside the salt room, and his efforts were rewarded generously.

Just like he hoped, he saw plenty of meat suspended from hooks along the walls and from chains hanging from the ceiling. What he *was* surprised to see was, in addition to sea monster meat, there was dried beef! The village must have slaughtered one of the cows before they left.

Come to think of it, there were only three web bundles in

the ruined pen, meaning one of the cows was unaccounted for, since there were four when he left. Beef jerky tasted a whole lot better to him than sea monster jerky, so he was elated to find some.

He wondered why there was so much food here. He knew that a large portion of the meat they harvested was dried for preservation, but once the salting process was completed, the product would be taken beneath the Keep to be stored with all the other food. If the sea monster meat harvested from the last sea hunt hadn't been taken there, that must mean the drying process wasn't completed before the evacuation.

Castor wished he knew how long it took to dry cuts of meat this size, because that might have given him some sort of time frame for when the evacuation occurred. While he didn't know when the cow was slaughtered, he knew that the sea monster was killed four days before he left the village. If he knew how long it took to dry the meat, he could more or less figure out how far he was behind the group.

Surveying the room, he realized that there was surprisingly too much jerky to take with him. That is, if he had to carry it normally. Triumphantly, he shrugged off his backpack and set to carving up the large cuts of meat into more manageable strips, starting with the beef. He stuffed it all into his bag, which steadily vanished its contents as he worked, and even treated himself to a celebratory lunch.

Eventually though, to Castor's surprise, he noticed that his bag was no longer vanishing its contents. Confused, he felt around the bottom of the pack before realizing that it must be full. He was a bit disappointed; he had assumed the storage space was infinite. He was reluctant to stuff the physical part of the pack; he needed to be able to move hastily after all. But while he *did* manage to clear out most of the salt room, Castor still felt bad for leaving any food behind. He even considered removing some of the other supplies stored in the bag in favour of bringing more jerky, not that he had much else.

He quickly decided not to though. Castor really wanted the extra clothes he had packed, if only to tear up and use as bandages, and there was no way he would give up either waterskin, not after what happened in the ravine. He would fill them both when he got the chance. Everything else was too small to make sense ditching to create more space.

A large part of him wanted to leave the seeds and the crystals here for safekeeping, but Castor didn't know what the future had in store for his village. The Torians may never be able to return here, as sad as that was, and he couldn't bear the thought of his efforts being wasted.

No, he would deliver them to his sister and Lord Tolam personally. Only then would he be satisfied.

Although he was trying to *make* room, he decided to take some salt from the piles sitting in the back of the hut. It would come in handy if he needed to perform a ritual or season his food. There were a couple of pouches in the room for this very purpose, and Castor filled up two. The pouches weren't waterproof like the water skin was, so he had to be careful not to fall into another river.

Actually, did the supplies stored in the bag get wet when the ravine flooded? After a moment, he remembered when he took the rancid bandages out to bind his leg wound. They were dry, he remembered. After a few half-hearted attempts, he realized he would have to take out all the jerky in the physical portion of the bag to do what he needed, so he dumped it all out onto his lap. But when he turned the bag inside out, his eyes widened when he saw that the number in the middle had gone back up to *eight*.

Castor's thoughts went into a frenzy. *How did that happen? What made it go back up?* The simplest explanation was that the number replenished itself after a certain period of time. If so, how long did it take?

He tried to remember when he last looked in the bag. He knew the number was still zero when he was in the ravine, at least until his last night treading. *Wait, I took some stuff out after I got hit by the wadom. It was still at zero then, I think.* Castor wasn't sure. He hadn't exactly been paying attention, but he didn't think the number had gone up at that point.

If time was the factor, then there was at least a six-day gap between when he last used the icons and today. That's what he thought at least, as he wasn't lucid enough by the end to be sure exactly how much time passed in the ravine. But maybe there was another answer. Did something else happen in between now and yesterday? Nothing came to mind.

His eyes never left the number eight in front of him. He was tempted, *so tempted*, to start messing around with the icons again, but he resisted the urge. He couldn't help but think there was a significance here that was lost on him now, and Castor knew the smart thing to do would be to wait for his sister to examine the design. Or, to at least keep a supply of numbers so that, if he ran into danger and needed a boost, they would be ready for him to use.

Decision made, he tore his eyes away from the icons and set to work, replacing some jerky in the storage space with the salt pouches. He withdrew the half empty waterskin he had been drinking out of as well, for ease of access, before dumping the rest of the excess jerky in.

Once he was finished situating himself, he slid back the deadbolt and carefully left the building. He was very grateful that the northeast entrance to the tunnels was almost right next to the salt room.

The evacuation plans were created to be used in a variety of scenarios, and not just ones that involved monsters. Years ago, no one expected monsters to overrun the continent to the extent they did, even after the Heroes disappeared. Lord Tolam was just as concerned with human threats, such as coordinated armies both from the land and sea. Therefore, a great deal of effort was put into disguising the entrances to the tunnels that extended underneath the village.

In a small, open space between buildings was a tent of sorts, which was white with red stripes that were so faded and discoloured that they appeared to be brown. It was once a permanent fixture in the marketplace, but it had been repurposed as a safeguard from prying eyes that might be able to glimpse this spot from a distance.

Underneath the tent was a trio of wells. Each one had a basic look to it, with a circular stone base, with a narrower yet longer cylinder stacked on top of it. Above that was a taller wooden structure, with a bucket and winch attached to it.

However, no one would mistakenly try to use the well to fetch drinking water because, on the wooden shutters that were typically included on a well to prevent small animals or children from falling in, someone had painted the statement: *do not use, water contaminated.*

They didn't look like entrances to a secret tunnel, which was the point. However, there were a couple things about them that might seem odd to a watchful eye. The most noticeable was that, for wells, they were all quite wide. Probably wide enough for two people to climb in shoulder to shoulder. Wells weren't usually that big. Also, the wooden structure above the well, which the bucket and rope were attached to, was quite higher than one normally would be. It was almost tall enough for a person to stand between it and the opening of the well, which seemed like it would take a lot more effort to use. In fact, for the winch to lock in place, the bucket would have to be pulled up higher than most people would be able to reach easily.

Additionally, it was unusual to see a contaminated well intact. Well contamination was a common problem, but those structures were usually demolished to prevent people from using them accidentally. The wooden shutters, even though they featured the painted warning, weren't even nailed shut. Still, even if a person noticed all three of these things, they would be unlikely to pay them any mind.

Each of these irregularities stood out to Castor, who knew their true functions. He opened up the shutters to the one closest to him. On the inside of each wooden door, there were thin chains that trailed down into the darkness. Along the side of the wall were two sets of metal rungs embedded into the stone which led down into inky blackness that even his sharp gaze couldn't penetrate.

With an apprehensive sigh, Castor grabbed the lip of the well near the path of rungs closest to him, his back and arms protesting before he even took his first step. However, before he truly began his descent, he glimpsed a building a block away that caught his interest. He decided that, even if he was tempting fate, it was in his best interest to check it out. Pulling himself back up, he stalked silently down the back of Guildhouse Row, which was on the main street, separated from the marketplace by the Keep. He wanted to visit the blacksmith's.

Chapter Seventeen
The Dark Below

The blacksmith was one of the largest guildhouses in Toriath by necessity. So much equipment was needed to properly forge metal, whether it be for a weapon, armour or anything else the village might need. Recently, most projects tended to be tools, both for farming and mining, and construction materials such as nails and brackets.

Most of the workshop was outside, because the process of heating metal created a lot of smoke. It was a fire hazard as well, and stone walls had been set up around the work area so that flying sparks didn't ignite any of the surrounding wooden houses by chance. Above the setup was a large tent-like roof made from oilcloth, suspended far above the reach of any wayward embers on tall wooden posts. Its purpose was to keep rain off their tools and unfinished projects.

The capabilities of the blacksmith's guild were greatly inhibited by the closure of the village because its members depended heavily on wood and other burnable materials to heat the metal for forging. Even though they had a surplus of metal, without fire they couldn't soften it. Trying to mould iron with only brute force was impossible for anything larger than Castor's hand, and it resulted in weakened metal.

Without the ability to harvest trees outside of the village walls, Musov, his apprentices and whoever else was tasked to help him had to rely on wood salvaged from other parts of the village. Most of the wood they still used came from demolished houses in the southwest quadrant, but lumber was sought after by most sects of the village. There had been talk of demolishing more abandoned houses before Castor left, since quite a few stood vacant, but he supposed they wouldn't have to worry about that anymore.

With the scarcity of fuel, all the workers would have to share the fire to complete their tasks, which Castor imagined didn't work so well. He could see tables and anvils grouped closely together around the forge, and tools, both the ones being repaired and the ones that the blacksmiths used to repair them, were strewn around haphazardly. Castor wondered if the smiths were in the middle of working on their respective projects when the call to evacuate was issued.

Castor didn't come here to look around the workspace. He was more interested in what he might find inside the guildhouse. Opening the back door, he was taken aback by the state of the interior, which basically acted as a combination of a storefront and a display. It was even more trashed than Mayson's house was, with wares strewn across the floor and displays destroyed. Musov, like many blacksmiths, most prominently displayed weapons. Those pieces often attracted the most attention from the public, and even though the guild no longer worried about making sales, there had been no reason to change the storefront.

Said weapons were the main reason Castor wanted to check this place out. He had been foolish to leave the village mostly unarmed, and if he could find something more suitable for him than his tiny knife, he should take it.

Near the main entrance, there was a barrel that contained discount swords. It had been kicked over, and its contents had spilled all over the floor. Castor always wanted a sword. They were the weapons of Heroes, and the weapons that the Noble Guard most commonly used. However, when he went to pick up the nearest sword, he soon realized that he wasn't fit to wield one.

He imagined that lifting a sword would be easy, but the damned thing was a lot heavier than it looked. It took quite a bit of effort just for Castor to pick it up, and whenever he tried to hold it straight, the end would dip towards the ground. He tried another, hoping that he mistakenly grabbed a sword that was heavier than normal. It weighed the same, and when Castor took an experimental swing, he was almost pulled off his feet.

Castor was still weak from his time in the ravine, at least he prayed that was the only reason. He was struggling enough before he had to carry anything other than his empty bag, but now it was mostly filled with food and clothes, and the physical weight magnified whatever was going on in his lower back. The dull pressure was already turning into an ache, and he only just filled the physical space of the pack.

Regretfully, Castor set the offending hunk of metal back on the floor. Even if he could feasibly swing the sword around, it was too unwieldy, and it would be miserable to travel with as he would have to carry it outside of the pack if he wanted to be ready to defend himself at a moment's notice. Surveying the room once more, he discounted anything larger than a sword for the same reasons. He doubted he could even lift a halberd at all.

He thought that a crossbow might be a lot more suitable for him. Castor liked the idea of being able to attack monsters from a distance. More specifically, he liked his body to be as far out of harm's way as possible. There was a crossbow on the wall to his left, and he had to drag over and climb on top of an errant crate to reach it.

Unexpectedly, the contraption was just as heavy as the swords he tried to wield. It was a bit more manageable since the weight was contained in a smaller area, as opposed to the length of a sword. It didn't matter if he could pick it up or aim it though. No matter how hard he tried, he just couldn't set the drawstring, even with the mechanism that was supposed to ease the process. No matter how viciously he cursed, he couldn't pull the lever all the way. He set it down with disgust and huffed.

The more he thought about it though, the more he realized that the crossbow, while appealing, wasn't a practical weapon for him either. In addition to the bow itself, he would have to take metal bolts to use as projectiles, which would just add to the amount of weight he had to carry. And he had no way to obtain more ammunition, so when he ran out, the crossbow became useless.

Also, now that he thought about it, were there even any bolts in the shop to begin with? A quick search revealed that, no, there weren't any. Well, that settled it. No crossbow for him. He could probably find bolts in the Keep's armoury, but he was already turned off to the idea of using the weapon.

Besides, he was uncomfortable with the idea of entering the Keep. Even though he knew the walls were thick enough to withstand a bombardment of siege weapons, he didn't want to tempt fate by venturing so close to the arachnas' vine. As opposed to other buildings, it was a lot more feasible for spiders to have made their way into the Keep because the doorways were considerably wider.

Castor was beginning to lose hope in finding a usable weapon. Everything seemed to be impractical, too heavy or both. Still, he continued searching. Along the back wall was a massive locked cupboard. Well, it was once locked, since one of the doors was ripped off its hinges. The missing door had a receptacle for a rotating piece of metal that was attached to the lock of the other door, but that seemed to have been completely bypassed in favour of brute force.

This cabinet held some of Musov's best works, and even some of his master's works that had never sold. Musov never even opened the cabinet unless an unmistakably wealthy customer came into the shop. About a decade ago, Castor once pestered Laseen, a blacksmith's journeyman who had moved out of the village before the arachna infestation grew rampant, into showing him its contents.

Castor was a little disappointed when he had seen them. He expected gold and jewel encrusted weapons, but they were just regular old iron. Well-crafted regular old iron, but that wasn't enough to captivate a child.

As expected, the cabinet was mostly empty. If someone had gone through the effort to force open the cabinet, it only made sense that they would take its contents with them. It was odd that Musov would bring all those weapons during an evacuation, but Castor supposed he understood. They were his most prized possessions, after all.

Still, he did leave some behind. Unfortunately, they were all weapons that Castor was unable to wield. Castor took a step forward to take a closer look at the images etched on the surface of a shield, and he felt a small shift underneath his foot. Mostly obscured underneath some pieces of armour that must also have fallen out of the cabinet was the tip of a blade. He kicked it, expecting resistance, and was surprised when the entire thing shot out from its hiding place and skidded across the floor.

Instead of a sword like Castor expected, the weapon was a considerably shorter dagger. Its double-edged blade was about two and a half times the length of the knife he currently kept in his belt, and only slightly narrower than that of a sword. From hilt to point, it was less than half a meter.

What was really strange about the dagger was its design, which was completely unlike any other piece around him. A fuller, a groove included to reduce weight, ran lengthwise down each side of the blade, and the hilt was wrapped with smooth, black dyed leather that was almost glossy in its perfection. Castor liked Sola and wouldn't say this to the man's face, but he didn't think the master of the tanner's guild was capable of making something as perfect as this.

No, Castor didn't think this dagger was forged in Toriath at all. Aside from the fuller, which Musov didn't include on any of the other pieces around him, the guard, which extended diagonally on just one side, had a lot more of a geometric look to it. The guards on weapons Musov crafted were all curved, and none of his apprentices would dare forge anything in a different style.

Musov likely got this weapon in a trade from a travelling merchant long ago. It didn't really matter why it was here though—Castor wasn't about to question his good fortune. The dagger, while heavier than it looked, was relatively easy for him to use while still granting him farther reach than his knife would. It was of very good quality as well.

As he gave the dagger a few experimental swings, Castor's keen ears picked up on a soft whistling sound that accompanied each slash. The weapon felt comfortable in his hand, and he liked the feel of the glossy leather underneath his fingers. He tried to spin it on the palm of his hand and failed, almost dropping it. Still, a satisfied smile tugged at his lips.

I think I found my weapon.

The small blade provided him a small modicum of safety, but Castor would much rather avoid conflict altogether. Therefore, even as he clutched the dagger in his hand, he still crouched down and remained as silent as possible as he left through the outdoor section of the forge and made his way back to the wells that disguised the entrance to the tunnel.

Climbing down the cold metal rungs was difficult for him. Castor wasn't usually afraid of heights, and he even enjoyed spending time on the wall, well above the expanse of greenery before him and the streets behind. For some reason, this felt different to him. Perhaps it was the inky blackness that obscured the bottom. He felt like he was descending into the unknown, and that made his heart race. He half expected the fangs of a spider to grab his feet and drag him down to the bottom, and he physically shook his head to rid himself of that fear.

Instead, he tried to focus on the feeling of the cold iron rungs. The metal bar rippled along its inner crease, and he rubbed the textured stretch with his thumbs to distract himself. He took the descent slowly as well, both to make sure of his security and to keep the bag from bouncing on his already abused back.

Attached to the inside of each of the wooden shutters was a single chain that formed a U. When he got close enough to its centre, he gripped the rung in his left hand even tighter, and with his right, he reached out and grabbed the chain. By pulling it, the shutters would shut above him to conceal the passage from any wandering eyes.

A large part of him didn't want to pull the thin chain. There was no one to hide the entrance from after all. But there was no reason not to. Eventually, he would go down far enough to be in complete darkness anyway, so he might as well do what he was supposed to.

Reluctantly, he pulled the chain sharply and the creaking wood slammed shut above him. The darkness was oppressive, and he became even more diligent with each passing moment. He would reach out with his foot to the next rung, and push against it for a couple of moments to test its stability. He would do the same with his other leg, and his hands. Unthinkingly, he even tested the same rungs twice when his hand reached a rung that his foot had already found stable purchase against.

Every step was sound, just like it should be. The bent metal rods had been hammered deep into the stone, and it would take a great deal of force to dislodge just one. That didn't matter to Castor. In his caution, it took upwards of twenty minutes to make his way to the bottom.

Castor had a miniature heart attack when he stretched out his leg and was unable to find the next rung. He felt along the rock wall frantically with his right foot to no avail. Then, after stretching out his right leg as far as he could while still maintaining an iron grip on his current rungs, he felt a rock floor instead of metal. He reached the bottom without even realizing it!

Immediately, the fear left his body, and he felt rather silly. It was pitch black, and he couldn't see his hand directly in front of his face, but he still expected some sort of indication that he reached the bottom. He supposed that, in an evacuation, there would be light that would allow a person to see the ground. In fact, that light *should* still be here for his own use.

He felt along the wall to his right, which he believed should be the direction of the opposite end of the tunnel. Castor didn't have to be afraid of falling off anymore, but his apprehension hadn't completely abated, and he really wanted to be able to see again.

After some searching, his hand reached a smooth object that seemed to be hanging off the wall. Castor carefully lifted the thing off its hook and traced it delicately with his fingers. He discovered a little latch, which he took between his thumb and index finger. With a quick motion, Castor ripped it away from the rest of the object. It snagged on something which stopped it, and Castor frowned. Slowly, he slid the piece back into place, and, with another sudden movement, he jerked it away again. This time there was an immediate effect. Several sparks popped into existence, landed on some sort of fuel and flared up into a small blaze, illuminating the tunnel around him.

The lantern Castor held featured a rather useful mechanic. Over the small pool of oil, which functioned as its fuel source, there was a drawer like contraption with flint on the bottom. By pulling it out quickly, it could generate sparks that would fall onto the oil and ignite it. By pushing the drawer back in all the way, the flint piece would cover the oil and smother it, extinguishing the flame and preserving its fuel. It was quite useful because it could be lit without having to rely on another match or firestarter. Castor still had his firestarter in his pack, but it would have been near impossible to use it to light the lantern in total darkness.

This particular lantern played an important role in the evacuation process. Its light would guide the villagers down into the tunnel, so they didn't have to descend blindly like Castor did. With so many people climbing at once, it was dangerous to be unable to see who was above or below them.

There was the time factor to consider as well. People would need to descend as quickly as possible, so no one was stuck at the top when the enemy breached their defences, and that was impossible if everyone was unsure of where to put their hands and feet. For these reasons, this lantern was supposed to stay hung up on the wall, where it could perform its job. However, since there was no one behind him, he didn't see a problem with breaking the rules by taking it with him. He needed to see where he was going. Castor was just grateful that someone extinguished the lantern instead of letting it burn out. It left some fuel for him.

The fire churned atop the pool of oil, and the darkness far beyond its reach roiled like waves in a storm. With a little bit of light, Castor could see the details of the tunnel a lot more sharply than most people would be able to, even though they were all tinted orange. The effect was surreal. He could see every crack in the stone, every furrow that marked the path of a pickaxe and every ambient mote of dust that was flung into the stagnant air with each step he took. Two details that interested him the most were the furrows in the dirt and the long, twisted rope that was suspended a couple of centimetres off the ground.

The uneven furrows were tracks left by wooden carts that had passed this way.

Wooden carts were positioned in this tunnel in the case of an evacuation, to be used for hauling supplies and other belongings. As time went on, and the possibility of the Torians abandoning their village grew, they had begun keeping these carts fully stocked as a precaution. Some people even used them as a general storage space.

Most of the carts belonged to Lord Tolam and contained important items for the villagers, such as food, communal supplies, tools and materials that would be needed to restart their lives somewhere else. The surviving guilds had carts as well, and ordinary families shared individual carts between them.

The tunnel was so narrow that people would have to move their carts in single file. Although he didn't check, he was sure that he could find several empty carts tucked away behind the point where he entered the tunnel. The carts would have been consolidated, and people probably would have had to shift their belongings to a different cart further ahead in the lineup, since there wasn't enough space to move around one that was to be left behind.

As he walked, he saw a number of discarded items in the dirt. The villagers surely searched their belongings as they travelled to make sure they were only taking what they truly needed. Anything that didn't make the cut would have to be left behind. Castor saw a number of books, clothes, and other assorted keepsakes that held nothing but sentimental value. He even saw what looked to be a chest filled with money.

The rope that Castor noticed was suspended slightly off the ground by hooks embedded into the wall. It was a solid black mass of twisted fabric that gleamed dully as his light passed over it. Castor was very careful not to bring his fire too close. The fabric was soaked in pitch and served as a sort of alarm system. If an enemy of some kind, such as a monster or even a human, entered the tunnel, then this rope would be lit. The fire would quickly spread across its length, and the direction the fire came from would let the refugees know what direction the threat was in. The rope was unburned, so they obviously encountered no danger once they escaped into the tunnel.

Castor's hopes for finding his fellow villagers down here dwindled by the second. If he was the captain of the guard, he would have kept some of his subordinates in the tunnel to keep watch. He was sure Bani would too. However, he held on to hope that he would soon encounter someone.

He passed another entrance, the one underneath the Keep. This entrance was just across from the area that served as the food locker. It was also considerably larger than the other two and featured a staircase rather than the metal ladder rungs. During an evacuation, guards were posted by this entrance to help those unable to make it down into the tunnel on their own.

The entire basement could be hidden under a massive trapdoor that Castor couldn't remember ever seeing closed. According to evacuation plan four, a couple members of the guard would have to stay behind to close and disguise it, before escaping to the northeast entrance to join the rest of the group. Again, Castor wasn't sure how strictly they would follow the plan, considering the odd circumstances. If they did, it was probably a good thing the giant spider blocked him from entering the Keep, as he wouldn't have been able to open the trapdoor by himself.

With the staircase behind him, Castor began to see passageways that branched off perpendicular to the main tunnel. These were the areas that miners worked hard to excavate each day, for multiple reasons. The first was to harvest stone. However, the most pressing issue was to dig for water.

Another consequence of the village closure was a major water shortage. Up until a couple of years ago, the village mainly got its fresh water for drinking and bathing from man-made reservoirs that were dug close by the outer walls. At the time, these reservoirs were perfectly located: right next to the farms, which needed a large supply of fresh water nearby to operate. Families kept their own basins for personal use within their houses, and children were often sent to refill them from the reservoirs as needed. Due to Toriath's climate, it rained quite often, so there was little danger of them running the reservoirs dry, although it did happen occasionally.

Like so many other things, the villagers lost access to the reservoirs when the gates closed. In response, they created cisterns to collect and store enough rainwater to survive and to perform most other necessary tasks. However, they could not collect nearly enough to grow crops within the village walls, especially during the summer. Therefore, their best solution was to create wells to procure water from underground.

Several people in the village's history had tried digging wells, and all of them failed. Quickly, the current generation discovered why. The groundwater level in this area was incredibly low, meaning they would have to dig a lot farther to reach water. Their solution was to create the wells underground, branching off from this very tunnel. The miners were in charge of maintaining them and creating new ones in order to keep up with the increasing demand, just so they could withdraw more water at once.

Castor turned into one of the narrow side tunnels leading to a well. This was a good opportunity to top off the waterskin that hadn't vanished in the pack, which by his estimate was over halfway empty. His spare was still full, but he had learned the hard way not to take any chances with his water supply. The water from these wells always tasted a bit off, so he chugged as much of the fresher rainwater as he could before refilling the skin.

This stretch of tunnel saw a lot more use than the northern half, which was evident from its appearance. It was a lot wider, and there were also alcoves where tools were kept, as well as other equipment such as spare carts for hauling away debris, extra lanterns and miscellaneous wooden pieces. Of course, these were just the objects that were left behind. Castor was sure that, as they passed by, the refugees took whatever they thought would be useful from this cache.

In addition to the tunnel growing wider, the ceiling grew higher the closer he got to the southwest entrance. Although it would be too slight for anyone else to tell, Castor could hear the difference with each step he took. His footsteps, which before seemed loud and reverberated through the small tunnel unpleasantly, became more flat and lower in pitch.

Castor knew he reached the southwest entrance when the tunnel opened even wider. The area up above was disguised as a storage unit near the wall, close to the stairs that Castor would climb each day to deliver the watchmen their lunch. This was considered the work centre of the tunnel, and Castor had been down here quite a few times for various errands. However, whenever he was here in the past, the chamber was always very well illuminated. With only his one lantern, the place looked almost haunting, especially due to the shadowy construct in the centre of the area.

A large system of pulleys was positioned around the wide hole along the wall that led up to the entrance. These were used to bring heavy loads, such as stone for construction and debris they needed to clear out of the way, from the tunnel up into the village. Any dirt or other waste materials would be catapulted over the wall, far enough away that they couldn't be used by the spiders to climb up into the village.

No one had any reason to travel beyond this point in the tunnel under regular circumstances. The first couple meters once held prepared evacuation carts so that they were out of the way of the tunnellers, but after that, there were no side chambers, or any features that held any utility for the village. As such, the tunnel immediately shrank back to the size of the northeast half, both width and height wise.

By setting foot in this segment of the tunnel, Castor felt like he was doing something forbidden. There were no rules banning any member of the village from entering this space, but no one ever did, not since the tunnel was first constructed. That was an odd time, Castor reflected as he walked.

It took six years to fully excavate this tunnel, and another to widen it out to become passable. Any villager who was physically able to do so was conscripted into working on the tunnel, even the members of the council like his sister and Lord Tolam himself. Each villager was assigned two days a week to work on the tunnel at first, but later that was upped to three days a week in order to complete the project more quickly. It was incredibly gruelling work, and it was a source of contention between many different groups. For example, the guards were exempted from the task for the first year, and many people grew bitter with them because of it. Due to that pressure, the captain of the guard made her subordinates pick up two shifts a week. Of course, people were angry with Lord Tolam for mandating this project, and the man nearly worked himself to death in response. He insisted on working in the tunnel every day until his body gave out. To this day, the man suffered from periodic coughing fits as a result of that time.

Feuds between individual villagers skyrocketed as well. If one person thought that another wasn't working as hard as they should, or taking too many breaks, then fights would inevitably break out. Also, at this time, people still had their regular jobs to attend to and currency still held value, so people who were conscripted felt bitter about being unable to lead their regular lives.

Some people dealt with this turn of events better than others financially, and the less fortunate became envious. That everyone was in a constant state of exhaustion didn't help matters one bit. Luckily, at this time the villagers still had their sources of food and water. They only lost access to those within the last two years. The project would have been impossible otherwise.

Time seemed to have no meaning in this tunnel. Castor didn't realize how much he relied on the sun to tell time, and with it obscured, it felt as if the minutes stopped altogether. He began to have a headache as well as his eyes automatically flew to every small movement around him, such as the dancing shadows, the dust that kicked up and each angular rock on the wall. He could now perceive a lot more than humans were meant to be able to, and his brain could only process so much without anything to distract himself. In order to cope, he zoned out, even closing his eyes for periods of time and using his free hand and the rock wall to guide himself.

In this state, he almost slipped and fell as the surface of the floor abruptly changed. Instead of the rocks and compacted dirt he was used to, he had stepped into a shallow pool of slick mud. It was apparent why as he looked at the path ahead of him. The tunnel began to slightly slant upwards, which meant that any moisture that made its way into the tunnel had rolled down to this spot. It also meant that he was nearing the end!

The tunnel led into a man-made cavern. If his people were still here, they would be waiting in that area. He took off into a run, and the slurping sound of his shoes against mud echoed off the walls. He was acutely aware that, even though his sensitive ears were perked, his foot falls were the only sound. Sure enough, when the tunnel opened, and he got his first glimpse of natural sunlight in a while, he could see that the cavern was completely and utterly empty.

Chapter Eighteen
Trail of White

For the second time that day, Castor broke down, even though he had already realized that the rest of the Torians had left the tunnels entirely. The lantern dropped from his numb fingers, hitting the ground with a clatter, and the fire petered out as fuel poured through the metal grates that protected it. Castor dropped to the ground as well as sobs wracked his body, which reverberated around the conspicuously empty chamber.

A beam of light shone through the gaps around the exit, and slowly moved across the floor as the sun set. Castor was supposed to spend this glorious night in his own bed, in his own house, with his own sister. It didn't matter that he could never have predicted the evacuation; he bitterly wished he never left. All his escapade netted him was some seeds he would never plant, some ambiance for rituals he would never use, and many injuries, both physical and mental, that he couldn't even comprehend the extent of.

He didn't just cry for himself. Outside of the protection of the village walls, it was doubtful that the Torians would survive long amongst the veritable army of arachna. He knew better than anyone how perilous the forest was, and, in a large caravan, they had no way to hide or outrun any monsters that might find them. They were probably dying in droves as he knelt here if they hadn't already been completely killed off by now.

Castor's gut hurt. His knees hurt, and his palms too. And he was just so tired. With nothing else he could do, he limply fell onto the dusty floor, and slowly cried himself into a fitful sleep.

The next morning, a despondent Castor awoke and mechanically ate some jerky. Not a lot, because he feasted yesterday in the salt room, and he didn't have much of an appetite anyway. Without the evening sun shining directly into the cavern, it was quite dim, and anyone other than Castor would have a hard time making out the room's features. He didn't want to linger here anyway, so he pushed down the piece of wood that blocked the entrance. He could have done so more delicately, and cautiously for that matter, but Castor couldn't bring himself to care.

He winced as light suddenly flooded the room, blinding him. Although Castor was slowly getting used to his sensitive vision, sudden changes in brightness still bothered him quite a bit. Gritting his teeth in frustration, he rubbed his eyes for a moment and turned away from the opening. That was another useless thing he got from his quest. This damned curse.

Aside from his inner turmoil, Castor did feel a lot better physically. His countless bruises were quickly fading, and the scabs all over his body, including the large patch on his shoulder, were itching, which signified that they were about to start falling off.

Castor wasn't grateful for whatever sped up his healing. It wasn't good enough of a consolation prize. Besides, there was still one injury that didn't seem to fade at all, and that was the pressure on his back. If anything, it was getting worse.

When the coloured splotches left his eyes, Castor could see the cavern completely for the first time. Castor hadn't been here since the tunnel's construction. Since the completion of the project was so critical, even he had been sent to work here. Castor couldn't even swing a pick hard enough to break stone in the present, and he certainly couldn't have six years ago either. All he could do was help move some of the debris into this area, and only a little bit at a time.

The cavern was actually on the ground level, it was just built in the midst of a man-made hill. The stone they excavated from the tunnel had to go somewhere, after all. This place was perhaps the most important part of the system because it would provide a safe place for the villagers to congregate during an evacuation. It was also the most difficult part of construction because it wasn't just about breaking rocks and putting them someplace else. This required thinking, planning and skilled labour, and there was only so much of each that could be spared.

Even though the structure holding the loose rocks and dirt overhead looked shoddy, it did its job well. If it wasn't sturdy, it surely would have collapsed by now under the might of Toriath's terrible storms. There were so many supports that it seemed like the ceiling was made of wood, and numerous columns were put in place to help bear the load. Castor noted absentmindedly that they were probably terribly inconvenient for the now refugees pulling their unwieldy carts.

Then, as he moved past one of the columns that blocked his view, Castor glimpsed something that made his heart race. A message painted onto the left-hand side of the wall in white.

Against his better judgment, hope began to blossom in his chest once again as he quickly strode over to the rocks stuck together with mortar and braced by two wooden supports. The message was short, in fact it was only two words.

Castor. Follow.

Apparently, that was all it took for Castor to start crying again, though this time his tears were coloured with something positive for a change. Although it was hard to tell with large brushstrokes on a vertical surface, the words were definitely his sister's. She had very poor handwriting, which was ironic because her profession relied heavily on drawing and writing. The bottom of the C was curved inward a bit, almost making it look like a G. The curves of the s were too narrow compared to the rest of the letters. And there were blots on the bottom of each of the Os because she always started drawing them from the underside for some reason.

He thought of the message she had drawn on the table, and

realized that, distracted as he was, he hadn't even noticed that she had left that message for *him*. Just as she left this one, for *him*. She even wrote his name!

Jayna had faith that he was still alive, even though all evidence pointed to the contrary. If she didn't, she wouldn't have even thought to leave a message for him. His sister truly believed that he was still out there, and that he would return to her, and she left him a way to do so! He assumed at least. After all, why would she have told him to follow, if she didn't plan on giving him something *to* follow?

Castor felt the fire reignite in his chest. Jayna had faith that he would survive against all odds, and now he had to have faith that she would as well. Even as she made her way through the arachnas' hunting grounds, he had to believe that she was alive, and that he could find her. That was all there was to it.

Every minute he wasted, the greater the distance between them grew. So, he grabbed his bag and set off immediately.

Walking out of the chamber, Castor stepped over the thin piece of wood that covered the entrance. He considered it for a bit, trying to decide if he should attempt to put it back up or not. The villagers obviously thought it was prudent to do so, even though they didn't know there was anyone behind them to protect. Castor decided to follow their lead, just so that other unfriendly creatures didn't take up residency in their escape tunnels. His people probably wouldn't return to the village for some time, if ever, but it wouldn't hurt Castor to at least try to prop up the disguise.

The wood was light for its size, but it was still cumbersome. He had to crouch down and put his entire body under the piece and stand up steadily, using his body as a fulcrum. With some manoeuvring, he was finally able to prop it back into place.

With it in its regular orientation, Castor could see that the already brown wood was painted with green, vertical brush strokes. The flimsy board didn't offer any protection; its purpose was to act as a facade. It was made to look like a small cliff face, and to complete the illusion, the village had grown a network of climbing ivy to cover it from the outside. Said ivy lay in pieces around the entrance, which they would have had to cut away from inside the cavern.

Castor imagined the villagers pressing against the door from the inside, trying to create a gap through which the guards could hack apart the overgrowth with their swords. Castor halfheartedly tried to fling some of the fallen vines back over the wooden frame, hoping that they would eventually grow back to encapsulate it once more, but he doubted any spiders would notice the now-blocked opening anyway.

The area that the tunnel opened into was cleared of trees in the general vicinity. Many of them had been used in the tunnel's construction, but a casual observer wouldn't have found any trace that they once existed. The villagers attempted to burn the stumps away, and they buried whatever remained. Through the years, grass had even begun to grow over the very slightly raised lumps that dotted the area.

Just as he was about to step past the tree line once more, he hesitated. Why was his throat so dry? Why was his heart beating so fast? *Why is it so hard for me to take another step?*

Leaving the village last time was easy. He was distracted by the adrenaline of sneaking out of the village, and he didn't know what he was getting into. How afraid he should have been. He knew, of course, that there was a high probability of death. That the chances he would return were slim. But he hadn't truly understood what agony the wild had in store for him, both physically and mentally.

By the gods, he knew now. He never thought he would have to take one step past the tree line again; that idea was the only thing that gave him solace even during his darkest moments. Now, there was no end destination. No sanctuary he could escape to.

It's not like I can stay in Toriath. Sure, I might be safe physically in the tunnels, but I'll run out of food eventually, even with all the jerky in the salt room.

Somehow, that reasoning didn't seem to help him at all. But then he took a deep breath. *I promised to be brave. I promised not to falter in the face of danger. Stay here or go back into the forest? I've already made my choice.*

Then, he forced himself to stop thinking. There was no fear, no helplessness, no forest at all. Only his legs and the ground beneath them. When Castor was afraid, he never really felt like he was in control of his body, and now he embraced that feeling. No matter what, he would keep walking. And as he marched on, his fear began to dull.

It didn't make sense to be afraid of a place, but it did make sense to be afraid of what inhabits it, so he soon fell back into the vigilant habits he had fostered over the last week. He constantly checked for movement in every direction and walked quickly between trees while lingering behind their trunks. But he smiled a bit at his internal victory.

Is this what they call being proud?

As he had hoped, he soon found Jayna's first track a couple meters straight out from the tunnel. Just a small splotch of paint that wouldn't even be noticeable if it wasn't white. But it was clear enough for him to see, and Castor began to feel confident.

Travelling through the forest felt a lot better when he wasn't walking aimlessly. It was a lot less stressful to follow a path, and Castor actually began to enjoy seeking out the white markers. They appeared about every five meters at first, but the distance between each slowly grew. It made sense; after all, Jayna would need to conserve her paint. She probably didn't have much with her, especially since she needed to travel light. Castor soon found it more and more difficult to locate each new marking, although Jayna graciously put some close together whenever the caravan began to turn.

Still, the forest wasn't a good place for someone to become completely absorbed in any single task. Castor began to encounter spiders once again, and he even saw a couple of vines, although they were all dead.

Castor was forced to abandon his trail when he saw an arachna through the trees. It was quite far away, but its path would bring it too close to Castor for his comfort. To compensate, he moved in a different direction, which led him farther away from the spider, but also his sister's trail. As frantic as he was to relocate the white markings, he didn't try to advance any further without confirmation that he was going in the right direction.

The problem, both with finding lost markers and knowing which direction to travel in, was orientation. If Castor followed one marker to the next exactly, there was no problem. However, since the marks were on vertical surfaces, in this case tree trunks, Castor could only see them from one side. If he walked towards that same tree from another side, the marking would be completely hidden from him, and he could easily walk past it.

Where the marking was on the tree also indicated where the next one was. If he faced the painted side of the tree, he would know that the next mark would be directly ahead. However, if he didn't have a marker in front of him and he got turned around, he wouldn't even know which direction to walk in.

This aggravating mistake was one that Castor was determined to only make once. From then on, instead of carelessly moving from one mark to the next, he took stock of his surroundings and noted landmarks, such as specific trees, bushes, and rocks. Also, as he faced each mark, he looked up at the sky and used the sun and Mount Kol, which was due south, to loosely gauge which direction he was travelling in. The refugees seemed to be heading in a straight path towards the mountain, but that could change.

Periodically, Castor also saw evidence of the carts that the villagers pulled with them, in the form of occasional ruts in the dirt or grass, and sometimes gashes in the bark of nearby trees. There was no road here, and the Torians probably had a devil of a time advancing through the forest. He was sure that the caravan was moving at a snail's pace, which gave him hope that, on his own, he could catch up with them soon.

He did wonder why the Torians didn't cut over to the main path that connected Toriath's gate to the highway. It would take them out of the way, especially if their plan was to head west like he thought it would be, but surely the ease of travel would make up for that lost time. *Maybe Lord Tolam was worried about being too exposed on the main road.*

Both routes had risks but moving so slowly was not conducive to the refugees' survival. The more time they spent, the more likely it would be for the arachna to find them, and the villagers weren't capable of escaping. If they ran away and sacrificed their supplies, they would only delay their deaths a short while, and even *that* wasn't a guarantee. They would have to fight when the time came, and Castor knew that they would be incapable of defending themselves without losses.

He was proven correct half an hour later, when Castor inevitably came across the scene of a battle. The first thing he noticed was a cart lying between two trees. One of its wheels was broken, which explained why it was left behind. No one was strong enough to drag a laden cart through the forest, and they couldn't afford to waste energy or slow the group down while trying.

The next thing he noticed, which caused his stomach to drop, were the three yellowish-white bundles grouped underneath the largest tree. After he made sure the coast was clear, he rushed over to them.

Horrifically, two of the bundles were human sized. Although he loathed to try and find out, Castor needed to know who was underneath. He needed to know his sister was still alive. With shaky hands, he withdrew his new dagger from his place under his belt and pressed its edge against the web.

It was quite dry on the outside, and it felt rather like trying to cut through a roll of thick twine. It must have been exposed to the warm, dry air for a while, which may have meant that the refugees were a lot further ahead than he thought. However, under that first layer, it began to get a lot more difficult to cut through, due to the material's elasticity. After a bit of work, the dagger plunged through into a cavity in the bundle.

Castor was prepared to see something disgusting. Bones, blood, bits of flesh. He was not prepared to see a shrivelled husk of a person, with little skin upon bones, no eyes, no lips or any other soft defining features. He was even less prepared for the dark brown slime that the corpse was suspended in, and the foul smell it gave off.

The moment it touched his nose, Castor instinctively dropped the remains and fell backward in his haste to escape it. It was putrid in a way Castor could have never imagined. It didn't smell like garbage, or sewage, or even rotten food, which was something he hadn't smelled since well before the famine began. All he could describe it as was exactly what it was. Liquefied human.

Still, Castor needed to identify the remains. Once the initial pungency, which had been concentrated within the confines of the web, had disbursed, Castor approached it again. There were no features that could indicate who the person once was. The clothes mostly remained, but they were so obscured under the dark muck that Castor couldn't even tell what they looked like.

Castor held his breath as he looked for some way to identify the cadaver, or at least to rule out the possibility that it was his sister, and he eventually found a determining feature atop its head. Its hair hadn't been dissolved, and it seemed to be long. Castor felt guilty for the amount of sheer relief he felt in that moment. His sister had short hair, and wore it in a rather unique style, so this wasn't her. Still, it was someone, probably someone he knew very well, and he couldn't find anything more specific to determine exactly who it was. There wasn't anything he could do about that though, so, even though he mourned their loss, he began to cut open the second one.

This time, he knew to hold his breath, but the initial punch as the fetid air escaped its prison still pervaded his entire being. It was impossible to tell the body's orientation within the cocoon, and Castor realized, after working hard to pry apart the web with his dagger and another stick, this one was upside down, and he made his cut far away from its head. Shuddering, Castor made to flip the corpse around, before he noticed that this body was wearing armour, which of course didn't dissolve like the flesh and skin did. Jayna wouldn't be wearing armour, so this must not be her. He tried not to think about who it might be instead.

He saw all he needed to. Castor grabbed his dagger and all but hurled himself away from the corpses, gasping for breath as he did so. The weapon was still covered in the sludge, and he did his best to remove it by plunging it into the ground again and again, hoping that the grass and dirt would wipe the offending bits away. He didn't want any part of that touching his body, both because it was disgusting and because it contained the spider's venom.

Aside from the two human-sized web bundles, there was another, much larger one. That must have been the spider that attacked them, which the refugees were forced to kill since they couldn't escape otherwise. Another arachna must have come after the event to wrap up all the bodies left behind, including its slain brethren. He wondered if the scavenger had been the one to web up the tree behind the corpses as well, and the canopy above it. It was a lot thicker than he was used to seeing, and it must have been difficult for the monster to get its webbing up so high. Maybe it thought more people might be coming.

Even though they were much bigger, the arachna still behaved like regular spiders. They built webs to trap unsuspecting prey, and Castor had seen plenty in the forest. However, they weren't very smart, and they couldn't comprehend that, unlike most animals, humans were able to notice and evade their traps. Still, the spider that made this might come back to check, so it would probably be best not to linger for too long, even though he had faith in his ability to detect something so large if it approached.

First though, he wanted to check out the cart the refugees had been forced to leave behind. Everything on here must have been incredibly important for them to have brought it along in the first place, but the most crucial stuff had surely been taken and placed on another cart. Still, it would be worth his time to check.

One of the first things he noticed was that it was nicer than the carts most people would be using. It was reinforced with iron in a lot of places, and the craftsmanship was markedly better. Those upgrades obviously didn't help it out much in the end, but they did signify to Castor that this cart belonged to one of the inner village council members, most likely Lord Tolam himself.

It was statistically likely that the cart belonged to him because most things used by the village were technically owned by the lord, and, as such, he took with him several carts that would be pulled by members of the Noble Guard.

Everyone else had one at the most, and many even shared.

On this cart, he found a wide collection of random items, most of them made of metal. Castor supposed that Lord Tolam was planning on constructing a settlement elsewhere. They couldn't survive as nomads for very long with all the monsters around, and iron would be the most difficult resource to come across initially. It was a real shame that they were forced to leave it behind, but as heavy as it was, Castor couldn't bring any of it with him.

Another thing Castor saw was a small collection of books, which seemed like an odd thing to prioritize in an evacuation. Their contents had to have been quite important.

Castor was the only Torian in his relative age range that could read. Most people simply didn't have any use for the skill, and the only ones who did either ran businesses or were learning to do so.

However, Castor grew up wealthy, and the son of a ritual master. He was groomed to be one of his father's successors, even though he didn't have the chance to learn most of the craft. Reading and writing were important skills for any master or apprentice because, even in the simplest of rituals, there were just too many parts to keep track of at once. Also, information on crucial topics such as matrix design and ingredient combinations were kept in indexes, which were useless to anyone who couldn't read.

Still, although he *learned* how to read, he hadn't needed to do so for upwards of a year, and many titles of the books before him contained words he didn't know. So, Castor leafed through their contents to try and see what they were about, and he stumbled across something that could be very important. One of the books, which was large, square, and bound in dark dyed leather, contained a collection of maps!

Maps were a rare commodity and had the potential to be lifesaving in this uncertain wilderness. Lord Tolam must have thought so as well, because Castor saw that quite a few of the pages were ripped out, presumably when he decided to leave the rest of the book behind. If Marak was to be believed, none of the maps Lord Tolam possessed were complete, but Castor expected that the ones that were taken were the most detailed, or the most geographically relevant.

Those left behind might still come in handy, so, following the Lord's lead, Castor tore out a couple, folded them and put them in his pack, making sure to switch them out with some jerky in the storage space for added protection. The first map he picked out had depicted the cities located on this continent along with all major roads, and the second contained major landmarks, such as the Kalival and, most importantly, necrovales. The last thing he wanted was to unknowingly stumble into one of those.

Castor scanned the other books to see if they held any more treasures, but they did not. The other books were on administrative and construction techniques, which would be useful for building a settlement, but not for him.

There was one last, strange thing Castor noticed on the front of the cart, directly behind the handles that extended out for the driver to push against. It was a small, opened chest which was completely square. The opening couldn't have held something much bigger than his fist, but it was heavily fortified. The walls and lid were solid iron and thicker than his forearm. It was unusual for anything to have a lock at all, but the one that secured the lid of this box was giant, with a deadbolt twice as broad as any he had ever seen. It was also fixed to the cart itself, which was probably why it was left behind when its contents were taken.

Castor had no idea what it could have held. Anything valuable in a monetary sense was useless, and he doubted theft would be an issue here. Maybe the chest wasn't to prevent theft, but to provide protection for something fragile. Fragile and very, very small. As curious as Castor was, the mystery of the chest's contents didn't matter. Maybe he could ask Lord Tolam when he caught up to him.

Deciding he had thoroughly searched the cart, Castor paid his last respects to the corpses behind them. He wished he could bury them, but he couldn't for the same reason the villagers didn't in the first place. It was unsafe to remain in one spot anywhere in this forest, and it would take too long to dig the graves. Still, Castor wished he could show them some sort of respect, since the spiders stripped away their identity in death. Without knowing who the victims were, it was difficult for him to feel any emotion other than disgust and a great deal of fear. This was what awaited anyone who fell victim to the arachna. He had known it before, but now he understood.

With that harrowing thought, Castor continued south, searching for the next mark Jayna left for him. Before he made it very far, something solid tapped him lightly in the head. Completely startled, heart in his throat, Castor whirled around, clumsily unsheathing his dagger and holding it tightly in both fists. It was unneeded. Just above him, lazily spinning around after knocking him on the forehead, was a small branch suspended on a loose piece of web from above. He had been so focused on looking near the ground for the next mark, he didn't see it.

He cursed out the offending piece of wood for startling him when he was so high strung and ripped it down. However, the sticky thread clung to his hand and the twig, and he shook his hand vigorously to rid himself of it. The twig came free, but the web didn't, and Castor had to rub his hand against the dirt to remove some of its adhesion so he could pluck it off.

I hate spiders.

Chapter Nineteen
Mortal Peril

Castor forged on. The painted markings his sister left him were growing less and less frequent, and they were smaller than they had been before. It took him longer to find each subsequent splotch of paint, and Castor was beginning to believe that the gap between him and the caravan wasn't shrinking, even though the refugees must have been moving at a snail's pace. If his vision was as poor as it used to be, finding each mark might have been impossible.

There were two possible explanations for Jayna's decision, and neither of them were very good. The first was that she was running out of paint, and therefore had to ration what she had more strictly. The second was that their end destination was a lot farther away than they thought and Jayna had to adjust her pattern so that she wouldn't run out later.

Castor hoped it was the second because, if Jayna ran out of paint, Castor would have to rely on following tracks. While the heavy carts left a noticeable impact on the land, even their tracks could be erased in an instant. This region of Alaya was known for its heavy storms, and enough wind and rain could easily leave him directionless. Castor didn't know how long he could survive here on his own, and while the future was still grim if he caught up with the other Torians, at least there was safety in numbers.

Goosebumps prickled the back of Castor's neck, and he

strongly felt as if something was watching him. It was hardly an unfamiliar sensation; he had been twitchy ever since leaving the safety of Toriath. However, the feeling was even more extreme now, probably because of the corpses. He found himself looking over his shoulder constantly and grew more annoyed each time he caught himself in the act.

It was a couple hours past noon, and, even under the canopy of the forest, it was still sweltering. Castor tried to ration his water the best he could, but he was sorely tempted to drain his waterskin in one go.

He came across another white mark on a tree at the far end of a clearing, and his heart sank as, just below it, he saw another human sized web bundle. It had only been a bit over an hour away from the first attack and there was already a second one.

Grimly, Castor approached and tried to cut the webbing away from where he thought the face would be. However, he found it to be immensely more difficult than the last two. In those cases, the outer facing layer of each was dry and in-elastic. On this corpse, the webbing was fresh, so it stuck to the blade itself and to his left hand when he tried to use it to brace himself. Also, instead of cutting, it stretched around his blade.

Frustrated, Castor tore free his left hand with all his might, eventually succeeding. It stung his palm, and some of the silk still stuck to his skin. He rubbed it against the ground to try and get the adhesive off, and although his attempt failed, the dirt at least made it so that he didn't stick to anything else.

With both hands, Castor took the dagger and used his whole-body weight to try and stab into the bundle, hoping to overcome the flexible cocoon. Not only was it fresh, but the webbing also seemed to be a lot thicker as well. However, after expending quite a bit of effort, the tip of his blade made it through, and bit into something hard.

Castor frowned in confusion. The other two bundles had cavities inside, within which laid the remains of the spider's victims. Angling his blade to the side to pry apart the webbing, he was able to see a small sliver of the bundle's contents. It looked to be a log of all things. Why the hell would a spider web up a log? Come to think of it, why was this webbing still so sticky when the last two already dried out?

Castor tried to pull out his dagger and failed. The excessive force he used had exposed too much of the blade's surface to the adhesive silk, and although it stretched a little bit, he could not pull it free. Castor had a terrible feeling about this, and in his haste to extract his weapon, he almost put his foot on the log to push it away as he pulled, catching himself before he could accidentally stick his boot to the web as well.

Suddenly, something hit him solidly on his back. He was still wearing the pack, so it didn't hit him directly, but the force knocked him forward. Castor had the presence of mind to twist his body so that he didn't fall onto the webbed log in front of him, and that quick thinking may have saved his life.

The forest, which had been utterly silent one moment ago, filled with the snapping of branches and an ominous chittering noise. Castor tried to stumble to his feet, but he was yanked down once again by his backpack. But now, Castor could see what was behind him.

It was a giant arachna. The spiders were already huge, but this monstrosity put to shame any Castor had seen before. Neither the arachna in the forest that took down the humanoid monster or the one inside the village could compare. This one, even with all eight limbs firmly planted on the ground, stood over four and a half meters tall. Its shortest limbs were considerably longer than the length of Castor's entire body, and its fangs were each the size of his head.

Castor barely resisted the strong urge to freeze in terror. Where the hell did it come from? The monster seemed to have just appeared out of thin air! How could he not notice such a large creature?

There was no time to question it. Using its front two legs, the spider reeled in a thick strand of webbing, and as it did so, Castor was dragged forward across the ground. The force he felt against his back was caused by the webbing the monster somehow attached. His backpack had prevented him from being struck directly, but he was still being pulled in. Quickly, Castor forced his arms out of the straps, which was a difficult thing to do while being pulled by them. But, he was able to free himself by sacrificing his supplies.

The spider saw that its target had extracted himself from its grasp, so it gave up reeling in the pack and rushed towards him instead. A giant leg knocked Castor off his feet again, forcing the air out of his lungs and leaving him sputtering as he rolled away.

Another leg stomped on his stomach, knocking the wind out of Castor and pinning him in place. But just as the breath left his lungs, something else shot out of him, like great pressure forcing a clog out the end of a tube. The clog wasn't some sort of object lodged in his throat; it didn't even come out of his mouth. Instead, it shot through his skin and into the giant limb that pressed him into the ground!

The effect was instantaneous. The arachna jerked away as if it had been struck, and without its weight on his stomach, Castor was able to take deep, gulping breaths.

Despite the force from the blow, Castor felt great. Better than great, actually. The aches and weariness that pervaded his being ever since he escaped the ravine, which didn't seem to be tied to any visible injuries, were gone completely, including the pit that had seemed to sit on the small of his back. He hadn't even realized, but he couldn't breathe as deeply before, even without the arachna standing on him. Whatever used to be blocking his airways was gone now, and he felt revitalized, even more so than he had been when he pressed the icons in the ravine!

He rolled to his feet, and found the arachna thrashing violently, heedless of trees and bushes it ran into. It looked like that... curse of some sort, which plagued him for days now, leapt from his body into the arachna's, and the monster was paying the price. It seemed like it was in excruciating pain, but the curse hadn't killed Castor, so he doubted it would kill the arachna either. With no means to press his advantage, not that he was brave enough to do so anyway, he used the distraction to turn around and run.

Leaving his pack and dagger behind was akin to suicide, but there was no way he could get them back from that thing. His only hope was to escape now and take his chances in the wilderness if he could get away. Sure enough, even before the trees had blocked his view, he saw the arachna's convulsions stop.

He barely made it another fifteen meters before he almost

ran headfirst into another web. Staggering as he forced himself to stop too quickly, he took off around its perimeter. The webs stretched between the trees, forming a fence with their trunks as natural posts. Frantically looking for an opening, Castor soon realized that none existed.

The white walls didn't look very thick, but they didn't have to be. Castor knew that, even with his dagger, cutting the fresh web would be nearly impossible due to its adhesiveness and elasticity. Without any tool, if he tried to pull apart the web, he would be completely stuck. And, even worse, the arachna would feel the vibrations caused by his struggles and could use them to locate Castor nearly instantly. He couldn't climb the trees the webs stretched between either because their branches had been purposefully stripped away.

Castor had heard of monsters that were strong, and fast. He heard of monsters that were venomous, and those that lured people in before attacking. He had even heard of monsters that were much bigger than this arachna. But never, ever, had he heard of a monster that was smart.

Smart was an understatement, in fact. The spider set a trap for him well in advance. It created this arena of webs, and removed any possibility of him climbing over. It even set bait for him, in the form of that web-wrapped log. Had it been watching him? Was it there when he cut through the bundles over an hour ago?

Did the monster plan to disarm him? And to take his pack? Maybe it had tried to push him into the webbed bait to weigh him down, although he avoided that one.

Gasps began to tear through his soon raw throat as he looked around wildly, while a sharp pain seared his chest. "No, no, no," he whimpered. "Not now."

He threw himself against a tree, stumbling to the ground as his calf muscles began to spasm. His vision was beginning to swim, which only added to his panic because if he couldn't see, he couldn't survive—

But what use was his sight? The arachna came out of nowhere. It was so large, there was no way it should have been able to take him unawares. He felt betrayed. Most humans relied heavily on sight, and Castor was no exception. But lately, he had begun to depend on it even more, both because of the dangerous environment he found himself in and because of its recent boost. For it to fail him so spectacularly was unthinkable.

Castor fought with his tightly coiling muscles, and he tried pushing himself into the tree he hid behind. The bark dug into his back painfully and Castor tried to use the sensation to ground himself. He suddenly realized he was biting down on the meat of his forearm, hard enough to draw blood, in an effort to just shut up. He also wasn't breathing at all. Without relaxing his jaw, he forced himself to breathe through his nose which brought almost no relief.

What a sad way to die. Curled up against a tree, crying like a child. How embarrassingly appropriate.

Then, something cool pinched his neck, and Castor flinched, his almost controlled breathing skyrocketing once more. The shock caused him to rip his arm away from his mouth, and when he did, he realized that the pinch came from his own arm. Specifically, his bracelet, as the metal medallion closed against the surrounding leather strap when he bent his wrist.

He stared at it, not really processing its image at first. But soon, his vision began to focus. The tarnished medallion gleamed dully, and his eyes followed the path of the twisting metal. It formed an X in the centre, and the nooks in the cross sheltered the greatest amount of grime.

The bracelet didn't really remind him of Tommygun or Karat anymore. He was long past even imagining himself as a Hero too, no matter how fervently he wished to be one when he was a kid. And he held no illusions that Tommygun actually saw something in Castor when he gave him the bracelet; it was just a trifle he gifted to some random kid who gave him a cookie.

Castor often fiddled with this bracelet unconsciously; he had worn it so long without taking it off that it may as well have been a part of his own body. He rarely looked at the thing anymore. But the last time he did... was in Mayson's house.

He had forgotten the words, truthfully. Something about bravery, strength. Not losing his head or giving up. An oath to not do everything he was doing right now. A large part of him didn't want to care. He was going to die anyway, did it matter how he spent his last moments?

He felt a strong sense of déjà vu, and some words floated through his ears, although he didn't quite remember where he had heard them. *If you haven't given up yet, and the alternative is death, then you should try everything, right?* No matter how futile it may seem.

And had he given up? It was a decision that both meant everything and nothing. It wouldn't change the end result, but it would define Castor as a person. Would he die a helpless coward? Or would he die like a Hero?

He liked the sound of the second one better. Even though there was no one here to witness his final act.

Castor realized his breathing had slowed and couldn't help letting out a chuckle, the action sending a pang through his sore chest. He almost felt at peace, and he was simultaneously resigned and determined.

Looking around, Castor realized that the arachna wasn't taking advantage of his moment of weakness. In fact, he hadn't seen it since he escaped its clutches, which was strange. It's not like he hid very well, preoccupied as he was.

His eyes flicked in every direction, especially up towards the canopy. With his mind clearer, he thought that, perhaps, he didn't notice the spider initially because it hid above him in the trees. He remembered, when he was hit by that web, he fell forward into the ground, so it stood to reason that the attack had come from above.

He even found the area that the monster might have used to climb above him. Arachna, and especially this gargantuan specimen, were way too heavy to climb up surfaces like normal spiders without using a web, but Castor saw two of the larger trees around the edge of the white perimeter smothered in silk. Even the gap between the two was covered in a thicker wall, and Castor supposed it took a lot of infrastructure for the spider to be able to climb up anything. However, even though it was in view of the bait, he had no idea how it managed to latch onto his backpack with its web.

Again, Castor couldn't help but chuckle at his desolate

situation. This was a lot of work for the arachna to go through just to eat one boy. He wasn't even very big. Maybe it had expected several people to come through instead of just him, so that it could catch and feed on a... large... group. Oh no.

Had this arachna found the refugees? Did it come back to hunt for survivors? He hadn't come across any other webbed up corpses, and his sister did leave a white mark on that tree. She wouldn't have had time to do that if she was fighting or running for her life.

But what if it killed them further along their path, and came back to search for others?

He shook the thought aside. He couldn't lose hope over a catastrophization he couldn't currently confirm or deny. Castor needed to focus on how he would survive now, not worry about the survival of others.

Why wasn't the arachna chasing him? That was the big question. Castor hesitantly peered through the trees and saw that the spider wasn't even in the clearing anymore. Searching the ground, he saw that it must have taken his pack and the log his dagger was embedded in with it. He scanned his surroundings intently, even the trees above him. Where the hell did it go?

Maybe it's afraid of me? Castor wondered. *Maybe it doesn't want to risk getting hurt again?*

Then, he realized something. There was only one place where the web boundary definitely didn't cover, and that was the path that Castor had come in through. Castor punched his thigh in frustration. Surely, the spider was there now, no doubt closing off his only escape. He had one chance to get through it, which was right after he realized he was being attacked. Instead, he ran blindly into the forest to have a panic attack, sealing his fate as the arachna's dinner.

He shook his head, refusing to go down that line of thought. *I'm going to die, I'm going to die,* he thought... reassuringly? He hadn't given up, exactly, but he had accepted reality and the peace it offered.

Castor ran back into the clearing, foregoing all caution. Sure enough, he could see through the trees that the spider was using to close the gap. However, its method for doing so brought him up short.

Ordinary spiders could build their webs in high places by climbing up the object's surface. Arachna couldn't climb, but they could jump far, so they would place their webs by jumping and attaching them high up. That's what the spiders used to do each night, up on the village walls. However, it seemed like this one was too heavy to even make it off the ground, so its body compensated by developing the ability to shoot its webs.

Shoot its gods damned webs. Castor couldn't believe it. The monster had curled forward up on itself, so that its giant abdomen was underneath its thorax. Web shot out of its end in spurts, but each one still connected to the last. This, he realized, was how it had initially struck him. From above him in the trees, it shot its web at him like an arrow. Or, more aptly, like the village's Bastardista, since it could reel him in just like the Noble Guard did their prey. If this thing had attacked his village, it could have breached its walls in a single night. But maybe its greater intelligence was the reason that it didn't try. It had no way of knowing how many people were inside, it could have been climbing into its own death.

The spider had nearly closed the entrance. Castor didn't notice the web boundary when he first entered the trap, and if he did, he must not have seen enough of it to become suspicious. Therefore, the boundary must have resembled a horseshoe before, with a wide opening. The spider worked fast, so now there was only an opening eight meters wide and it shrank by the second.

Even though his every instinct screamed at him not to, Castor picked up a stick and threw it at the monster. It fell quite a bit short because his depth perception was off and he didn't have the strength to hurl it that far. He grabbed another, errantly noticing that there were quite a few branches on the ground since they had been stripped off the trees, ran forward several paces, and threw again. This time it hit, but the beast completely ignored it and continued shooting its webs. Castor hollered and did it again and again. The beast sensed his desperation, and it knew why. It knew that there was no way Castor could break through its webs, and that once it closed this gap, he was its dinner.

Except, it never did. Once the gap was around five meters wide, it stopped connecting its web between the trees, and rolled back onto itself normally. Turning around, its three pairs of eyes rested on him, and Castor couldn't help taking a couple steps back. Still, the arachna refused to move. He threw another branch, but all his strength had left him underneath the monster's heavy gaze. Even as the twig hit one of its legs, it remained motionless.

It wasn't going to let itself be drawn away, he realized. It had left that opening for Castor to try and get through, and after a moment of thought he realized why.

If the spider closed off the entrance completely, it would have to chase him around the entire enclosed area before it could finally catch him. Castor was small and nimble, and the arachna was very much neither of those things. He remembered how much difficulty the ordinary arachna had navigating the forest quickly. It was the only reason he had been able to outrun them, even though they were faster than he was. The trees weren't as close together here as they were near the Glade, but this spider was considerably bigger than any other he had seen. He could probably evade the thing for quite a long time.

In other words, the spider was lazy. However, that worked well for him. All he would have to do is get past the arachna and he was free, for the moment at least.

Although, after all the intelligence it had displayed to far, it didn't make sense for the arachna to gamble like this. He was tiny compared to it, and no matter how fast the monster was, he could probably still slip past it. Also, the gap was too small for the arachna to follow him through, and although it could climb over the web, it would have to find a section sturdy enough to support its weight, which would give him an even greater head start.

Castor would have to be an idiot not to realize that this was just another trap. And that begged the question, should he spring it?

Yes, he should. If he wanted to die a Hero, that would be the way to go. In a move that would have given his past self a heart attack, he stepped towards the arachna.

Chapter Twenty
Head On

To a human with average eyesight, the spider would appear to be motionless, but Castor could see each of the tiny hairs on its legs vibrate ever so slightly as its muscles—*do spiders have muscles?*—tensed. It was poised to strike.

First idea, he thought. Bait it into a more favourable position. Like he did with the wadom. He picked up a slightly heavier branch, eyes never leaving his opponent. The end was sharp from where it had been broken off its tree, but he doubted it would do any damage against the spider's exoskeleton. Still, it was better than nothing.

He took one deep breath, mentally steadying himself. Then, he darted in towards the arachna.

The creature didn't even hesitate, darting to meet him head on with a speed that something of its size shouldn't be capable of. He hoped it would lead with its fangs, which would force it to move farther away from the opening and allow him to duck out of its field of vision. Unfortunately, the arachna was smart enough to realize this. Instead, it reared back and tried to stomp on him with its two front legs. When Castor danced out of the way, it swatted at him again, and again.

He refused to back away, even though he was barely able to dodge the heavy blows. He needed to keep the monster engaged so that it was less likely to notice he was leading it away from the opening ever so slightly.

Too slightly. Before long, the arachna let up on its assault, and steadily backed up to its original position. Panting, Castor rubbed his forearm. He had dodged all its attacks, but one had gotten a bit too close, and a razor-sharp hair drew a long scratch along his skin. It was shallow enough that it didn't bleed, but it still stung.

"All right, you stupid animal," he said with a cocky smile that he didn't really feel. "What are you, afraid of me after that little shock from earlier? I'm going to kill you." He was beginning his second plan: make the arachna angry. That was what eventually got the wadom out of the water, after all.

Either the arachna was good at keeping its composure, or it didn't understand what he said. That was fine either way; Castor's taunts were weak to say the least.

He strafed around its massive body, poking at its legs with his stick, and jumping out of the way each time it struck out at him. It seemed too disciplined to give him an opening with such pitiful attacks, only turning enough to keep him within its admittedly impressive field of vision.

Soon, Castor became more frustrated than the monster he was trying to antagonize. "Move, damn you!" He growled, and thrust his makeshift spear with much greater force than he had previously.

The branch skated off its hard armour, redirecting to a spot between its back left legs. The force Castor committed to the blow made him stumble forward, and he felt a slight crack and heard an alienlike shriek. In an instant, the arachna was upon him, and Castor, already destabilized, hurtled to the ground.

He rolled frantically, trying to keep himself underneath its thorax and out of reach of its fangs and thrashing legs. He had actually hurt the monster! Its exoskeleton must have been weaker in between each of its sets of legs.

Grasping the branch he had dropped, he brought it up just as the creature slammed its abdomen down to pin him in place. Again, the branch slid off the hard, curved material, redirecting the force the arachna supplied to another weak spot on the other side this time. It shrieked again, and this was his chance.

Diving forward, he surged towards the opening just out of reach. The arachna whirled around in the blink of an eye, its fangs stretching above him, and he could dodge but—

He threw himself to the ground, rolling clumsily away from the attacking monster and the opening in the web because, just in time, he saw the arachna's trap. A couple strands of web pulled taut against the trees that marked the border of the exit.

It was a tripwire; Castor was sure of it. The strand was too thin for most normal people to notice, and even he would probably have missed it if he wasn't as focused. While the web wasn't thick enough to hold him for very long, it would have made him stumble or even fall entirely.

This was the monster's insurance, Castor realized. By blocking the upper portion of the opening with its body, it would have forced him to slide against the ground, or maybe it would have even pushed him into the trip line. And as soon as he fell, the arachna would have pounced.

Suddenly, Castor didn't like his chances at all. Sure, he might have accepted his inevitable death, but he wasn't going to throw his life away so recklessly. It looked like it would be impossible to get through the exit while the arachna was alive, and even though he identified one of its weak points, he knew he had no chance of actually killing it.

He would try though, if he had no other option. But for now, he cursed at the chittering monster and staggered away. Sure enough, it didn't follow him. The arachna was confident that he wouldn't find another way out of its trap, but Castor wasn't going to give up without trying.

The first thing he considered was digging under the barricade with his hands. He chose a spot underneath one of the walls and tried to dig into the ground with his fingers. The soil was packed together, and it took a lot of effort to make any progress. He even broke a couple nails on his now filthy fingers. In a moment of inspiration, he got a branch and tried to use that to loosen up the dirt. It didn't work quite as well, but at least it hurt him less.

However, after quite a bit of work, he encountered an even greater resistance. Tree roots. The solid wood created a boundary that he just could not get around no matter how hard he tried. The trees the web stretched between created their own barrier underground, and Castor couldn't break through with his bare hands. Even if he had tools at his disposal, it would probably take a full day to do so.

Castor took a deep breath to calm himself once again. Maybe he could try a different spot? He might be able to find two trees that were far enough apart that their roots might not block his escape. However, it took him so long just to dig that last portion, and Castor didn't know how much longer the arachna would wait. At any time, it might decide to close the opening and come after him, and he would lose his chance to find some means of escape.

Going under the webs wasn't an option. But what about above? Castor had initially dismissed this idea because the spider had purposely stripped the branches off each tree within the boundary. At least, it stripped off all the branches it could reach. However, since it was substantially taller than Castor, the branches that remained were all well out of Castor's grasp. Still, he searched each tree, concentrating on the ones near the boundary. He looked for one with a single, specific feature, and, with elation, he found it.

The tree in question was tall, like its fellows. The trunk wasn't incredibly thick, but that suited his purposes. What really made it stand out to Castor was that one of its upper branches extended slightly over the silk barrier. If he could climb up to that point, then it was possible for him to jump over to another tree on the opposite side.

It wasn't a good plan by any means, and it presented a lot of risks. The branch in question was a lot thinner at the end, and probably couldn't withstand all of his weight. He would somehow have to throw himself off it, latch onto another tree, and then climb down that one very quickly. He couldn't just jump straight down to the ground because, even if he made it over the wall, he wasn't safe. The spider would definitely pursue him, and the web wouldn't be much of an obstacle because the arachna could just climb over the silk. If Castor dropped down from that height, he would break his legs at least. And if he missed and fell back onto the web, he wouldn't break anything, but he would be immobilized and at the mercy of the giant arachna.

This was all assuming that he could make it to the branch in the first place. Like all the other trees, the lower branches had been completely stripped off. However, Castor had an idea about that.

For the first time since he landed in this mess, he began to feel a faint ray of hope. And with it, a kernel of dread. Already, the almost peace he had felt was melting away, because what if he did survive now?

As soon as his feelings turned into cognizant thoughts, he laughed.

"I've gone insane!" he realized. Why did it take him so long to figure it out? He didn't know if it was from the isolation, the danger, the loss or the pain, but sometime in the last week, his mind had just broken. The sudden panic attacks should have clued him into that. So what should he think? What should he feel?

One thing was for certain; he wasn't going to listen to a crazy person. He was alone here though, so what would someone else tell him? What would Jayna want him to do?

Live, idiot.

Right. He would try.

Castor had very few resources available to him, just the materials lying around him and the clothes on his body. Luckily, that was all he needed for his plan to work. Castor undid his belt and looked at it consideringly before deciding it was too short to suit his purposes and regretfully looping it around his neck for safekeeping. Then, in annoyance, he removed his shoes and took off his pants, leaving him clad in only a shirt and his undergarments.

The arachna might be smart when it comes to killing, Castor thought ruefully, *but it doesn't seem to know much about humans. Does it even know what clothes are, or does it just think they are a part of my skin? Does it know I can take them off?*

Walking up to the tree, Castor grabbed the waist of his pants with one hand and swung them around the trunk of the tree. Then, he grabbed the ends of the pant legs so that he and the garments formed a circle around the trunk and pulled it tight. He had seen older kids do this a long time ago, back when they could still explore outside the village walls. They never used their own pants of course, usually rope or other stretches of cloth. However, he had to make do.

He wrapped the excess fabric around his hands, to get a better grip and increase the pressure on the tree. He wished his pants were longer, but there wasn't anything he could do about that except hold one pant leg in each hand instead of doubling it up, which he was reluctant to do. He was afraid that the pants would rip if he did that, although there was still the possibility of that happening anyway. That was yet another risk with this plan.

He quashed his fear and replaced it with grim determination as he began to pull himself up the tree. He had positioned himself so that he could peer around the trunk in the direction of the spider, but he soon found it very difficult to concentrate. Pulling himself up the tree vertically was difficult. Castor wasn't very strong, and, for the millionth time, he cursed this fact. By the time he made it only three meters off the ground, his arms were already incredibly sore. However, the alternative was death, so he persevered.

The bark was rough, and Castor was sure he had scratches and splinters down the length of his arms and his bare thighs, which he used to help support his body. Each pull he made dragged his skin against the wood, and it felt as if he was being sawed into. To cope, he zoned into the pain, feeling each flare as it travelled through his body. Because of this, he completely stopped checking his surroundings. He missed the first couple sounds of leaves and twigs crackling in the distance, and the insectoid chittering. But he didn't miss the shout the spider made when it saw what he was doing.

The noise was somewhere between a squeal and a hiss. When he heard it, Castor, who had become so engrossed in his task, almost let go in shock. Looking past the trunk, he saw the arachna approaching at full speed! His pace had slowed a bit before as he zoned out, but he once again began to work frantically to pull himself up the tree as fast as he could.

Panic shot through his body like lightning. The arachna barrelled towards him, and it didn't look like it was going to stop! Sure enough, it collided straight into the tree, creating a tremor that shook Castor like a leaf. Even though he prepared for it, the force almost threw him off, which was what the spider wanted. Backing up once again, the monster rammed the tree again, but without its momentum, Castor wasn't rattled nearly as much.

Castor was over five meters up the tree, which put him out of the spider's reach. Or so he thought. Suddenly, the monster reared up on its four hind legs. Castor yelped and tried to pull his own legs up as much as he could, but the spider's front left limb brushed his shin. With the weight of the massive spider behind it, even the glancing blow nearly knocked him off. The sharp, needlelike hairs over its exoskeleton left gashes in his skin, and rivulets of blood ran down his foot and dripped onto the forest floor.

The spider couldn't stay in that position for long before gravity caused it to slide back down. So, it backed away and lunged again. Castor dodged the next lunge and tried to hold himself even tighter against the tree, hoping that doing so would make him more secure. However, that was an even worse idea, because the vibrations that shook the tree made him hit his head a couple of times on the trunk. He was dazed for a moment but caught himself before his grip could loosen too much. When the spider went down again, he used the opportunity to climb higher up the trunk.

When the spider came up again, one of its front legs came right below Castor's foot, and, instinctively, Castor used it as a step. By placing his leg onto it and relaxing the tension of the fabric, Castor jumped off the spider's outstretched leg. This move bought him a third of a meter, which, although it seemed inconsequential, meant everything for Castor. Even if the spider stretched as far as it could, he was out of its reach. The vibrations, while they might delay him, wouldn't stop him.

After two more attempts, the spider seemed to realize this as well. However, it wasn't out of tricks just yet. The arachna backed away a couple meters and extended its legs to their maximum height. Then, it rolled backwards onto its abdomen. With a start, Castor realized it was going to shoot its webs at him. Hurriedly, he tried to shimmy around the trunk, putting it in between himself and the webs. He needed to keep moving. The lowest branch that hadn't been pulled down was just over a meter above him.

A blur of white shot past his face, and he ducked behind the tree, bumping his head once more in his haste. Soon another followed, and he quickly tried to shift around the tree once more. Not only did he want to be out of the arachna's line of sight, but he also wanted to be in a position that, when it was time to reach out to the next branch, he could easily do so.

There was a pause in the web shots, and, looking down, Castor could see that the spider had uncurled itself, and moved to a new position to shoot from. Castor used this break to move diagonally up the tree, advancing and hiding simultaneously. It was a lot more difficult than moving up in a straight line though, and it used a different set of muscles, but given how tired his other ones were, that was almost a good thing.

The arachna renewed its bombardment. The projectiles were moderately fast, but they were rather inaccurate. The spider probably had a general idea of where they would go from practice, but there was a lot of distance between its eyes and the opening on its abdomen, and it must have been hard to aim something so far from its line of sight.

He was so close to the branch, and he didn't know how much longer his arms could hold out. He needed the relief the branch would give him, and once he could stand on that, he could climb up to the next one without using his pants as support.

Then, as he tried to make one last pull, he was horrified to find that he couldn't pull the fabric up anymore. Craning his neck, he looked around the trunk and saw a white mass attached to the brown cloth.

Castor had been so preoccupied with trying to keep his body hidden that he paid no mind to another target. One that, if it was stuck to the tree, would also halt his progress. His pants!

With them stuck to the trunk, he was forced to try and make it to the branch from the position he was in now. It was *just* out of reach, and if he weren't so sore and exhausted already, he might have been able to fling himself upward to catch it. But his arms were already trembling from exertion, and they were liable to give out at any second.

Still, he had to succeed. There was no other choice. He did have one tool to help him though. The loose leather belt that hung around his neck had been an annoyance for all of his climb so far. In fact, he would have taken it off and dropped it if he was able to let go of the fabric without falling off entirely. However, it might just save his life now.

The spider web that had pinned his pants to the tree actually helped him with this next part. If it was just the pressure of the fabric against the tree that held him up now, he would fall off as soon as he let go with one of his hands. With it held up by another source, he was able to let go with his dominant right hand, while just holding on with his left arm and his thighs. He shook out the strained and battered limb for a moment.

Around him, web projectiles continued to shoot, their ends trailing like streamers behind them, until the arachna saw that they had missed and cut them off. However, he was in a good position, and they all missed by a substantial amount.

Castor unwound the belt from around his neck and tried to loop it around the branch above him. It took a couple tries, but he eventually managed to do so. Then, with his right hand, he grasped both ends of the belt and began to pull himself up. His life was now in the hands of this hemmed strip of leather, and mercifully it held up. It was a good thing he was so light after all.

With a considerable amount of effort and pain, he pulled himself up onto the branch. Then, the entire tree shook again, and Castor, with all limbs wrapped around the branch, held on for dear life. It seemed like the arachna realized the futility of continuing to shoot webs and decided to go back to its initial method of trying to shake him off. Unfortunately for Castor, vibrations were more dramatic at the end of long objects, like trees. He felt each tremor even more harshly than he did before, and Castor had to be quick if he wanted to take his next step.

He didn't even have time to consider his actions when, as soon as the arachna stepped away once again, he stood up on the branch holding onto the trunk for support and jumped, not giving himself the chance to be scared about it. He caught the next branch and secured himself just in time, as the spider struck again.

The branch above him was his ticket out of here. As soon as the spider retreated again, he made his way up, mentally steeling himself for this next part, which would be the most dangerous. He would have to jump off the thinner end of this branch and cling on to another tree outside the barrier without falling too far to injure himself. Then, he would have to run away as fast as he could to escape the arachna, which could just climb over its own web wall with little effort.

Before he could act, the monster struck again, and this time, he heard a loud, all-encompassing snap that shook Castor to his core.

Castor's heart froze when he heard that noise below, and the prolonged crackling that followed. His world began to tilt downwards. The monster, through its repeated lunges, had broken down the tree!

He scrambled across the branch even as it began to slant upwards. The wood fibres down below clung at one another, trying to delay the inevitable, and their failure was heralded by the sound of splitting lumber.

He tried to stand while still grasping the branch in front of him. If he jumped and caught onto the branch of the other tree below him past the webbing, he would be free! He was just about to make his attempt when the spider lunged against the tree one final time.

And everything collapsed.

Chapter Twenty-One
Passage to Nowhere

Castor clutched the wooden branch below him with both arms and legs, hugging it against his chest like a lifeline even as he and it fell backwards. He didn't think, he was too distracted by the terrible feeling of falling.

Despite the strength with which he held onto the branch, Castor was still sent flying when the tree struck the ground. With no means to control himself, he gracelessly flipped backwards once in the air before hitting the ground, where he rolled to a stop over the sparse grass.

Shell-shocked, Castor lay on the ground for nearly a minute before his mental faculties returned to him. When they did, he frantically pushed himself to his feet, his left hand instinctively coming up to cradle his right side which he had first landed on before rolling away. His ribs were bruised at the very least. It wasn't nearly his only injury, but it was the most painful.

He was still in danger. The spider hadn't attacked yet, but it was just a matter of time. He had to get to the exit, which he hoped to the gods was still clear. The fall had left him completely discombobulated, and Castor would later mark this as another disadvantage to enhanced sight and hearing. He involuntarily attempted to focus on everything as he fell, and the spinning images made him even dizzier than they would normally have made someone. Similarly, the wind whistling in his ears as he spun sounded as loud as a bugle call, and even after he stopped there remained a faint ringing sound.

Through his raging headache, Castor tried to orient himself, looking for both the way out and the spider. He identified the movement of long, dark brown limbs some meters away and yelped, ducking behind the nearest tree. He prepared to bolt at any second, but as his vision and hearing regained focus, he began to hear something odd. They were reminiscent of the low sounds the spider made earlier, but they were shorter and garbled.

Castor peeked out from behind his hiding spot, and as his eyes fixed on the source of the noise, he slumped back to the ground in relief.

The massive spider was pinned under the tree that it had collapsed. No, pinned was the wrong word. Its entire right side had been crushed, its exoskeleton unable to take the full weight of the fallen lumber. All four legs on that side had been nearly ripped off, while the four on the left scrabbled futilely against the dirt.

Pale blue liquid pooled under the tree and ran across the ground like water welling up from a spring. Castor's village had combatted the arachna for many years now, so he knew that, even as alien as it looked, the liquid was the spider's blood.

Cautiously, Castor walked in a wide circle around the arachna to make absolutely sure that it was no longer a threat. Looking straight down the log, he could see the spider's main point of injury. The tree didn't completely sever the creature's legs, it had flattened the exoskeleton, pinning what remained underneath the tree. Struggle as it might, the monster could not break free, and even if it did, the injury was too great. It would just die quicker.

The tree must have fallen directly on the arachna's rounded abdomen before the slanted surface diverted it onto its legs. Massive cracks ran out from the main point of impact, where jagged pieces of hardened brown armour had torn free of their original placement. The iron defence that made the spiders so difficult for the Noble Guard to fight now worked against the beast. The sharp fragments, which reminded Castor of shattered glass, dug into the spider's insides, most likely severing many important organs.

Though the wound was fatal, the spider's death would be a slow one. The fact that it didn't die when the tree first hit it, and the fact that it still had the ability to struggle as it did, indicated that its heart, brain, or other vital parts hadn't been hit. However, even if by some miracle it survived the wound itself and the blood loss, it had been permanently rendered immobile. The four legs on its right side were squashed and pinned underneath the trunk, and it would starve at the very least.

Stuck to the back of the dying monster's abdomen with a web were two objects: Castor's pack and the log with his dagger stuck in it. Castor couldn't help letting out a soft hiss of laughter at that, which caused pain to shoot through his injured side. He had already seen that the arachna had confiscated both items, but Castor didn't have time to dwell on it as he was desperately searching for his escape. Did the beast attach the objects to itself as another form of bait? Or did it just want to make sure he couldn't find them?

The spider's abdomen didn't have much range of motion normally, so even as the monster violently convulsed, it remained rather stationary. Castor was reluctant to approach the beast at all, even in its vulnerable position, but he needed his stuff back. He had no idea how long its death rattle would last, and he didn't want to remain out in the open. It was possible that the sound of the tree falling, or the noises that the spider now made, would attract one of its brethren, and he held no illusions that he could fend off or even escape another arachna in his condition, even if it was normally sized.

He started with his dagger. Figuring it would be impossible to pry the entire log off the spider, covered in webbing as it was, he tried to wrench the dagger itself out of its confinement.

Trying to do so with both hands was a mistake. Pulling anything with his right arm brought a fresh wave of agony that brought him to his knees. So, when he collected himself, he tried again with just his left. It was difficult without his dominant hand, but after wiggling it for a couple minutes, he worked the blade out of its place.

Removing the pack was more difficult. The arachna had wrapped it in a couple strands of webbing to secure it to its body, and the flexible leather made it so that he couldn't use leverage to remove it like he did with the dagger. Frustrated, Castor eventually started to work loose soil into the sticky silk, trying to remove some of its adhesion, and, after several minutes of hard work, he succeeded.

Hurriedly, he took out the only spare pair of pants that he packed and put them on, grateful that he had the foresight to bring a change of clothes this time around. After a minute of searching, he found his belt around a branch of the fallen tree as well, wincing as he had to bend down to retrieve it. If he just needed it to hold up his pants, he might not have gone through the trouble, but he needed a place to put his dagger. He found his shoes, which were much more important, around the base of the tree.

The arachna's cries grew steadily softer by the minute. Castor realized that he had never gotten a good look at the thing until the tree fell. He had been so focused on either running away or climbing the tree. Looking at the beast now, he saw swirling patterns covering its exoskeleton. They were the same, deep brown colour, but they contrasted because, unlike the rest of the armour, which was glossy and reflective, the designs were matte.

These patterns reinforced the idea that there was something more to this creature other than its remarkable size, but Castor just couldn't bring himself to care now. His chest hurt with every deep inhale, so to compensate, he had to take shallow, unsatisfying breaths. His nerves had barely settled down, and he was wary of another attack. The webs that trapped him would be no obstacle to any other spider that might find this area. He turned to limp away, and then two things happened simultaneously. The arachna succumbed to its wounds. And, a large crack rang out through the clearing.

Castor wheeled around to the sudden noise behind him. There were no spiders, but he looked up just in case. *Did the fallen tree break another on its way down?* Then there was another crack, and his focus was drawn to its origin.

It was the tree in the back of the clearing, the same one his sister had marked in white paint. That tree wasn't anywhere near the one that had been felled, and, to his knowledge, the spider hadn't touched it at all. However, it was cracking, and in a completely bizarre fashion. A fissure ran vertically up the trunk instead of horizontally like it should have. The unnatural cleft quickly grew in length until it ran about two and a half meters up the trunk.

And then, inexplicably, the crack *opened*. It didn't swell to encompass more of the tree trunk, it was as if someone was parting a curtain, but made of solid wood and accompanied by a cacophony of snapping timber. And, in its place, there was now a triangular space filled only by a wall of oily darkness.

Castor cursed in shock and leapt back, stumbling over the uneven clods of grass as he did so. He ducked behind a tree, in a desperate bid to hide from whatever monster that might emerge from that abyss. But nothing came out.

The shadow had somehow completely wrenched apart the wood without destroying it. Four meters up, it even looked like a completely normal, healthy tree. However, the area below it couldn't look any less inviting. The opening was black except for an orange pinprick in the centre, which looked like it was far away. However, that was impossible. A quick glance past the tree made it clear that this was no tunnel, no matter how much it appeared to be. It couldn't lead anywhere, there wasn't any space.

Even more ominous was the area around the opening. The grass all around the tree had died, and even the bark of the tree that surrounded it looked ashen and cracked. Patches of mould grew way too quickly over its rough surface, and sap dripped down like drops of blood.

Castor cursed repeatedly in bewilderment under his breath, unable to fathom what was going on. He needed to get away from the opening quickly before it ate him, or something.

At least, that's what he told himself. However, the shadow was entrancing. It seemed to ripple like a sheet in the wind, and Castor had to force himself to look away. Then, he grew scared that it would attack him with his back turned, so he looked over his shoulder and was mesmerized once more.

After a couple minutes, he gave up trying to fight his curiosity. With a sigh, Castor walked back to the shadow, reached down, snatched a twig from the ground and poked the wretched thing. To his bewilderment, the twig passed through the black wall as if it wasn't even there, as if shadow was all it was. But darkness didn't act like this. Real darkness didn't have a border, it faded into light.

Castor kept pushing the twig slowly, trying to find an end that he couldn't reach. He hesitated right as the tips of his knuckles were about to enter the shadow, and then he kept going. The darkness didn't feel like anything either, and it didn't even obscure his hand.

Now, as unfathomable as it was, Castor was forced to accept that this *was* some sort of tunnel. The blackness wasn't some solid mass, but the result of meters of darkness that extended into this abyss. Although he had already checked, he once again circled the tree. Its width hadn't changed, it was still less than a meter in diameter.

Striding back around to the entrance, he jerkily shoved his whole left arm into the entrance, before pulling it out quickly. Then, he poked his head in. That orange dot he saw was something in there, some distance away. Probably a light source of some kind. He didn't know how that made him feel. A light source presumably meant people, and while he didn't really *want* to meet anyone who lived in a shadowy cave in the middle of a tree trunk, they might be able to help him, or perhaps provide him with a place to stay the night.

Or, they could kill or eat him. Monsters couldn't make fires, could they? At least, spiders couldn't. Even that arachna that had nearly killed him, while it was probably smart enough to figure out how to do so, didn't have the proper appendages to build and start a fire.

Castor shook his head. He couldn't believe he was seriously considering this. But the potential reward was tempting. He didn't relish the idea of trying to travel in his current state, and there was no guarantee he could find a remotely suitable place to rest. Night was still hours away, but his progress would undoubtedly be slow.

With trepidation, he slowly entered the tunnel, clutching

the wooden doorway with his left hand as he did so. And when he went as far as he could while still keeping a hand on the opening, he stopped. Then, steeling himself, he warily withdrew his hand.

Castor was most concerned that, once he entered the tunnel, the entranceway would close behind him as suddenly as it first opened. It didn't, however, and, when Castor was finally convinced it would remain open, he hesitantly continued onward, still frequently checking over his shoulder just to make sure.

"Hello?"

Castor called into the darkness. His voice cracked, and he suddenly realized that this was the first time he had spoken at full volume in a very long time, aside from the occasional scream. He tried again, a lot more clearly this time. His voice reverberated through the passageway, but there was no response.

The tunnel seemed to stretch a lot longer than it should, although Castor questioned his metric when he reminded himself that it shouldn't be able to stretch any distance at all. He found it impossible to tell how much time passed without counting the seconds, which he began to do after a while. The orange glow grew slightly larger with every step he took until he could make out the red and yellow hues accompanying it, and the fluttering of the flame itself.

The entrance, which was now far behind him, remained open. He could still see the white sunlight peeking through it. Every couple of minutes he called out once again, but he never got any response.

Finally, after Castor counted twenty minutes in addition to an unknown amount of time before then, Castor could see the end of the tunnel. The passageway opened into a large, domed chamber, and there were even more flames previously obscured by its walls.

He felt the heat of the fire as he reached the mouth, and, as he edged around the chamber's perimeter, he could see five pillars arranged in a circle within the room. On top of each pillar was a fire, and Castor couldn't see a fuel source for any of them. It was as if the pillars themselves had caught on fire, and the element defied its very nature by refusing to spread any further. They gave off no smoke either.

There was another, shorter column in the centre that was not on fire, although it glowed faintly. And, of course, there was no one in the chamber other than himself. The walls were dark and glassy like obsidian, and there were no other side tunnels for anyone to hide in.

This entire area felt malevolent, and nothing about it made sense. Castor walked past the fires to take a closer look at that centre column and immediately felt the searing heat of all five. Although it didn't truly burn him, it was uncomfortable to stand amongst.

Suspended above the centre column, by some means unknown to Castor, was the source of its glow. It looked like a mass of dark red liquid, boiling violently inside of a vial. Although, the vial itself didn't exist, and the liquid conformed to the shape of a container even though there wasn't one. Another contrary aspect about the liquid was that, although it appeared to be boiling, there was no steam. The entire, inexplicable *thing* bobbed gently up and down half a meter above the column which, unlike the taller ones on fire, looked to Castor like an abstract hand. The five, pointed fingers reached up towards the bubbling liquid like a victim that was about to drown.

Castor had only ever seen one thing like this before, and it was in the cave that bordered the Glade. Their images were nothing alike; that one had resembled a flower. However, both gave off the same ethereal sensation. The glow, one pale green and the other a dark, wine red, was unlike anything he had ever witnessed elsewhere. They were both translucent as well and possessed that same sense of intangibility. Although, he must have been able to touch that flower in some way for it to impact him as it did. The final tell for Castor was that they both levitated in the same manner.

The flower was both a blessing and a curse, and Castor still hadn't really worked out his feelings about it. The suffering it caused was the second worst thing he had ever felt, right behind his final day in the ravine, and the margin was small. It had knocked him unconscious for an entire day, and it left him debilitated for even longer. Nonetheless, he would have undoubtedly died days ago without the gifts it imparted within him, even though he didn't truly understand what they were.

Besides, he didn't even know what effect the vial could have on him. Would it make his sight and hearing even sharper? Would it do anything at all?

One thing was for certain. He couldn't afford to become incapacitated now, not with his injuries. He knew that if he encountered any more monsters in his current state, he *would* die. The only thing he had going for him was his ability to detect and evade enemies, and anything that might hinder his capability to do so had to be avoided, no matter what benefits it could potentially have in the long run.

Still, Castor thought. *It would be a shame to leave it behind.*

Maybe he could take it with him? One of his fellow villagers might find as great a use for it as he did with the flower.

It was worth a shot. He figured that the liquid wouldn't affect him if he didn't touch it himself, so he took a spare shirt from his bag and drew his dagger from its place under his belt. His impromptu plan was to use his dagger to guide the liquid onto the cloth, which he could then wrap up around it. This was, of course, based on the assumption that it wouldn't act like normal liquid and seep into the fabric.

Admittedly, Castor didn't think this through very carefully. He was tired and in pain, and this unsettling chamber made him duly anxious. Luckily, his reckless actions didn't backfire on him too spectacularly, although the outcome was one that he didn't expect at all.

As soon as he reached out to poke the floating liquid with the tip of his dagger, it instantly vanished. Nothing but the light from the five fires around him remained in its place.

Castor blinked in surprise. Reflexively, he looked around, half expecting it to have reappeared somewhere else, and his careless twisting of the torso caused blinding pain to shoot through him once again.

Gritting his teeth and glaring at the space that the liquid once occupied, he decided that he didn't care. That thing was more trouble than it was worth anyway, and its disappearance probably saved him one hell of a headache, perhaps literally.

There was nothing left in the chamber other than uncomfortable heat, so he made his way out. The walk back through the corridor was just as long as he remembered it, although now, instead of fear, he just felt annoyance.

He considered staying the night here, but only briefly. While it might be a bit safer than sleeping out in the open, the only exit was still right outside what might become a hotbed of spider activity soon. Also, even though Castor noted gratefully that the exit was still open now, there was no guarantee that it would remain so indefinitely. Those were just the logical reasons why he didn't want to sleep here, and he had plenty of illogical ones as well. Besides, there were still several hours of daylight left, so he should be able to find someplace suitable in that time.

A wave of relief hit him as he finally limped out of that tunnel. He refused to look back at the shadow as he walked away, carefully skirting around the still husk of the giant arachna that came so close to killing him.

He couldn't help looking back at the corpse as he left it behind. It was truly remarkable he made it out alive and uneaten. Once again, he was saved by pure luck. The same could be said about most of the challenges he faced on this quest, he realized. The only reason he found the Glade was by being chased into the river. The only reason he escaped the ravine was because of the storm that lifted him out. And the only reason he was alive now was because the tree snapped and fell on the arachna.

It was a strange thought because he certainly didn't *feel* lucky. He was shambling through the forest alone, and in considerable pain. He may have survived, but at what cost?

Did he even deserve to be alive now?

Then, he remembered. He had escaped the arachna before falling into the river and finding the Glade. He had persevered in the ravine for an entire week, spirit bent but not broken, before the storm lifted him out. And now, in the face of an overwhelming foe, he had *acted* instead of giving up. His plan might not have worked as intended, but at least he had the presence of mind to make one, right? And now he was alive, while an arachna many times his size was not. A smile tugged at the corner of his lips, stretching out a cut on his cheek. It stung, but he barely paid it any mind.

Castor set off on this quest to bring seeds to feed his starving village, and ambiance to save his sister, sure. But he also set off to prove he wasn't useless, both to others and himself.

He got the seeds. He got the ambiance. And, was he useless?

He stepped through the gap in the web, grateful that the arachna hadn't closed it off before it noticed his impending escape, and the white wall finally obscured his view of the monster's still form.

"Heh." He let out a short chuckle, ignoring the searing pain that accompanied it. "Quest. Quest, quest, quest."

Castor had just realized he had been calling this venture a quest this whole time. He had never really thought about it.

I guess I never actually gave up on becoming a Hero.

Epilogue
What Rests Beneath the Mountain

Castor trudged on. He was relieved to keep finding paint marks, as that confirmed that his people were still alive, but locating new ones seemed to be getting more and more difficult. Jayna must have been steadily spacing them out.

Exhausted and in pain, he found concentrating on even a single thing to be nearly impossible. He needed to split attention between *three* things though: the markers, any monsters that might appear, and any place that he could safely rest for the night. He estimated that he had about three hours before nightfall, so he kept an eye out for any space that would allow him to hide for the night.

Then, a spider appeared in the distance. Castor halted completely, hiding behind the nearest tree as completely as he could manage while still observing the approaching arachna.

This might be it, Castor thought in fear and sadness. He couldn't run, his body just wasn't capable of it now. And he couldn't switch to a hiding spot that was farther away because he didn't have faith in his ability to do so quickly and quietly.

The monster steadily closed the distance between them, stopping and swaying a half second in between each step like the creatures normally did when they weren't in pursuit of prey. It clearly hadn't noticed Castor yet, otherwise it would have been moving a lot more quickly.

Hidden by the tree trunk, Castor slipped his dagger out from under his belt, and immediately noticed something odd about it. It hadn't changed colour per se, but the sunlight that reflected off the gleaming metal seemed to be tinted red.

Just like the liquid in the chamber, he realized. There was no time to consider what that might mean, because the arachna was still slowly approaching. He stroked the handle of the changed dagger and the feeling of smooth leather against his fingers brought some small measure of comfort. Castor had no confidence that he could take down an arachna in a fight when he was in peak condition, and now he couldn't even use his dominant hand. Maybe he could take it by surprise if it came too close.

He couldn't look out from behind the tree anymore, the spider was too close to risk it. He marked its position mentally and used the sound its steps made against the grass to judge its distance. Where could he strike? If he blinded the beast, then maybe he could escape, even at his current speed. It had three pairs of eyes though. Would he have to slash all of them?

Castor readjusted his grip so the blade faced downward, and prepared to reach out from his hiding place and drag the dagger across the top of the spider's head. Then, all of a sudden, he heard it stop.

Abruptly, the spider broke into a sprint. Heart pounding, Castor readied himself, knowing that he would only have one attempt. However, his fear turned to confusion as he realized that the spider was actually running away from him. Not directly away; a quick look revealed that the arachna was heading in the direction he had come from.

He didn't have much of a chance to wonder why. A moment later, a deep boom sounded, so loud that he felt the earth tremble underneath his feet. Castor whirled around, easily determining its origin. A cloud of dust formed a halo around Mount Kol, many kilometres away. The mountain had been part of the background for so long, Castor had nearly forgotten its existence.

There was another boom, even louder than the first, and Castor was knocked off his feet. It felt and sounded like he was standing on a giant drum that had just been struck. Wide-eyed, he looked past the tree to the giant mountain.

Then, its peak *exploded*. Giant boulders were flung with such ferocity that some even reached past the point where Castor now cowered. A ring of dirt and smaller rocks were flung even further, and dust hung in the air for a moment, before a strong gust, once again emanating from the mountain, forced it all away. Leaves and branches were stripped away from trees, and many were toppled, unable to withstand the wind pressure. Castor lay flat on the ground in a bid to escape being flung into the air, heedless of the agony from his side that flared through him.

Then the sound came. A roar, louder than anything Castor had ever heard, blasted from the mountain. His sensitive eardrums burst immediately, and Castor himself cried out as the blood that freely poured out was whipped away by the wind.

Despite the pain he was in, and the devastation all around him, he couldn't look away from the mountain, as its summit seemed to stretch upward like wet clay being pulled by a potter. Then, Castor realized with even greater horror that it wasn't part of the mountain. It was an unfathomably titanic, scaled, ferocious, *enraged* monster.

Acknowledgements

Special thanks to:

Hannah, my partner, my soundboard and inspiration. Without her, this book would never have been written.

My family, and all their continued support.

Carter, whose help in the early editing process was invaluable.

Catherine, and the rest of the Brain Lag staff, for indulging me.

And Edmund McMillen, who I have never met, but whose games continue to be a great inspiration.

An avid reader, D. Holden Kennon, born in Orlando, Florida, always knew he would become an author. He even started writing his first book at age ten (although it was *suspiciously* similar to one of his favourite novels at the time). He adores crafting immersive worlds, complete with intricate magic systems and rich histories, and has spent years developing this series, The New Heroes of Kairodor, before finally putting pen to paper at the start of the pandemic. Holden believes that, even in fantasy worlds, humans are still human, and he hopes to facilitate discussions concerning real life, human issues he is passionate about, including mental health, systematic oppression and inequality, gender and misuse of power.